Praise for Hsi-wei Tales

Hsi-wei Tales is an imaginative, vivid creation that brings historical Sui Dynasty China alive: the rich, the educated, the politically privileged, the working class, and the poorest of the poor, all are tied together by a humble, itinerant shoemaker who is a skilled craftsman and a famous (yet unassuming) poet. He has the wisdom of the careful observer wed to the humility of someone who is unaware of his gifts. He values the shoes he makes more than his poems, but his poems and life have the loveliness one finds in work that is finely crafted. He is a wanderer, a lover of simple things, and has the gift of finding beauty and joy in conversation and interaction with anyone of any class, as long as they commit themselves to embracing the world. The stories are deceptively simple, with depths that repay more than one reading. Characters are finely drawn with delicate brush strokes that one would expect from the best of ancient Chinese artists and calligraphers. Hsi-wei is a welcome guest whose presence is more than ample payment for allowing him to visit.

- Michael L. Newell, poet, whose most recent works are *Meditation of an Old Man*, *Standing on a Bridge*, and *Traveling without Compass or Map*, both from Bellowing Ark Press.

Robert Wexelblatt's latest wisdom gift is his collection of stories about the peasant/poet Hsi-wei, a survivor of the short-lived Sui Dynasty, a time of wars and outrages in which rulers used their subjects as so many bricks to build a great wall. Still, courage, wit, and beauty make their appearance in *Hsi-wei Tales*, nourishing a troubled world and helping to preserve some of its more admirable inhabitants. The vagabond poet plays a role in the balancing scales of society as nature balances the seasons of the year. Rogues are outwitted, worthy lives plucked from danger, pretension and falsity revealed.

As the ever modest Hsi-wei notes, "at its best, poetry is language made unforgettable." Both the poetry and the prose in these tales offer gem-like images of nature—"a steady thing," Hsi-wei tells us, "punctuated by seasons of peace and war, plenty and famine"—and a changeless humanity that are deserving of contemplation and a delight to read.

- Robert Knox, author of the novels *Suosso's Lane* and the forth-coming *Karpa Talesman*.

Dear Hsi-wei, from your ancient land of misted mountains and still lakes where you cross borders and thresholds full of strife, leaving poems and peace in your wake, I welcome you to our time. We need your unassuming wisdom and keen observations, your straw sandals and your quiet dedication to justice. For as you write "apparent stability is really the ceaseless/setting right of countless imbalances." Welcome, Hsi-wei. Long may your poems be sung!

- Elizabeth Cunningham, author of *The Maeve Chronicles*, *The Wild Mother*, etc.

Published by
Regal House Publishing, LLC
Raleigh, NC 27612
All rights reserved

ISBN -13 (paperback): 9781947548930
ISBN -13 (epub): 9781947548947
Library of Congress Control Number: 2019941550

Interior and cover design by Lafayette & Greene
lafayetteandgreene.com
Cover art © by Svetoslav Tatachev
Author photograph by Boston University Photo Services

Regal House Publishing, LLC
https://regalhousepublishing.com

Printed in the United States of America

Hsi-wei Tales

Robert Wexelblatt

Regal House Publishing

Hsi-wei's Skull

Chen Hsi-wei was born in the latter half of the sixth century, at the close of the troubled period of the Six Dynasties and at the beginning of Sui rule. His verses, though original, are characteristic of the times, except for his frequent use of vulgar idioms and southern dialects. Recently a curious manuscript of Chen Hsi-wei's has come to light.

According to a brief preface added by an unknown hand, it was at the request of a certain lady-in-waiting that Chen wrote this account of one of his well-known but perplexing poems, popularly called "My Skull" after the final words of the fourth stanza. Evidently composing this explanation especially inspired Chen Hsi-wei because he supplied something more than was requested, virtually an account of his becoming a poet.

Freely translated, the poem reads as follows:

In Pingyao, as they began to lash my back and chest,
I could just hear little girls chanting "Rice-Bowl-Rice":
Through green doors, across red pavement, that jolly song.

When they dragged me off to be questioned in Nanyang
Melancholy music wafted from Three River Tavern,
Just the sort to make barge men soften like medlars.

I curled up contentedly by a great sow near Chuchow,
No less warmed than she by our soiled straw,
Our cradle rocked by Feng's fierce horsemen tramping by.

Wuchow's streets ran with festive dragons, crackers burst,
Women warbled, children cheered, babies bawled as
General Fu ran his so-eager finger over my skull.

Honored Lady, deeply touched by your request, I rush to

1

fulfill it. Please overlook my awkwardness, put it down to my haste to gratify your curiosity.

You must first know that I was born a peasant. My people lived in a village not far from the capital. In fact, you may have at some time enjoyed a banquet supplied from our farm which used to be famous for its ducks.

There was nothing unusual about my rearing or indeed about me, save for one peculiar capacity which I will mention presently.

In those first days of the new dynasty the Empire was still riven by strife. Warlords threatened the peace on every hand. Ruthless bandits terrorized the countryside. One of the greatest problems with which the new government had to cope was the getting and sending of letters and dispatches. Under the conditions of the period, no postal system could be counted on.

It happened that the Emperor's ministers needed to get a message through to our southern army. Apparently, nothing less than the survival of the Empire itself depended on the safe delivery of this message; moreover, disaster could be counted on should the information fall into the wrong hands. But to get to the southern army, a messenger must pass through vast lawless lands and many regions under the thumb of one or another warlord.

The Emperor's ministers knew that an armed force sent south with the message would only call attention to itself and, whatever its strength, was bound to fall prey either to warlords or bandits. Nor could couriers be trusted, for they were only too likely to be captured along with the message. I am told that the stratagem adopted was suggested to the First Minister by an old scholar who had come across it in an obscure history of the Chou dynasty.

A decree was put about the vicinity of the capital that the Emperor required a healthy young man with three qualities: bravery, illiteracy, and fast-growing hair. Rewards were promised to any family that should supply such a man.

You will recall my mentioning that in my youth I possessed only one noteworthy peculiarity. This was that my hair grew so quickly it needed cutting every week. While I cannot claim to have been especially brave, I certainly could neither read nor write.

Peasants are not only illiterate but also poor, My Lady. My parents were poor indeed, and when they heard the decree of the Emperor read out in the marketplace they did not hesitate to bundle me off to the capital. They even gave me a duck for the Emperor's minister. I carried it on my back.

Of course I was not the only peasant lad to show up in the palace's outermost courtyard on the appointed morning. There were scores of us. The guards, who instantly relieved me of my duck, made us wash our faces in great vats of water then lined us up in ranks. "Stand straight!" they roared at us and we did so for half an hour until a group of distinguished personages issued from a doorway. I wonder if you, My Lady, can imagine our awe when I tell you that the First Minister personally walked among us and, as we had been forbidden to kowtow, looked directly into our faces. I had never seen anyone like him, so grand and wise, so haughty and disdainful, draped in silks and taking little steps on shoes that elevated him well above even the tallest of us. We trembled before him—beneath him I should say, for the tiled roofs of the palace, the height of its walls, the scornful regard of the First Minister, everything looked down on us and made us feel stuck to the earth like beetles.

Many were dismissed at once. Some looked weak, had coughs or boils. Some were too fat, had bowed legs or thin hair. A few city boys, dressed up by their parents to look like peasants, in terror of the First Minister confessed that they could read. They too were sent packing. About forty of us remained. We were conducted into one of the palace's stables. The place looked to me vast enough to hold my whole village. Here we knelt six at a time. A small patch on the back of our heads was shaved. Then we were each issued a tiny bowl of rice with a few vegetables and locked into the stable for the night with our guards. Anyone heard groaning with discomfort or complaining about the food was immediately seized and sent away.

Those of us who remained were fetched out at dawn and told to race to some privies several hundred yards away. Note was taken of our speed. Nature's call being particularly insistent that morning, I ran faster than most. Once we had accomplished what was necessary at the privies, the guards again commanded us to wash in the vats of water, except for our heads that were to be kept dry. Once again we were arranged in ranks. "On your knees! Bow your heads!" yelled the guards. This time the First Minister did not participate. Instead, we were examined by clerks who held rods to the shorn spots on our heads. Each clerk had a scribe behind him to record our names and the results of the night's growth.

An hour later, two guards escorted me trembling with fright into the palace itself. I walked through magnificent galleries, down burnished and lacquered corridors into a magnificent room with a high teak desk and many opulently cushioned couches. On one of these couches, raised upon a low dais, reclined the First Minister.

I kowtowed.

"Explain matters to him in plain language," said the Minister gravely to one of his attendants.

This the attendant did and plainly enough. The crucial message to the army in the south, the communication on which the whole of the Empire depended, was to be entrusted only to me. There would be no scroll to deliver, no words for me to memorize. Scrolls can be taken away, memorized words divulged either in one's sleep or under torture. No, the message was to be inscribed in indelible ink on my shorn skull. The moment my hair had grown back sufficiently to hide it, I should depart for the south. I would travel on foot but as rapidly as possible and as inconspicuously too. I was to be given barely enough money for the journey and should take on the role of a peasant lad forced on the roads after being thrown out by his family. I must expect to be threatened, captured, even tortured along the way. At all costs, though, I must get through and never tell anyone except General Fu himself about the secret message on my head. The general would himself write a message for me to take back.

This, they told me, was the command of the Emperor himself and therefore my mission was divine.

Perhaps you can imagine how dumbfounded I was yet also how proud. It was as if I had been suddenly shown some special merit in myself. Looking back now, I wonder how many of us boys might have listened to that speech, felt the same shocked pride, how many were sent into the cauldron of the warring states, and whether I was just the only one to make it all the way to Wuchow and back. I wonder also about that message I could not read but which I, in a sense, was. I wonder how essential it actually was, and whether it arrived in time. In Wuchow General Fu said nothing to me. I might have been a scroll. He simply directed a scribe to paint a few characters on my freshly shaved skull and kept me under close guard for the few days it took for my hair to grow back.

And so, My Lady, the poem about which you were so gracious as to be curious merely records a few images from my journey. However, the first of my travels introduced me not only to the vastness of the Middle Kingdom and the variety of its peoples, but also to the grandeur of civilization and the cruelty of barbarism. I learned something else as well. I learned the diversity of tongues and what I might call the weight of words.

I returned to the capital as illiterate as when I had departed so many months before but with an inextinguishable burning to become educated. I who had borne language on my empty head yearned to master its secrets. That is why when the Emperor's clerks offered me gold and land and concubines I begged instead to be taught. This made them howl with laughter. They must have informed the First Minister because he sent for me.

5

"I am told that all peasants dream of land and money and women. Why do you, a peasant, wish to be educated?"

Though I lay prostrate before him, I replied with an audacity I must have somehow picked up on my journey. "Your Excellency, would you consent to surrender your education, to forget not only all you have read but even how to read, for land you could not describe, wealth you could not count, or a woman with whom you could not intelligently converse?"

The room grew hushed at this unheard-of temerity, but lucky for me the First Minister, notwithstanding his contempt for peasants and despite his haughty smile, replied seriously. "I see your education has already begun, boy. Very well. We shall see that it continues, but there shall be no land or gold or women."

There was never, My Lady, a truer prophecy.

I was assigned a stern tutor, the Master Shen Kuo, with whom I spent the next eight years at hard intellectual labor. I seldom saw my parents, though they did me honor for the gifts they received from the Emperor. My first nephew is named Hsi-wei.

In the end I became a poor poet, which is just what I wanted to be. I believe the happiest moment of my life was the first time I overheard "The Yellow Moon at Lake Weishan" sung in a tavern by some students far gone in their cups.

Yet I confess to you here, My Lady, how little has altered since my fate was first decided. A poet too is a sort of messenger from the Emperor; he too must remain faithful to his mission, inured against the hardships of his travels. To this day I still make my way through the wide world in search of General Fu with mysterious characters I myself cannot always understand inscribed upon my skull.

How Hsi-wei Became A Vagabond

Once again Hu Zhi-peng had brought a small gift. This time it was a pomegranate from the south, quite a rarity in the days when Yang Jian had yet to unite the two kingdoms and declare himself Emperor Wen of Sui.

Tian Miao sat up straight, her back not touching the chair. She thanked Hu humbly and sincerely but didn't know what to do with her hands or, indeed, her life. She prepared herself to receive Hu's guidance; for he never arrived with presents alone; there was advice as well.

When Tian Miao became a widow at the age of seventeen Hu Zhi-peng had been of great service to her. He helped her secure the small house in which she lived and the one hundred *mou* of land which he then arranged for her to lease to two peasant families. Hu had also found her a servant, Jingfei, a decent if garrulous peasant widow of forty. Miao was obliged to be grateful to the merchant.

Hu had been a business associate of Miao's husband and had been a frequent visitor to the Tian villa. As a second wife, Miao had exchanged hardly a word with the man; but, after her husband was killed by bandits on the road to Chiangling, it was Hu who had come to her aid. He was an intelligent and discreet man and, like her late husband, almost fifty years old. Miao told herself she could feel secure with him because he already had two wives. So she was disconcerted when Hu, making himself at ease on her couch, said, "A pomegranate is hard on the outside but inside there is much sweetness. Do you know, Miao, people sometimes say that's how I am, too. Perhaps it is a compliment. What do you think?"

"You have been kind to me, Zhi-peng. To me you have been nothing but sweet."

Hu seemed to content himself with this guarded answer.

"Ah," he said, "I nearly forgot my other surprise" and pulled from the sleeve of his silk robe a small scroll. "Imagine," he said tossing the scroll up and down, "a peasant has set up as a poet."

"Really?" asked Miao absent-mindedly. She was still unsettled by Hu's comment about himself and pomegranates.

"Oh yes, indeed. I have here copies of some his poems. It seems they're being circulated by the young man's teacher, Shen Kuo, a most remarkable man. I'm told he is proud of the young peasant the way a dog-trainer is of a pup he's taught to stand on its hind legs."

Miao frowned prettily. "Do you know how this peasant came to be educated?"

"I do," said Hu, striking his thigh, "and it's a fine story. I'll tell you and then, if you wish, I'll read you one of this Chen Hsi-wei's poems."

"Yes, please," said Miao, glad not to have to speak of her gratitude or her guest's sweetness.

Hu told the story of how, four years earlier, during the most chaotic period of the war, Hsi-wei had been chosen to deliver a critical message to General Fu's army in the south, a secret message that could not be allowed to fall into the wrong hands.

"They used a stratagem some scholar found in a dusty history of the Chou dynasty. The First Minister put out a call for illiterate peasant boys with fast-growing hair. Volunteers were tested and a few were chosen to be sent south. Their heads were shaved and the message inscribed on their scalps. As soon as their hair grew back they were dispatched to try to reach General Fu. This Chen Hsi-wei was the only one to get through, or at least the only one to return alive. He was offered money and land but—astonishing for a peasant—he begged instead to be educated."

"I think I can understand," said Miao in her soft voice.

"Really?" Hu was genuinely surprised.

"Chen Hsi-wei must have passed through all sorts of dangers carrying on his head words he couldn't understand. I expect he wanted to learn to read, to understand the mystery, and to be able to write down what had happened to him, to record the images inside his head."

Hu nodded, pleased that Miao, who spoke so little, was engaged by his story. "You may well be right," he said.

"He must have seen a lot on the roads," Miao added.

"Yes. The first of these poems is about just that, what he saw."

"May I hear it?"

"Of course." And Hu read Miao the poem which later became known as "My Skull."

"What do you think of the poem?" asked Miao, who liked it very much. She felt sympathy for the peasant boy, lashed in Pingyao, hiding from Feng's cavalry in Chuchow. She could hear the music from Three River Tavern and the chanting little girls.

"It's rather crude, and he mixes in southern idioms."

"Are all the poems about his adventures on the road?"

"No," said Hu. "The last one is quite peaceful and settled, a kind of survey of the city. But the boy can't resist being excessively personal. At the end he mocks himself, which I do like."

"Would you please read that one to me?"

"If you like, certainly." And Hu read her a poem Hsi-wei had written only two weeks earlier.

Tendrils thin as new snakes
undulate upon the inlaid table.
No desire for sudden noise
disturbs the Lord Shi-yeh
taking green tea with his friend.

In the scarlet bedchamber
a man turns to his wife
and speaks of some incident
long past. Her gentle nodding
is like sunlight on gold roofs.

The family sits in the garden.

From the railing of the foot-bridge
the littlest child pushes pebbles
into the shallow running brook
while two ducks stop to watch.

In his study underneath the
dumpling shop of Mrs. Shang-kiu,
the wretched student Hsi-wei
paints these images in his
bumbling bird's-foot characters.

Miao found the poem charming; in fact, she liked it even more than the first but sensed that Hu would not be pleased to hear her say so.

Hu put the scroll back in his sleeve. "Miao, I've been thinking," he said cautiously, "thinking about your situation. It's true you could live here as a widow; you're not wealthy but there's enough to get by. Still, it will be a poor and lonely sort of life for you, a dry life. I think as the world does."

Miao stiffened. "How does the world think?" she asked without needing to.

"It thinks pretty young ladies of good family like you ought to be married, of course."

Miao fumbled with her useless hands.

"I, for instance," drawled Hu, leaning back on the couch, "have only two wives, as you know. I can easily afford another. You would get on well with Sulin and Meili; I'm sure of it. They'd make a pet of you."

For a moment Miao thought Hu meant to get hold of her property; but then she admitted to herself that, while he was a man of business, Hu was also honorable and not exceptionally greedy. Besides, what did her property amount to in the eyes of a man like him? Then she recalled the way he had looked at her in her husband's house, the intensity of it.

Tactfully, Hu got to his feet and arranged his robe. "Think it over, Miao…as you enjoy the pomegranate. I am not impatient.

Meanwhile, will you do me the honor of permitting me to call again?"

"Of course," whispered Miao, looking at the hands lying heavily in her lap.

When Tian Miao told Jingfei about Hu's offer, the woman laughed. "So," she said, "he's got to the point at last."

"You knew?"

"My dear Lady, only a seventeen-year-old who didn't care for his horse's face and camel's feet would have failed to notice his intentions, and even then she'd have had to work at it."

Miao confessed she had been dreading just such an offer from Hu. A third wife, and of another merchant more than twice her age and even uglier than the first one! "But I owe him so much," she said, to be just.

"Never mind about that. It wasn't out of the kindness of his heart that he helped you. You ask me, another part of his body had more to do with it."

"You dislike him?"

"Yes," drawled Jingfei. "I suppose I do."

"Yet I believe Hu Zhi-peng is a good man. And he isn't wrong about the lonesome life a widow can expect, is he?"

Jingfei just grunted.

"Since my mother died, my father takes no interest in me. My brother is in the army down south and I can't say if he's alive or dead. Except for Hu Zhi-peng, I'm alone."

"Except for Mr. Hu and me."

Miao smiled. "Tell me, Jingfei, have you heard talk of a young peasant who writes poetry?"

"I know plenty of young peasants but none that can tell a poem from a pisspot."

In the days that followed, Miao often found herself thinking of Chen Hsi-wei, of his sufferings, even his maladroit calligraphy. She would have liked to know whether the secret message was still inscribed on his scalp. She wondered what his voice was like and whether he was fat or thin.

Finally, one morning she sent Jingfei to seek out the dumpling shop of Mrs. Shang-kiu and to ask if this Chen Hsi-wei were really living in the basement.

Jingfei was back by noon with a terse report. "He lives there all right."

"Did you see him by any chance?"

Jingfei almost smirked. "No, dear Lady. The great poet was out. The peasant too. As it's winter and there aren't any flowers to smell, I can't think what he was doing."

Miao withdrew to her bedroom.

It was with a feeling of effrontery—freedom mixed up with transgression—that, the following morning, she took up her brush to write out an invitation. Miao had to still her hand.

Hsi-wei was not pleased by the invitation Mrs. Shang-Kiu delivered to him when he returned from his lesson with Shen Kuo. Since the Master had taken it into his head to scatter abroad copies of his first poems, there had been half-a-dozen such invitations, none of which he was in a position to decline. The meals were all excellent; but the fine people who wanted him at their homes treated him as an upstart, a butt for their dull wits, or a curiosity to be shown off to guests. From her name he knew this Tian Miao was a female. All the previous invitations had come from men, third ministers, teak merchants, and the like. He pictured a bored dowager who desired a novel diversion to impress her circle of rich old women. With a sigh, he wrote out his acceptance and went to look for the usual boy, the one who loved to hear about his adventures, to deliver it.

It was nothing like the grand villa he had expected. A peasant woman met the poet at a low door and, without ceremony, invited him in. The furnishings were comfortable, but sparse and rather worn.

Jingfei had resolved to treat this Chen as an equal and so she spoke to him, not rudely, but familiarly, even with some fellow-feeling.

"So you're the peasant-poet. Well, you certainly dress like one—a peasant, I mean; I've no idea how poets dress. But good for you, I say. Why shouldn't a poet be a peasant and a peasant a poet? See you write plainly, though, and not just about flowers either. Come, come inside. My dear Lady will join you in a minute or so."

Miao left her bedroom a little flustered. If Hsi-wei was surprised by the modest house, Jingfei's cheeky greeting, and the absence of a flock of silk-clad crones, Miao was equally taken aback by the poet's appearance. She had been anticipating someone meaner, less dignified, shorter, with either too much hair or too little. But here was a tall, straight-backed man of twenty-one, half-peasant and half-lord.

The two looked at one another and each felt it was a moment outside of time. Such things really can happen.

"I'll bring the tea," mumbled Jingfei and withdrew, amused by the two young people standing stock still.

"Thank you for coming," said Miao at length.

"And to you for the honor of being asked to do so," replied Hsi-wei, and he made a bow of the sort he gave his Master and third ministers.

At this moment, Miao took a step toward the couch but the hem of her robe caught on a loose fitting of a chest and she faltered. Hsi-wei leapt forward and caught her as she fell. This little contretemps may explain a passage in the poem known as "Women and Rubies."

Perfection, being cold and lifeless, is suited
Best to precious stones and ice crystals;
While nothing is more fetching than a moment
Of clumsiness in a woman one loves.

Though little was said that evening, both relished every minute. Hsi-wei praised the food; Miao his verses. Miao remarked on how cold the weather was; Hsi-wei that the war would have to wait until Spring. Even Jingfei managed to hold her tongue.

Through the winter, the young people saw one another every other day. They would walk by the frozen river or stroll through the deserted Pavilion of the Five Virtues. Hsi-wei told her about the poor village in which he had spent his boyhood and how, when the call for illiterate boys with fast-growing hair was read out, his parents had sent him off to the capital with a duck to give to the First Minister. He told her about the tests—the running, swimming, keeping quiet under pain, the hair-growing measurements—how the boys had been housed in a stable. He explained his gladness at being chosen, not knowing the risks. She thrilled at his stories of escape, his resourcefulness, how he had hidden among the pigs, how cleverly he had talked his way to freedom when he was taken prisoner.

Hsi-wei felt discontented with himself after speaking of these things to Miao; it was too much like boasting, no matter how he played up his luck and down his courage. And yet, in her presence, boasting was just what he felt like doing. He yearned to tell her how those courtiers who had laughed when he turned down money and land in favor of learning no longer mocked him, how his stern Master, who had grumbled and cursed when Hsi-wei was sent to him for instruction, had come to treat him nearly with respect and exploited his pupil's poems to advertise his own skill.

As for Miao, she was simply infatuated with Hsi-wei. Now it was she who out-talked Jingfei, going on about his stories, his good manners and humility, his sensitivity, repeating his comments on the people at court, his opinions of the war, his accounts of how people lived in the south.

"Enough!" cried the exasperated Jingfei one day. "If you really mean to marry a penniless peasant boy, dear Lady, then do it. But please give me a little peace."

The mention of marriage reminded Miao of Hu Zhi-peng, who still visited once each week and brought presents each time, most recently a little jade Buddha. He had explained that this Buddha was the founder of a religion which had come over the mountains and was spreading throughout the north. "Doesn't he look jolly and wise?" he asked her. "You don't often find the two together."

Hu found out about the time Miao was spending with Hsi-wei but he waited for the right moment to put an end to this rivalry. He considered carefully how best to approach the young peasant. Hu was neither a violent man nor an unjust one; moreover, he sensed that threats, empty or genuine, were likely to achieve the opposite of his aim. He thought the matter over thoroughly, weighing what he had learned of the character of this Hsi-wei, until he had settled on what he should say to him. One afternoon he accosted Hsi-wei as he was leaving his Master's house.

"Chen Hsi-wei, my name is Hu Zhi-peng. I am a merchant and, without boasting, can say a successful one. Perhaps Tian Miao, a young lady in whom we are both interested, has mentioned my name to you?"

Hsi-wei said that she had and always with respect and gratitude.

Hu was relieved; he had anticipated something different, most likely bridling resentment. "That's good," he said. "I'm glad to hear it. Let me speak plainly and to the point. I have offered to make the lady my wife; this would not only assure her security but also her place in decent society. Forgive my bluntness, but, as we both know very well, you can offer her neither." Here Hu took Hsi-wei by the arm and scowled at him, hoping to imply some sort of unpleasant consequence. "Do you understand me?"

Hsi-wei said nothing. He shook off the older man's grasp and, by way of reply, simply nodded and went on his way.

The new year celebrations were well past and winter was drawing to an end. Crocuses broke through the unfrozen earth. As the air grew warmer and softer, the court busied itself with preparations for the year's military operations. Miao and Hsi-wei continued seeing each other; they read old poems aloud and spoke about the Buddha, whose teachings appealed to them both.

With his usual tact and patience, Hu did not pressure Miao for an answer but neither did he allow Miao to forget about his suit. He had an ally in Jingfei who, despite having become fond of the young peasant, made it clear that in her opinion Miao ought not to reject the merchant for the poet. She gave her reasons, too, and at length.

As for Hsi-wei, he had been troubled ever since the conversation with Hu. Though perhaps there had been the faintest hint of a threat, in fact the merchant had appealed to his reason and his love. He did love Tian Miao dearly and the thought of losing her was like being dismembered. And yet more and more the conviction grew in him that he was on the wrong path. The merchant was right to argue that he was in danger of ruining Miao's life. What troubled him nearly as much was that he was going against something in himself. It had to do with his poetry and with his adventures on the road. He did his best to resist his vocation and wanderlust as he did Hu's level-headedness; nevertheless, as the first white and pink blossoms appeared on the fruit trees, his misgivings overwhelmed him. Every day became a torment, especially those he spent with Miao, and the nights were worse. In the end, he decided that the only solution was for him to leave the city. He could not give up Miao and still live near her. The night on which he resolved that he had to leave Miao, his Master, and the life he had lived for four years was terrible. He lay in his basement under the dumpling shop and wept.

Hsi-wei could not look Miao in the face and say he was going away. Feng's cavalry had not frightened him, but for this he lacked the courage. Instead, disgusted by his weakness, he wrote a poem for Tian Miao, the one that has become popularly known as "The Cruelty of Springtime."

Blossoms unfold overnight.
Hills change from ugly brown to
The pale green of Lingnan jade.
The weightless air bears intoxicating
scents of manure and turned soil.
Ducklings waddle behind their mothers,
plop into ponds refreshed by rain.
Horses stamp on the dried-out roads.
Armies begin to march.

I too take to the road in springtime,
indifferent to peril, ineptly sealing up
a heart fissured by departure.
I suppose in springtime all men must
go to war, each in his own way.

Hsi-wei's Famous Letter

In a reply to an inquiry from the Prince of Sung, Chu Juyi, one of the compliers of *The Bronze Lantern*, explains why, despite its fame, he chose to exclude Chen Hsi-wei's "Letter to Yang Jian" from the anthology. "This poem," he writes, "is nothing like Hsi-wei's other work. It lacks his customary tact, subtlety, and indirection. Usually, the poet fixes his eye on details of the world and lends them a patina of use and familiarity through his verse. He writes of quiet moments and ordinary things. The interminable wars going on in his youth can certainly be felt in his poems but they are fought offstage, as when he concludes a description of early spring by writing *Horses stamp on the dried-out roads. / Armies begin to march.* Hsi-wei's meanings are like shadows cast by mountains, trees, and those small objects he disposes with such care. The "Letter to Yang Jian," on the other hand, could hardly be more blunt, its purpose more obvious, its violence more brutal. Even knowing the letter is signed, I still find it difficult to believe it is the work of Chen Hsi-wei. The clue as to why the poet abandoned his accustomed manner in the 'Letter' may lie in a tale told about how he came to write it and why he circulated copies of it throughout Northern Zhou." Chu Juyi goes on to relate a remarkable, probably fanciful, story about the composition of Hsi-wei's renowned open letter to the future Emperor Wen.

❧

The village of Kuo-ling lay on the old road between Ch'angan to the west and Shan to the east. The place was hardly large but it could boast an inn called Tong Yun, The Red Clouds. What travelers spent kept the village afloat even in hard times.

18

Consequently, the innkeeper, a fat widower named Chung, was highly respected.

On arriving in Kuo-ling, Hsi-wei went directly to The Red Clouds and asked this Chung for his humblest accommodation. As he was addressing the innkeeper, he happened to glance into the cool shade beyond the portico. Atop a bright red sideboard, he saw a painted clay statue, a smiling Buddha. Hsi-wei remarked on it.

Chung clapped his hands together. "Ah, my happy Buddha. You recognized him, yes? Three years ago a pair of monks converted me, though I'm still looking high and low for enlightenment. Those monks were making their way back from a pilgrimage to the West and, according to what they told me, the statue was made someplace beyond the T'ien mountains. The good monks, of course, had no money for lodging, nor would I have taken any. All the same, they insisted on making me a present of the statue. Would you care to look at my little Buddha more closely?"

As they were going inside Hsi-wei told the good-natured innkeeper that he had studied some of the many Buddhist texts available in the capital. The Regent, it was said, had taken an interest in promoting the Buddha's teachings.

Chung was delighted to hear this, said a blessing for the Regent, then began asking question after question of the road-weary poet. Could he say whether the Regent himself was a Buddhist? Did he sit under a tree to meditate? Had he spent any time at a monastery? Did the esteemed traveler himself believe that the Buddha was really a rich prince who renounced wealth and pleasure? What exactly is meant by the Buddha-Nature and could he possibly repeat the Eightfold Path? "It's shameful. I've already forgotten five of the precepts!" the innkeeper confessed with a self-deprecating laugh.

The two men settled in the lobby with its polished wood pillars. There were many cushions scattered about, some new, others worn to tatters. Chung ordered a girl to bring them tea, then, later, vegetables and rice. The poet and the innkeeper talk-ed until nightfall when Hsi-wei tactfully reminded Chung that he needed to sleep and a place in which to do so.

"My apologies! I was up there in the celestial ice mountains. Well, I have only two rooms available, but they are the finest. Take your pick."

Hsi-wei explained that he hadn't sufficient funds for such a fine accommodation, nor did he require one; a corner in the stable would do for him. "However," he added, "if anyone in Kuo-ling stands in need of new straw sandals, I'll soon have money, though hardly enough for one of The Red Clouds' fin-est rooms."

"Young man, this evening's conversation has been a pleasure for me, like rain after a drought," said the innkeeper touching three fingers to his forehead. "Your words are wise, learned, and, if I may say so, beautiful. Take either of the rooms and pay whatever you like."

By city standards, of course, the room was neither large nor well furnished. Then again, to a man who had been living rough and on the move for more than a year, it was both.

Before retiring, Hsi-wei opened his pack. He laid out his tools and the notice he would post by the well. Then, as he did night-ly, the poet carefully unrolled the oil-cloth in which he kept his ink stone, brushes, and supply of paper. After that, he undid the leather binding of his small library, the precious scrolls he had taken with him when he departed the capital. These in-cluded *The Consecration of the Lamp*, *The Five-Pillared Pavilion*, two Buddhist tracts, and copies of his own early poems. Rolled up tightly in the middle of the latter was a brief note from the Lady Tian Miao which it was the poet's habit to press to his nose each night.

Since taking up the life of a vagabond, Hsi-wei always fell asleep quickly, stretching out where he could. That night— on a proper cot, under a freshly aired blanket, between solid walls—he slept deeply. Yet in the hour just before dawn he was awakened. He heard a woman's voice loudly whispering his name over and over right up against his ear, though he felt no breath. When he opened his eyes he saw standing by him in the moonlight a thin woman. She was chalk-white and wrapped in a colorless cloak. As the only illumination was that of the moon, at first he thought the appearance of the woman's face must be a trick of the shadows. Yet her face was not in shadow but in full moonlight. It was smooth and pure white and all its features appeared to have been washed away, like a pebble worn smooth in a river. There were no eyes, no nose, not even a slit that could pass for a mouth.

Hsi-wei started up.

"Don't be frightened," said the woman in that unnaturally loud whisper. "I'm not here to do you any harm, Hsi-wei."

The woman was not close to him yet he could hear her whisper plainly; she spoke so clearly and yet she had no mouth. "You must be a ghost," he mumbled fearfully.

"You are a poet, Hsi-wei. The time will come when your poems will be known everywhere. But you are also a peasant, not from the lordly class."

"Hardly famous nor likely to be, but, yes, I'm certainly a peasant."

"Then you know what we suffer, affronts that are never written down, crimes that are never avenged, injustices never made good."

"Yes."

"Listen to me. I come from the village of Xin Cai Cheng in the province of Chiennan. All of us were loyal to the Duke of Daxing, our lawful ruler. He treated us justly, even after he was raised to be Duke of Sui and Regent. Maybe our loyalty to him is the reason, if there was any reason at all, why three months ago the rebel General Yuchi Jiong and his men attacked our village. They killed all our men at once, and every boy, even the babies. My husband, my son—both of them were dead before

I could grasp what was happening. Then that terrible Yuchi, armed all in black, joked that the loss should be made good. He ordered his men to rape us, even the youngest girls. I fought my way to him and begged on my knees for mercy. For this I was, by the General's command, twice raped, stabbed four times, and thrown down the village well."

"That is horrible, horrible."

"I haunted Yuchi Jiong for two months. I came to him at night but he was so drunk I could hardly wake him, even when I shrieked. So I frightened his wives and concubines until they all begged him to let them to leave. 'Good riddance,' he said. 'I've been hankering for fresh meat anyway.' I scared a servant carrying an oil lamp so that she would drop it and set fire to Yuchi's tent, but the guards quickly doused the flames. And so I've come to you, Hsi-wei."

"I don't understand."

"I want you to write my story. To make it into a poem. I want it to be read everywhere. I want everybody to know what this Yuchi did and what he is. I ask this as a favor, a favor a live peasant can do for a dead one. For many, many dead ones."

The faceless woman didn't wait for Hsi-wei to reply. She simply vanished.

When he woke in the morning, Hsi-wei felt troubled but convinced himself the visit from the faceless woman was simply a bad dream. He washed his face, went to the village well, set up his sign, took a dozen orders, purchased two *dou* of straw on credit, then returned to the inn to begin making sandals.

The innkeeper brought him some food and asked to sit with him. He had thought of more questions to ask about the Buddha. And so the evening passed, with Hsi-wei working and chatting with his landlord. Then, having completed six pairs of sandals, he retired to his room.

In the middle of the night the ghost returned.

"Hsi-wei. Hsi-wei, wake up. Wake up!" It was the same loud,

uncanny whisper which seemed to come from beside his ear. "Hsi-wei, will you do it?"

When Hsi-wei paid up and said farewell to Chung, he handed the innkeeper a copy of the "Letter" with the request that he lay it on the red sideboard by the Buddha's statue. Then he took up his pack and headed up the highway. At each village he left behind not only new straw sandals but a copy of the "Letter." Hsi-wei knew that the illiterate peasants would not be able to read what he had written but hoped that educated travelers—clerks, assistant governors, deputy ministers, merchants—would see it and might even read it out to the villagers. Above all, he hoped that eventually one or another would see that it reached its exalted addressee, the Duke of Daxing and Sui, the Regent Yang Jiang. In this manner, as he went on his way, Hsi-wei spread seeds of outrage in obedience to the bidding of the faceless woman.

Tales of atrocity were, alas, hardly uncommon in those days; but there is a difference between vaporous rumors and hard verses. At its best, poetry is language made unforgettable, untouched by time as gold is by fire. The "Letter" spread. More copies were made by unknown hands in distant towns and before long it became known throughout Northern Zhou. At last, his First Minister presented a copy to Yang Jiang himself, along with the news that the peasants were demanding that this Yuchi Jiong be punished. "Here in the capital, Lord," said the minister boldly, "we've considered the activities of this renegade a minor annoyance, but I can assure you that in the countryside your loyal people are speaking of little else."

The Duke read Hsi-wei's poem and nodded.

"My loyal people," he said. "Loyalty is a spoon with two handles. Very well. The peasants are right. It's high time we dealt with this man."

Yang Jiang chose to lead his troops himself, wanting to be seen at their head. He pursued Yuchi for a month before catching up with him in Iwu, a place three days' march from Chiangling. At the sight of the Regent's pennants and his cavalry, Yuchi's army dissolved. He himself fled with a few henchmen in the direction of the T'ien mountains. The Duke sent a detachment of horsemen in pursuit. At each village and hamlet, the horsemen inquired about the rebel and those who had seen him were quick to tell what road he had taken.

When the detachment galloped into the small village of Hofei, the captain made his usual inquiry about Yuchi Jiong. This time the peasants were silent. Then a burly fellow strode up to the captain and unrolled before him a copy of Hsi-wei's "Letter." Trailed by the entire population of the village, he conducted the soldiers to an abandoned well.

Pointing into the well he said simply, "There."

A Letter from the Humble Chen Hsi-wei to the Most Honorable Yang Jian, Duke of Daxing and Sui, General of the Army, Regent of Northern Zhou

Like famished tigers on stunned sheep,
the fires leap at the roofs of parched thatch,
his soldiers on the defenseless peasants.
Yuchi Jiong raises himself in his stirrups
and surveys the scene, a black oak amid scorched walls,
broken bamboo, crushed cabbages, slain oxen, dead men.
The chests of Yuchi's pike men heave, their faces are
black with ash and sweat. Slaughter is hard work,
but they carry out Yuchi's pitiless command.
"To make widows is good, men," shouts the general
from his high horse, "but the place needs peopling.
It's only fair that you make mothers too."
Mixing with the shrieks of dying pigs and fleeing geese,
the soldiers roar, break ranks, drag out women and girls.
One new widow fights off bloody hands, ceases keening
over her slashed husband and lifeless son;
she rushes at the general in his black armor,

throws herself in the dust before his horse's hoofs.
"Lord, spare the girls at least. Surely it's enough
to have made us destitute orphans and widows."
Yuchi Jiong looks down on her with contempt.
"What presumption!" he growls and motions to two guards.
"Rape the bitch then toss her down that well."
Thus did the rebel Yuchi Jiong deal with the loyal
village of Xin Cai Cheng in the province of Chiennan.

Hsi-wei's Justice

Though Emperor Wen had reunited the Northern and Southern Kingdoms and brought an end to years of ruinous war, even he could do nothing to improve the weather.

That April the province of Hotung was muddy and much of it flooded. People huddled inside waiting for the sun to come out, but storm followed storm so that planting was delayed. It was during one of these cloudbursts that Chen Hsi-wei trudged into the village of Kuyuan just after dark.

The previous week he had been in the provincial capital of Loyang. During almost four years on the road he had kept to the countryside, living among the peasants, reminding himself daily that, his education, time at court, and poems notwithstanding, a peasant is what he was too. To support himself he made straw sandals and, along the way, wrote his poems.

In Loyang, Hsi-wei learned something that surprised him and about which he felt ambivalent. He discovered that his name was known, and not as it had been in the capital, as that of an upstart who got himself an education and had the audacity to compose verses.

On arriving in Loyang, Hsi-wei had gone into a ramshackle tavern incongruously calling itself The Inn of Divine Pleasures where he hoped to find a place to sleep. While he waited for the innkeeper, a large, boisterous man dressed in a formal robe burst in, a regular to judge by the way he was greeted by the other customers. He turned out to be a third minister who liked slumming to get away from both work and home. He noticed the young stranger sitting patiently in the corner straightaway.

"Ho! I see we have a traveler," he said, looking Hsi-wei up and down, "and by the look of him he rides the two-legged horse."

The man pointed to a low stool. "Bring that over here, young fellow. I'll buy you some wine and you can tell me all about where you've been."

Hsi-wei moved the stool next to the man and considered his appearance at closer range. He looked like those old women whose faces turn round and whose skin stretches tighter as they age. It was a genial countenance, though the small eyes were shrewd. The man emptied his cup as quickly as a bargeman and introduced himself as Third Minister Kwan.

"The country around here's plagued with brigands and robbers," said Kwan. "Happen to come across any of them? First Minister would be obliged for any useful information."

Hsi-wei said he had been fortunate in that respect, or perhaps he was merely too poor to be of interest to robbers.

"Lucky indeed," said Kwan and slapped Hsi-wei on the back. "You wouldn't be one yourself, would you?" Then he laughed, so Hsi-wei did as well.

"I've told you my name. What's yours?"

"Chen Hsi-wei."

"What? Chen Hsi-wei?"

"Yes."

"Well, there's a coincidence. Do you know you've got the same name as this poet everybody's been talking about? Don't suppose you've ever heard of a poem called 'Yellow Moon at Lake Weishan'?"

Hsi-wei was astounded. "You know my poem?"

Nothing would do but that Hsi-wei should be a guest at Kwan's villa and that the author of "Yellow Moon" be presented to the First Minister the next morning.

The First Minister appeared to be quite thrilled. It wasn't that he himself was crazy about poetry, he explained, but his wife was an aficionado and was quite taken with those verses of the peasant-poet that had made their way from the capital into Ho-tung.

"She likes 'Yellow Moon' but I prefer 'My Skull.' More adventures, more manly."

So Hsi-wei had enjoyed two days and two nights of luxury and adulation in Loyang. On the second night, a banquet was given by the First Minister so that wife could show the poet off to the richest and most important people in the town. Hsi-wei was reminded of those dinners he had endured in the capital after his teacher Shen Kuo began to boast of having turned a peasant into a poet and circulated his early efforts. Still, there was a difference. In Loyang there was no condescension or at least not much, and sharper questions about his poems. Nevertheless, just because everything was so pleasant and his bed was so soft and his clothes so dry, the food so toothsome and the compliments so flattering, Hsi-wei itched to get back on the road and into the countryside, sodden as it was. *I suppose*, he said to himself with amusement, *I'm not comfortable being comfortable*.

"At least wait until these terrible rains end," said Kwan when Hsi-wei announced his intention of leaving.

"Yes, do stay a little longer," begged Mrs. Kwan.

But with many bows and fulsome thanks, Hsi-wei took his leave. On departing, he gave the Kwans two pairs of straw sandals and a copy of "Yellow Moon at Lake Weishan" in his own hand.

Hsi-wei knew nothing of Kuyuan or even that Kuyuan was the place he'd stumbled into. He was unaware that it was the chief town of the district and could boast of five taverns, two inns, and half-a-dozen elegant villas. In the murk and rain, the town appeared to him a mere hamlet, as small and dark as the inside of a child's fist. In fact, he had fetched up not in the town proper but a farmstead on its outskirts. He was weary, wet through and, seeing a light inside the low dwelling, decided to try his luck.

The man who answered his knock was about Hsi-wei's own age, closer to thirty than twenty, sturdy and smiling.

The poet asked his usual questions. "Would you have any space for me? A corner will do, or perhaps you have a stable?" Recalling the coin purse the First Minister had pressed on him in Loyang, he added, "I can pay."

"Come in, come in. It's a wet night," said the peasant with an easy courtesy that Hsi-wei rarely encountered. "We're just sitting down to eat. We'd be honored if you'd consent to join us," and he took a step back to make way for his dripping guest and his soaking pack.

Hsi-wei bowed. "Many thanks. My name is Chen Hsi-wei."

"You're welcome, Mr. Chen. I'm Shin Liang." The peasant bowed slightly then nodded his head toward a young woman by the hearth. "My wife, Mingmei, and our son, Tung," he said with a chuckle.

Mingmei put her hand to her mouth. She laughed too, and her laugh sounded like a silver bell. Then she touched her hand to her stomach and said, "It could be our daughter Bao." Bowing to Hsi-wei, she said, "Off with those wet things, Mr. Chen. Liang—don't you have some spare clothing for our guest?"

"Yes, yes. Of course, of course."

The meal of rice and vegetables was hot and well-seasoned. It tasted good to Hsi-wei who was thinking that he felt more at home with the Shins, who had no idea who he was, than he had with the Kwans, who did. Yet this was hardly surprising. Though writing poems exhilarated Hsi-wei, it was always a relief when the peasant put aside the poet.

"Are you on your way to visit relatives?" asked Mingmei courteously.

"Alas, no."

"Business then?" said Liang.

"Not that either."

The Shins exchanged a puzzled glance.

Hsi-wei smiled. "There's no mystery. I'm simply traveling."

"Not going anywhere?"

"Maybe everywhere."

"But it's not safe," said Mingmei seriously.

"That's true," added her husband. "Only last week Fen was attacked on the road from Loyang."

"Then I'm a lucky man. I've just come the same way."

The Shins asked about the city, which they had never visited. Perhaps they really were curious, but Hsi-wei felt they were only being polite.

"Loyang's a fine town. The main streets have stone paving and there are many splendid villas, too. But there are also rough neighborhoods and these take up most of the town. It's the same as elsewhere—the poor outnumber the rich."

"That's so," sighed Liang.

"The rich are powerful and not always fair,' said Mingmei with some heat.

"Look," said Hsi-wei, fishing the coin purse from his damp pack. He had already decided to give them all his money. "I can see you're troubled. Your generosity is obvious but, as I said, I insist on paying. Perhaps this will help."

"No, no," said Liang, refusing the purse.

"Then put the money aside. For Tung…or Bao."

"Money isn't our problem, Mr. Chen," said Mingmei looking at the floor. "At least not yet."

"Ah, so there *is* a problem."

"Nothing to worry our honored guest."

"Too late for that," said Hsi-wei. "Please tell me."

Liang explained. "The land here is good and this house is solid. We rent from Assessor Lai, the most important man in Kuyuan."

"In the whole district," added Mingmei.

"The rent is a little high but in the four years we've been here we've never been late in paying."

"Assessor Lai himself has twice visited," said Mingmei with some pride, "and had nothing but praise for how we've cared for his property. We've even made improvements."

"We've extended the house and given the shed a new roof,"

said Liang. "But," he continued, "a week ago one of the Assessor's servants showed up with a message from his master. He said we're to be out of here by the end of the month."

"But why?"

Mingmei answered. "Everybody knows it's because the wife of Assessor Lai has nagged him into giving our place to her useless nephew. That's the long and the short of it."

Liang wanted to be fair. "I don't think Assessor Lai is a bad man. Only he is sometimes ruled by his wife." He smiled at Mingmei, to show he did not mean to disparage the influence of *all* wives, just one.

Hsi-wei noted that Mingmei's tone was bitter while Liang sounded defeated. "This is most unfortunate," he said. "It isn't right. I'd like to think about it a little. If you'll allow me to stay a day or two, tomorrow I'll buy some straw and make sandals; I think better while I work. Perhaps I can come up with something that will help."

The Shins were too courteous to point out that an itinerant maker of straw sandals was unlikely to be able to resolve their difficulty with the Assessor. Instead, they made up a bed for Hsi-wei and told him he was welcome to stay as long as he liked.

"Until the end of the month anyway," Mingmei added, anxiously caressing her stomach.

The next morning's weather was gloriously fair. Hsi-wei followed his usual procedure; he walked into the center of town and set up to take orders for straw sandals. Once he knew how much would be needed, he would buy straw, always plentiful and cheap. What was not customary was that he should proclaim the sale not only of sandals but of poems. The peasants in the market square found this funny. They certainly knew what poems were—indeed, no one could recite verses from memory with more feeling than a peasant—but they were, of course, illiterate. For them, poetry was an oral art; the poems they knew they had learned by heart as children.

Hsi-wei, normally shy, soft-spoken, and secretive about his

writing, shouted out: *New straw sandals! New poems! Fresh footwear and verses! All orders quickly filled!* People gathered around, some to order sandals, as their old ones had been ruined by all the rain, but more to make fun of the cobbler who was trying to sell them poems.

"Do these poems cost more or less than the paper they're written on?"

"Chiang here's too embarrassed to ask, but he wants to know if you've got any poems that cure sciatica and impotence."

Hsi-wei played along. A scene was what he was after and, before long, he got what he wanted. Two young men in formal robes were attracted by the crowd and the noisy laughter. They pushed their way to the front and demanded to know what was going on.

"This fellow's offering us two buckets, only one of which has handles," said a droll peasant.

"How's that?" asked one of the officials.

Another explained. "He's selling sandals, which can use, and poems, which we can't."

"Poems?"

"Yes, sir. And he's a sandal-maker!"

The two officials stepped up to Hsi-wei.

"You've got books of poems?"

"No, sir," said Hsi-wei. "Only sheets of paper. The poems written on them are my own."

"Let's have a look at one."

Hsi-wei, thinking of his recent experience in Loyang, handed the official a copy of "Yellow Moon at Lake Weishan."

The man began to read:

Weishan lies cool and still as a forgotten bowl of tea,
the moon immobile as a yellow disk embroidered
on a gown of black silk heavy with pearls...

The man laughed and turned to his companion. "But this is 'Yellow Moon at Lake Weishan'!"

"Yes, sir," said Hsi-wei.

The pair of officials exchanged a few words then turned to Hsi-wei. "Are you claiming to be Chen Hsi-wei?"

"Yes, sir. I am Chen Hsi-wei."

One of the men threw Hsi-wei a couple of coins and went off with the poem.

Within an hour they were back with an imposing middle-aged man in a yellow silk robe and high black hat. Everybody made way for him.

"I am Assessor Lai," the man announced to Hsi-wei, who made a respectful bow. He considered asking the grandee if he would care to order a pair of straw sandals then thought better of it. This was no time for offensive jokes.

"A great honor, Assessor Lai."

"Can you prove you're the poet Chen Hsi-wei?"

"I don't suppose it would be easy to do, sir. You might send for the First Minister in Loyang. I was his guest at dinner last week."

"The First Minister?"

"Or Third Minister Kwan. I had the honor of spending two nights at his villa."

The Assessor seemed nonplussed. "Describe them," he demanded.

This Hsi-wei did in detail, and, for good measure, their villas, and then their wives as well.

"Your poems are becoming well known, Chen. People are talking about them. If what I've heard is true, you performed a service to the state and the reward was an education. They say you lived for some years in the capital."

"Yes, all that's true."

"So why are you traveling around making straw sandals?"

"Ah, how can I explain? Someone of your station, sir, is justly considered an educated man. I, on the other hand, will never be more than a peasant with an education."

It was really this clever reply that convinced Assessor Lai that Hsi-wei was truly who he was. *I can hardly do less than the First*

33

Minister in Loyang, he thought, and insisted that Hsi-wei be his guest during his stay in Kuyuan.

"I'm overwhelmed by your kindness, sir, but I already have comfortable lodgings for my brief sojourn."

"Very well. But you must come to dinner. I insist. The gentry will be curious; they'll want to meet you. My wife in particular."

Hsi-wei appeared to have compunctions. He pinched the sleeve of his jerkin. "I'm afraid I lack proper attire."

Assessor Lai waved off this objection. "Suitable clothing will be provided." He drew a servant to him. "I have pressing business now. Just tell this fellow where to deliver your robe. He will be bringing it and conduct you to my residence—let's say at sundown. Is that agreeable, Chen?"

Hsi-wei bowed, as if giving in reluctantly.

There were eight guests at the banquet in addition to Hsi-wei. Assessor Lai's wife, Pang, quickly found a way to inform him that she was a daughter of the Suo family. Even allowing for how the Shins' story might have prejudiced him, Hsi-wei found the woman unprepossessing. He had seen her like in the capital, women of the Hundred Families who insisted on two things: being the center of attention and having their own way. They typically overestimated the worth of a family name and underestimated actual achievement. Hsi-wei guessed that, in her view, Mrs. Lai outranked her husband.

Lai Pang looked at him dubiously but not, he sensed, because she questioned his identity. Rather it was because she was torn between entertaining what passed in Kuyuan for a luminary and the exasperating fact that this celebrity was a peasant.

"Mr. Chen," she said with formality, "welcome to our home. I have invited a few of the most distinguished members of our little community. They would like to meet you. I hope you don't mind?"

Hsi-wei bowed low, ill-at-ease in the stiff, too-large silk robe. He tried to appear as obsequious as Mrs. Lai doubtless expected him to be. "A great honor," he mumbled.

At dinner he was seated between the Lais. People asked for details of his dangerous trip to the South during the wars, made famous by his poem on the subject, when he had carried the important message to General Fu inscribed on his scalp.

"Is the message still there?" one woman wished to know.

"I suppose it is, My Lady," replied Hsi-wei. "However, you should have to shave off my hair to be entirely certain."

This elicited general amusement.

"How did you come to write your first poem?" asked Mrs. Lai, less from curiosity than to demonstrate her superiority by posing a serious question.

"That is no easy matter to explain," said Hsi-wei to his hostess. "Late one night I was doing the copying my master assigned me to improve my wretched calligraphy. I had to write out one of the *Eulogies of Shang* from the *Shih Ching*. When I finished the piece I found myself still writing, writing something new, almost as if I had become one of the ancients. It was a very peculiar feeling."

"Do you find writing poetry difficult?" asked Assessor Lai. "I could never manage it myself."

"Sir, on my travels I encounter many people. One day, I met a skilled carpenter, a man much admired for his tables, and I asked him the same question. 'Is it difficult for you to make your tables?' The carpenter reflected for a moment then answered that he would be pleased if people said of his work that it was easy for him but, at the same time, that it was terribly difficult."

After a moment of bewilderment, the Assessor laughed. Then everybody else did the same.

A carefully made-up woman of a certain age with lively eyes, one not concerned to appear serious or particularly interested in poetry, asked just the question Hsi-wei had been hoping to be asked.

"Mr. Chen, I understand you visited with the First Minister in Loyang last week."

"That is so, my Lady."

"Poetry is well enough, but I wonder: did you hear any good stories in the capital?"

"Stories?"

"You know. What people there are talking about."

Assessor Lai drew smiles from his guests when he leaned toward Hsi-wei and said in a loud whisper, "*She means gossip.*"

"Well, as a matter of fact, there was a story. People at the First Minister's banquet had a lot to say about it, too. Apparently, it's the talk of the Court, a scandal."

At the word *scandal*, everybody came to attention the way students do when the master says *for example*.

"A scandal?"

"I suppose so. It has to do with the Duke of Shan, a noble from far in the South, and his wife."

"Never heard of him," sniffed Mrs. Lai.

"Oh, do tell us the story."

"Yes, what happened?"

The table fell silent, expectant, already pleased. Hsi-wei paused, then began the story.

"The Duke of Shan had a retainer, Quon Ju-yi, who was married to a beautiful woman named Niu. This Quon was universally respected as a brave and loyal warrior, scrupulously honest, and learned beyond his station—in short, an excellent man. By his merits, he rose in the Duke's service until he was put in charge of the cavalry—the men and their pay, the horses and their provender, all their equipment, plus the maintenance of the barracks and stables. Quon carried out his duties punctiliously and the Duke was well pleased with him."

"What about the scandal?"

"Be patient. Didn't he say Quon's wife was beautiful?"

"It seems the Duke's chief wife, whose family traced themselves all the way back to the Sung dynasty, had a nephew. This nephew was a useless fellow given to dissipations of all sorts. He had fallen into debt because of his free spending and gambling. The Duke's wife was determined that her nephew should have Quon's job. Her husband, who knew nothing of this nephew's character, nevertheless resisted, arguing that it would be unjust to remove the worthy Quon, even for a relative. But his wife persisted, ceaselessly nagging the Duke, pointing out the superiority of her family to his, reminding him of the size of her dowry, and bursting into tears. Finally, she accused him of carrying on a liaison with Quon's young wife. The Duke protested that this was not true, but his wife said she would believe him only if he sent Quon away and replaced him with her nephew, whose invented virtues she praised to the skies. In the end, to restore peace to his household, the Duke gave in and did as his wife insisted. He sent Quon away and replaced him with the nephew."

"That was unwise," said one of the men judiciously.

"I'll bet his wife was jealous of that good-looking Niu," one of the ladies commented with relish.

Hsi-wei resumed. "Perhaps you can guess what happened next. Not only did the nephew make a mess of his duties, but he embezzled as well. He stole from the soldiers' pay, sold the horses' fodder and even some of the horses. He also failed to maintain the stables and barracks, then he bribed the Duke's accountants to keep it all from their Master. In the end, of course, everything came out. The Duke was furious. He banished the nephew and put his first wife into the apartment of his lowest concubine whom he then married and put in her place."

Hsi-wei could feel Lai Pang becoming angry as he told this tale; her body seemed to give off heat. From the corner of his eye, he saw his host's hands clench into fists. The rest of the company, however, was delighted with his story and discussed it with gusto for nearly an hour after which the party broke up.

As he took his leave, Assessor Lai and his wife looked at Hsi-wei with uncertain frowns which he affected not to notice. After many profound bows accompanied by expressions of gratitude and admiration for the meal, the house, and the distinguished company, he promised to return the silk robe first thing in the morning.

"One thing, Mr. Chen," said the Assessor.

"Yes, sir?"

"Where is it that you're staying?"

"I have the honor to be accommodated by a most worthy family. Perhaps you know them? The Shins?"

Early the next morning, Hsi-wei made his way to the Assessor's residence. His knocking was answered by the same servant who had guided him the previous evening who said that his master Lai Zhong was already out and his mistress not yet up and dressed. Hsi-wei handed over the robe, neatly folded, brushed, and pressed by Mrs. Shin, and also a small bundle wrapped in burlap.

"I would be obliged if you could see that your Master receives this package."

"Certainly, sir."

The bundle contained two pairs of straw sandals and two sheets of paper. On one he had written a new poem; the other was a note to the Assessor and his wife:

Honored Sir and Madam,
I do not often have cause to regret my poverty but today is one
of those occasions. There is little I can give you in recompense for
your great kindness to me and what I have to offer is poor indeed:
merely these two pairs of sandals and a poem. The sandals I made
yesterday afternoon, the poem late last night. I beg you to accept
these unworthy gifts with my thanks. I shall be leaving Kuyuan at
sunrise tomorrow and will always cherish the memory of your generous
hospitality.
Chen Hsi-wei

The remainder of the day Hsi-wei spent completing the last three pairs of sandals and, with the aid of a local boy, delivering all the orders he had received. So, he was not at the Shins when Assessor Lai came in person to apologize and withdraw his eviction order.

The poem Hsi-wei wrote for Lai Zhong and his wife Pang is the one that has become known as "Justice":

Lord Zhang Siyu paced grumpily until
his second wife set things right with
no more than a small adjustment to his sash.

Meiling waited until her brother got up
to pee then moved her toy duck
to the right side of her yellow pillow.

Wu's mother-in-law looked at what her son's
new wife had done: nothing in its proper place.
Uncomplaining, she put all the pots to rights.

The world's a wavering rope-walker whose
apparent stability is really the ceaseless
setting right of countless imbalances.

Hsi-wei's Grandfather

One summer afternoon my grandfather took my hand and walked me all the way to the Pavilion of the Five Virtues. I couldn't have been more than five years old at the time. Did he speak to me about the five virtues? I expect he did. To lecture on obedience, courage, humility, thrift, and honesty was the usual purpose of bringing children to the Pavilion. My grandfather was a lean, strong man, a real soldier who always stood erect, who marched rather than walked. I was rather frightened of him.

As we stood outside the pavilion, he pointed up. "Hsi-wei, look at those clouds. Clouds are the sky's thoughts. When it is thinking of joyful things, you see clouds like these, billowing white ones shaped like morsels of laughter. But on other days the sky is, as people say, of two minds. That is what it means when you see clouds that are white but also others that are gray. When the sky is grieving you see rainclouds. When it is recalling something that makes it angry the sky fills with thunderheads.

"What would you say the sky is thinking today, Hsi-wei?"

I was a little boy. I said I didn't know.

"Well," said my grandfather pensively, "to me the sky today looks sad, as if its mind were brimming over with shameful memories and bitter thoughts."

"Bitter thoughts? What are bitter thoughts, Grandfather?"

"Thoughts the sky would prefer to drive away with sunlight."

That was the day my grandfather taught me to look at clouds.

In my ninth year Grandfather became anxious that the war threatened our province. He decided that we should go north and take refuge at an inn where he was well known. I remember my mother crying when we left our house, how she touched the objects we left behind, especially the humblest, her pots and kitchen utensils. The inn was hard by Shulin-Lan, the Blue Forest. As it happened, the fighting veered to the south and we only stayed a week. While we were there my grandfather, who now seemed to me a little less formidable and slightly more affectionate, asked me to accompany him on a walk through the forest. Shulin-Lan was thick with beeches, just the kind of trees that invited a boy to climb them; but, of course, it was most famous then as now for its pines.

As we walked my grandfather spoke a little about the war—or, rather, he spoke of war in general. He called it the worst of all catastrophes. "Floods and earthquakes kill thousands, but they don't degrade people. War disgraces the victors no less than the defeated—usually more."

It surprised me to hear my grandfather speak this way. I had thought him proud of his service and his general's many victories. I had yearned to ask him about his experiences; now I sought an explanation for his words. I wanted to hear about the battles in which he had fought, how he had become a hero, what he had done to be rewarded with a fine red house and rich flat land, why he was so respected by the proprietor of the inn where we were staying and feared by its servants. But, when I looked at his rigid figure and stern face, my courage failed me.

"Look at these pines, Hsi-wei," he said suddenly.

I looked. Before us was a stand of colossal trees, trunks thick as three men. Reaching higher than a pagoda with five eaves, their tops dissolved in mist. The ground beneath them was soft with brown needles, punctuated with huge cones.

"A tree must battle its way through dirt and rock toward light. Even the meanest sapling has to be ambitious. The ones who fare best steal water and light from the less determined. These tall pines are simply the most merciless. Notice how no other trees grow beneath them."

"Is it the same in war, Grandfather?" I ventured to ask.

He took a step away from me. "It's time to turn back, Hsi-wei," he said. "Your mother will be worrying about you."

It was my eleventh winter. Grandfather had been losing weight all year long and now his skin hung sallow and loose on his bones. He no longer stood with legs wide apart, fists on hips, surveying the household like a commander reviewing a regiment. His face was contorted with pain, and he seemed to me full of anxiety. I could now easily lift his sword which, as a child, I had longed to wield. Now I could heft it and he could not.

He lay on a couch by the window most of the day. I would sit with him for hours. He was the first to hear my earliest verses and, in his way, he encouraged me. "That's not entirely terrible, Hsi-wei. Keep it up and you might become a real poet and starve in exile."

He grew weaker daily. Mother took to speaking in hushed tones. Father drew me aside and told me to prepare myself.

The winter deepened. Grandfather's hands and feet were always cold.

One afternoon I came in from the shed and saw that he was shivering on his couch, even though the fire had been built up and the room was intolerably close. I pulled the thick blanket aside and lay down beside him. I took his icy hands in my own.

"Look," he said. "Look at the snow, Hsi-wei."

I raised my head to peer out the window. It was true; snowflakes had begun to fall and were coming down faster every second. The air was so still they plummeted, like silver coins.

"Is the snow covering up the sty, the midden?" breathed Grandfather.

"Yes," I said, squeezing his hands more tightly in my desperation to put into them the warmth of my own.

"The snow will cover up the mud," he mumbled weakly, "the privy, the manure."

I could feel him dying. His eyes were closed and the face that for months had been so full of anguish and regret began to relax. "Snow is the sky's purest offering, oblivion," he whispered in my ear. His breath fell on my cheek as softly as a butterfly. "For at least a little while it will bury all that one has done wrong. It is beautiful, Hsi-wei, the snow. Beautiful to forget everything… be forgotten."

After he died we laid him out and began the funeral rituals. All of us bowed to say our farewells. Only I dared to touch him. He was cold but his hair was warm. Even today I can feel the warmth of my grandfather's hair.

Hsi-wei and the Tale of the Duke of Shun

What follows is an explanation of a recently discovered poem-letter dating from the Sui period. It was sent by the poet Chen Hsi-wei to a friend he made in the vicinity of Hsuan, Ko Qing-zhao, thought to be a painter of pastoral scenes. To understand Hsi-wei's text requires some knowledge of the nearly forgotten figure of Chang Yan-lu.

No one can be certain about the truth of the ancient tale of how Chang Yan-lu became the Duke of Shun. Without faith in its veracity a story will be judged less as history than as a made-up tale: is it credible? faithful to human nature? does it make me think or wonder; above all, is it both pleasing and significant? Of course, everyone must decide such questions for himself. However, if the story of Yan-lu were not pleasing it would long ago have been lost to our people's imperfect, albeit long, memory whereas, in fact, it has been retold many times and over many centuries. Proof that it is a meaningful story is that it has given rise to disputes and has even been the cause of bitter feuds. That is why it is held to be a dangerous story, not to be told to young children. Surely a story that is both inflammatory and often repeated ought to be granted some merit, whether it is true or not.

According to most sources, Chang Yang-lu's father was a petty landowner in Zhou, holding the rank of count, second class. His land lay in the north and, while extensive, was arid and unproductive. Yang-lu was a second son. Though the title and land had to go to his brother everyone acknowledged Yang-lu's superiority, even his brother. The boy was well-built, athletic, quick with numbers, a precocious apt pupil who produced elegant calligraphy. He excelled at all martial exercises and games of strategy; he was able to speak easily with either a peasant or a scholar, and to impress both. Despite all these gifts, he aroused affection more often than jealousy.

Yan-lu's mother had a cousin in the capital who had attained the rank of a third minister. Through him, a place was arranged for Yang-lu at court. With tears being shed on all sides, he was sent off to the capital at the age of fourteen.

Yan-lu was politely received by his mother's cousin, welcomed warmly by his extensive family, and given a room in their villa. He was appointed as an assistant in the Ministry of Cloud Cavalry which, in addition to horses, had charge of food storage and road maintenance.

The boy quickly distinguished himself by adding up a *dan* of rice more rapidly and accurately than anyone else and by riding the most fractious horses with reckless grace. In short order, he was promoted.

According to one version of the story, Yan-lu was rewarded by his superiors with an invitation to join the gentry in the silver pavilion at the annual Lantern Festival. In the course of the evening, Yan-lu found himself standing near a group doing traditional riddles. A lady complained that the riddles were so traditional that they had grown stale.

With the audacity of his youth, Yan-lu spoke up. "Pardon me, My Lady, would you like me to ask you a new one?"

The lady was surprised but smiled. "What? Have you just made one up?"

Yan-lu bowed low. "Two, My Lady."

People gathered around, including the Cloud Cavalry Minister himself.

"Well, what's the first?" asked the lady, intrigued.

"What can turn everything around without moving itself?"

"What indeed?" asked the Lady with a giggle, glancing around at her friends who all shook their heads. "It appears we need a hint, if you please."

Yan-lu looked at the lady in her carefully coiffed hair and silk gown which was cut rather low. "It is something you see at least once every day."

"I've got it!" exclaimed the Minister. "It's a *mirror* and I assure you she sees it *twenty* times a day."

Everyone laughed except for the lady, who happened to be the Minister's first wife.

"Let's have the second riddle," said the Minister, who had enjoyed solving the first and discomfiting his haughty wife.

"Well, Your Excellency, try this: When I slap you, I slap me. And when I hit you, my blood flows. Who are *you?*"

The Minister's deputy, who seldom left his side, made a shocked face and grumbled. To speak to the Minister of slapping? Imagine! To his mind it was this impudent boy's blood that ought to flow.

But the Minister was not in the least offended. He requested that Yan-lu repeat the riddle and asked his deputy if he knew the answer. The deputy scowled and shook his head. Then the Minister asked his first wife if she knew, but she turned away and pretended not to have heard.

"Well, then, I give up. What's the answer?"

"A mosquito, Excellency."

"Ah, a *mosquito*. Of course. Splendid!"

The boy grew into a tall young man and his reputation rose with his stature.

One day the First Minister sent for Chang Yan-lu. The First Minister was a crafty man feared for his ruthlessness, high standards, and intelligence but esteemed for the same qualities. Yan-lu was conducted by two guards through courtyards he had never before seen and down a red-painted corridor to a wide and well-appointed inner chamber. On a dais sat the First Minister. Yan-lu at once put his forehead to the floor. The First Minister gestured to the guards to leave the room. Only after the doors were shut tight did he address Yan-lu.

"By all accounts you are a gifted and brave young man. I am informed you are now seventeen. Is that so?"

"Yes, Excellency. Seventeen."

"We have a challenging task for you. It will be difficult, but I ask it in the name of the Duke, to whom you have sworn allegiance."

The Minister explained that the recent death of the Duke of Shun had brought his young son to power. Shun was growing in strength and, with a new ruler of unknown temperament and ambition, might prove a problem. In short, the Minister had to consider the probability that Shun would attack Zhou in the near future.

"You will be provided with documents proving that the Duke has treated your family unjustly. You are to take these to Shun, declare that you detest Zhou, and beg to be taken into the service of the Duke of Shun, even in the lowliest capacity. We rely on you to distinguish yourself in Shun as you have here and so to attain a position giving you access to information that will be vital in the event of war."

For the sake of this plan, the Chang family did have their land confiscated by the state, though, after a few months of privation, they were given a smaller but more profitable estate in the south.

Yan-lu did as instructed and was taken into the service of the youthful Duke of Shun in which he rose quickly. After only three years, he was appointed third deputy to the Minister of the Green Jade Gate. This was approved by the First Minister, a kindly man who, during their interview, treated Yan-lu in a fatherly manner. In this new position, he accompanied the Duke, who was only two years his senior, on hunting forays and then on a punitive expedition to the western border. On the way to the frontier, the column was ambushed and, in the ensuing fight, Yan-lu saved the Duke's life. As a consequence, he became the Duke's favorite companion.

According to some versions of the story, shortly after this expedition Chang Yan-lu married while in others he remained single; however, all agree that he grew fond of the Duke and of the people of Shun. As for the young Duke's political objectives, he could find no indication of any aggressive intentions with regard to Zhou; quite the contrary, in fact.

Yet war did come.

Zhou's First Minister persuaded his Duke that Shun was a clear threat and the time had come to eliminate it by annexing their neighbor. With a man of their own in a position of confidence in the court of Shun, they could rely on having a decisive advantage.

A distant cousin of Yang-lu's father, a rural bureaucrat, was sent to Shun, ostensibly to visit him and give him news of his family. When they were alone, the cousin said, "I've been sent by the First Minister to deliver this" and drew from his robe a sealed scroll. "Don't ask me anything about it. I swore not to open it. All I know is that I am to take your reply back with me in the morning."

The scroll did not say that an attack was imminent; however, the questions it posed made the Minister's intentions clear enough. Shun would soon be attacked and without warning.

Yang-lu spent a terrible night, torn between two loyalties. He did not sleep and wrote nothing until dawn was breaking. When he did write, he wrote falsely.

The following day, after seeing the cousin safely off, he begged a private audience with the Duke and his First Minister. He told them the whole story, not leaving out his personal struggle.

The Duke was too furious to speak but the First Minister remained calm. "Why did you decide for us?" he asked.

"Three reasons," said Yan-lu. "First, because you are the more worthy. Second, because you are not the aggressor. Third, because I have come to know you."

The Minister suggested to the Duke that Yan-lu be given a commission in the cavalry and sent to the border with two generals to strengthen the defenses.

The fighting began within weeks. Yan-lu led his men so well that he was acknowledged as Shun's best field commander. After repulsing the initial onslaught, the army of Shun crossed into Zhou. Meanwhile, in the capital a treacherous official, bribed by Zhou's First Minister, poisoned the Duke of Shun and his First Minister as well. In the panic that followed, he declared himself ruler. He sent orders for the army to withdraw from Zhou and signed them as Duke of Shun.

Yan-lu met with the other officers and they resolved to ignore these orders. Instead, with Yan-lu at its head, the army swept across the plains of Zhou to the capital. When the troops reached the palace, they found it empty. Yan-lu drew up a proclamation to the effect that Shun and Zhou would henceforth be united for the benefit of both. The bulk of the army remained to pacify Zhou while Yan-lu, at the head of half the cavalry, wheeled around and made for the capital of Shun. News of his approach preceded his arrival. The Second Minister, who had gone into hiding, managed to organize loyalists among the guard who could foresee what would await them on the return of Yan-lu. And so, before Yan-lu and his horsemen arrived, the usurper had been arrested and beheaded. The late Duke of Shun had neither children nor brothers and so, instead of the desperate battle he expected, Yan-lu was asked by the remaining ministers to become Duke of the united Shun and Zhou.

From a position that had been precarious and divided, Yan-lu now unified his two countries in his own person. According to the most popular accounts his reign was progressive, prosperous, peaceful, and long. He was even-handed with all, favoring neither Shun nor Zhou. After his death many legends were told of his wisdom and the people gave him a new title. Putting their children to sleep mothers would whisper to them, "May the Duke of Good Dreams visit you tonight."

Four years after leaving the capital and taking up his vagabond life, fashioning straw sandals and poems, Chen Hsi-wei arrived in the city of Yun. He was recognized in the market as the young poet-peasant of whom people were talking and word was sent to the governor who invited him to a banquet that very night.

The feast was in honor of a far more celebrated visitor to Yun, the Court chronicler Fung Chu-li. At the reception before the meal, the Governor introduced the two, formally praising both. The older man looked Hsi-wei up and down, taking in his youth and the borrowed robe made of woven linen rather than silk. When he spoke he did so as rudely as he had scrutinized Hsi-wei.

"Forgive me, but I cannot share in our host's high opinion of you, young man. If I cannot think well of you, it is not only because you are a peasant," he went on, "it is still more because you are a poet. What irritates me about you poets is just what you brag of most—I mean your so-called imagination. While claiming to see the profound insides of things you ignore the exterior facts which, while they may appear too plain for you, are nonetheless true. History is solid rock; a poem is merely a mirage."

Hsi-wei did not respond to these insults. He simply smiled at the chronicler's using two metaphors, gave a bow, and moved to the other side of the room. However, over dinner, he did reply in his own way. One of the guests had raised the subject of loyalty and the chronicler spoke of Chang Yan-lu.

After clearing his throat, he spoke pompously. "When loyalties are divided they must always be resolved, for good or ill. I am reminded of the famous Duke of Shun. Though he died almost a thousand years ago his life remains the best account we have of such a dilemma being resolved in a happy fashion."

Hsi-wei, one of the few at the table who knew the story, spoke up. "Perhaps I am too ignorant and that is why I am uncertain about the Duke of Shun. But I have heard that people do not all see the story in the same way. Even where they agree on the facts—or that the facts *are* facts—they do not agree on their meaning."

The chronicler was not pleased by this turn in the conversation and decided to bully Hsi-wei.

"That is ridiculous. There is nothing to argue over, once the facts are known."

Hsi-wei replied, "Pardon my using a comparison that might be thought poetic, but it seems to me that facts, like peonies and lilies, can be arranged in various ways. Where one makes a bouquet meant for a young lady, another will weave a funeral wreath."

"Nonsense," said the chronicler at the same moment that the Governor said, "Go on."

"Well," said Hsi-wei, "when I was living in the capital, my tutor entertained several scholars. As it happens, they fell into arguing over the story of the Duke of Shun. One said the popular ending cannot be believed, as it is too neatly happy. The bad are punished, the good rewarded, and the two dukedoms are married like a prince and a princess at the end of a fairy tale. His view was that, having won the war, Shun oppressed Zhou, and the story was exactly the kind victors always like to give out. Another insisted the story was not about divided loyalties but betrayal. He pointed out that Yan-lu had sworn allegiance to the Duke of Zhou, legitimate ruler of his homeland. He shirked his duty and was the cause not only of his country's defeat but its disappearance. Nothing more damnable, he said, and added that he had more sympathy for the banished Duke of Zhou than the poisoned Duke of Shun. Another observed that both dukes came to disastrous ends. He said the story is actually about the evils of war which so often harms victors as well as vanquished. In his opinion, if Yan-lu was a hero at all, it was not because he won the war of Shun against Zhou but because he foreclosed the possibility of all future wars between them."

"Ah," said the Governor, "that's quite a range. And what was your master's opinion?"

"Well, Excellency, my master was not the most optimistic of men. He saw the story as one about high politics carried out by the all too customary methods of murder and treason. He argued that the character of Yan-lu may have had some historical source but was obviously an imaginary figure, invented to trick the people into believing that what is ugly and selfish is pretty and magnanimous."

The banquet came to an end shortly thereafter. As they were departing, Hsi-wei went up to the chronicler to say that it had been a great honor to meet him. Though Hsi-wei was sincere, Fung felt provoked. So he gave the poet yet another and still more passionate lecture on the supremacy of his profession.

And that is how Hsi-wei came to write the following:

Hsi-wei's Letter-Poem to Ko Qing-zhao

Just yesterday I encountered Fung Chuan-li, the renowned chronicler.
Pointing to a coffered ceiling he declared, "The present is fleeting,
not to be caught, and the future unknowable; but the past—the past is
as firmly set in place as iron spikes have made this roof beam."
I bowed courteously, a peasant thankful for this lesson on the
objectivity of truth. I did not wish to offend and so refrained
from remarking, "Beams burn. Surely you know some future
emperor is going to make a bonfire of your elegant chronicles.
The past, rewritten in a moving present, only appears still."

What is beyond dispute in the tale of Chang Yan-lu?
As it recedes, the past softens into poems up for interpreting.
Did Yan-lu make a good choice or a treacherous one?
Was he a hero to Shun, a villain to Zhou, the savior of both, or a
usurper loyal only to himself? The tale is so ancient one may ask
if there ever was a Yan-lu, or even a hostile Shun and Zhou.
Like snowstorms and heat waves, so many dynasties have blown
over Zhong guo, that it scarcely matters now. What counts
is that people like the story—and what they make of it.

The Sadness of Emperor Wen

In his fortieth year, Chen Hsi-wei's wanderings brought him to the town of Yemanrem Damen in the western province of Yangzhou. It was here that, almost miraculously, a letter from his old friend Ha Chan-jui reached him.

Yemanrem Damen was once little more than a rough outpost of the northern empire. As suggested by its name, Barbarians' Gate, it had endured frequent incursions and been the scene of many battles. Now, thanks to the peace imposed by Emperor Wen, it prospered; indeed, it had grown so large that it had its own governor.

When this official was informed that Chen Hsi-wei had arrived in his town, he ordered the poet be found and invited to his villa, courteously but firmly. The governor personally greeted Hsi-wei and insisted that he remain as a guest at the villa for as long as he chose. Knowing of the poet's eccentric mode of living, he added that, if he wished, Hsi-wei could go to the marketplace and solicit orders for straw sandals from the peasants. However, he could not tolerate the poet putting up in any rude accommodation in some mean inn or, worse yet, a stable. It would, he argued, be a blot on his honor, that of Yemanrem Damen and all Yangzhou.

Hsi-wei, no longer young, gave in with a good grace. Such honor had been offered to him increasingly in recent years. In the larger provincial towns, his name was more often known than not and he was received with a kind of deference, especially by the high-born. He was aware that the gentry esteemed poetry not so much because they really loved it as because they had been taught to do so by their Confucian tutors. Hsi-wei was uncomfortable with these welcomes. He was himself a peasant and understood very well the peasants' impatience with artistic refinements. Like them, he believed the wealthy overvalued things like poetry. Though writing was Hsi-wei's chief reason for living he felt it was a private compulsion and hardly meritorious. He did not make too much of his art because his reasons for writing were not altogether edifying. He wrote because when he did so he was never bored. He wrote to relieve his feelings. Some poems are like the inclined planks at the edges of ponds to drain the excess water. Hsi-wei often wrote because he couldn't help it. Then too he wrote because he admired the poets who had come before him. Writing was a way of paying them tribute and entering their company, albeit humbly, at the very back of the hall. Finally, he wrote because his old teacher, the strict Shen Kuo, had bragged about his early verses—just as a trainer will show off the tricks he has taught his dog.

Early on the morning after his arrival, Hsi-wei made his way to the town's marketplace, posted his sign, took orders for sandals, and bought straw. Then he returned to the governor's villa to set to work. A servant met him at the gate. She said, "Sir, His Honor wishes to see you at once."

The governor was waiting in the lobby.

"Hsi-wei, a courier from the capital arrived today with a packet of official dispatches. There were also a number of private letters. One of these is addressed to you."

Hsi-wei was astonished. "To me?"

"I've been told that you don't plan your travels, but did someone know you'd be here?"

"No, sir."

"Then it really is quite remarkable. But I've been thinking about the matter and it occurred to me that copies of this letter may have been given to many couriers in the hope that one might reach you—much as, if the story's true, several messengers with shaved heads were once sent to General Fu in the south."

"My Lord, do you know who sent me this letter?"

The Governor smiled and handed Hsi-wei a scroll tightly

wrapped with red silk ribbon. "The letter is from the Emperor's palace and it is under seal. Here, see for yourself."

Hsi-wei took the scroll and, excusing himself, took it to his bedchamber.

The letter was from Ha Chan-jui. More than twenty years before, he and Hsi-wei had both been students of Shen Kuo. Chan-jui was from an old aristocratic family but had nonetheless befriended the peasant boy who had made the famous trek to the south and then astonished the court by turning down all material rewards, begging instead to be educated. Now Chan-jui had risen to the rank of Third Minister.

The letter explained that for some time copies of Hsi-wei's verses had been arriving in the capital and had been received with general approval. "In fact," Chan-jui wrote, "you've become famous all over again, old friend." Chan-jui went on to tell Hsi-wei about his two wives, his seven children, and the sort of work he did. But most of the missive was an account of conditions in the capital and especially in the palace. "On the one hand, conditions here are excellent. You would not recognize the place; it has more than doubled in size. Charming new villas have been built, also gardens, pavilions, public parks, two new bridges. Our storehouses hold enough food to last fifty years. The government runs with an efficiency and honesty not seen for three hundred years."

And yet, despite all this, Chan-jui confided to his friend that he was uneasy. "The Emperor is not happy. The gossip is that he is beset by guilt and some nameless fear. People say that the Emperor is henpecked by his wife and that he is on bad terms with his sons. Death has claimed almost all his old companions and the rest have been driven off by his wife's jealousy and the machinations of his sons."

Chan-jui also explained something Hsi-wei had observed in his travels.

"The Emperor has turned away from the teachings of Confucius. In your travels you must have observed the new monasteries and Buddhist temples. These were erected at the Emperor's command and with his support. Out of faith, but also, I suspect, fear, he has now ordered something unprecedented. A series of religious observances are to be held throughout the Empire to mark his next birthday. With his own hands the Emperor has sealed holy relics in a hundred jars. These are to be carried into every province by the most distinguished monks. On the day, they are to be enshrined in the new temples according to a ceremony devised by the Emperor himself. What people say is that, by this extraordinary act of public piety, he hopes to relieve his apprehensions and guilt, and to lay up a vast store of karma to see him through the lives he has yet to endure. Let us pray for that fortunate consequence."

Chan-jui's letter affected Hsi-wei deeply.

The Governor sent for him. "So, Hsi-wei, what was in the letter?"

Remembering his friend's seal, and understanding that discretion was called for, the poet gave his host the most cursory account of its contents. Pleading indisposition, he politely declined the governor's invitation to share the family's meal, withdrew to his room, and lay down. When a serving girl looked in, he begged her not to light the lamps. The letter had taken away his appetite for both food and work. He lay in the gathering dusk recalling his adventures in the south, the humiliations of his education, his strange life in the capital, the good and bad people had known there, and finally, with a sorrow that pierced no less deeply for all the years that had passed, he thought of the Lady Tian Miao.

It was lucky, the poet reflected, that Chan-jui did not know that story or he might have written of her marriage to Hu Zhi-peng, the number of children she had borne him, whether her beauty had faded. But mostly he thought of the Emperor Wen, his impatient, scheming sons and jealous wife, and of the desperation that had led him to this fantastic birthday plan.

Whether the melancholy that stole over him was his own or

the Emperor's Hsi-wei couldn't say; however, his sadness grew darker by the moment, just like his bedchamber. In the end it was this sadness that belonged both to him and the Emperor that impelled Hsi-wei to compose the poem that has become known as "The Emperor's Sadness."

How rarely do we care to feel the cares others, discern
the precise shade of darkness that overshadows the exalted.
It is a mean thing to suck sweetness from one's bitter soul.
The homeless suppose anybody with a roof must be in
heaven; the hungry are sure the laborer gobbling up
his small bowl of noodles leads a life of incessant joy.
But the Emperor, surely he must be the happiest of all.
How exasperating when folk tick off the reasons why
we ought to be happy. O, Divine One, happiness
is not the guzheng's accompaniment to the melody
of your attainments, nor the sum of your riches.

Can it be that only the unhappy are worthy of happiness?
In this borrowed room the pain of heaven's mandate
is beyond my imagining, the guilt of its getting and keeping.
Yet your Empire may be as happy as it shall ever be.
How it would have delighted me to receive a letter telling
of your gladness. How I would rejoice to read that, reclining
on his raised couch in the innermost room of his high
palace at the center of a capital with paved streets,
silk-robed merchants, comfortable villas, graceful
pavilions, gardens of grass and lilies, that at the heart
of a city that has stored food to last fifty years, at dusk,
surrounded by his family, the Emperor stretches
and smiles at the prattling of his children's children.

Hsi-wei and the Hermit

One of the remarkable things about the Sui period poet Chen Hsi-wei is the way fame caught up with him. He began life in a poor village near the capital, was selected as a courier to the south during the wars, returned alive, turned down the money, land, and women he was offered, asking instead to be educated. A hard master was ordered to take the boy on. To improve his pupil's weak calligraphy, Shen Kuo put Hsi-wei to copying the ancient masters. Almost without willing it, the boy began to emulate these poets, composing new verses of his own. Seeking to promote himself, Shen Kuo circulated his pupil's poems at court as curiosities. Never before had China seen a peasant-poet. Then Hsi-wei fell in love with the young widow, Tien Miao, who returned his love but was being courted by a rich friend of her late husband. To spare Miao from being attached to a penniless poet of no family and with no prospects, Hsi-wei took to the road, supporting himself by making straw sandals and leaving behind him a trail of verses. These poems proved popular; they were copied and spread across the country. So the time came when Hsi-wei's name was known to people in many of the towns into which he wandered and even some of the small villages. If they got wind of Hsi-wei's arrival the leading gentry were quick to offer him hospitality. He was no longer a novelty but a figure whose presence conferred a measure of prestige on his hosts. Yet he continued his vagabond life just the same as when he was unknown, fashioning his straw sandals and poems.

During his travels through the province of Chiennan, Hsi-wei arrived in Hongchun, a town that was prospering under the peace of Emperor Wen. As was his custom, he made his way to the marketplace and set up his sign advertising sandals. On this occasion, however, he had two competitors, neither of whom was about to welcome a third. These men hated one another. Only the month before they had brawled and knocked over the dumpling stand of a Mrs. Chin. For this they were fined and sternly warned by Peng Chaoxiang, the local magistrate. As a result, the sandal-makers were cautious about the best way to drive out this new competitor in the dusty clothing. They approached each other with hesitation but soon made common cause, put their heads together and prudently decided—though it went against their nature—to try a friendly line.

Hsi-wei stood up as the two came over, thinking they might be customers.

"How do you do, young fellow? I can see you're a traveler," said the first.

"Yes, welcome to Hongchun," said the other with a forced smile.

Hsi-wei thanked them for their welcome. "Do you gentlemen want new sandals? My price is good."

Indeed, the price Hsi-wei quoted was half theirs.

"No," said the first, "we don't want any sandals."

"You see, we're sandal-makers ourselves. We supply all of Hongchun."

"Oh," said Hsi-wei, grasping the situation.

"Yes. And so, as you can see, there's no point in your sticking around," said the second, who was unable to keep a threatening tone from his speech.

"Yes, we recommend you be on your way. But we're reasonable men," said the first with a show of affability. "No doubt you could do with a few coins for your journey."

Hsi-wei politely declined the offer.

At this the second man drew himself up and clenched his fists. "Look, if you don't clear out, I'll see you regret it."

At that moment, Constable Ying, who was in the market buying radishes for his wife, saw what was about to happen and strode over.

"Enough," he said. "Have you two already forgotten what Magistrate Peng told you?"

"He only warned us about fighting with each other," said the second man truculently.

"Don't split hairs with me," retorted Constable Ying, then turned to Hsi-wei.

"You. What's your name?"

"Chen Hsi-wei, sir."

"You're obviously not from around here. Where *are* you from?"

Hsi-wei pointed down the road.

"A vagrant, eh? A trouble maker? I think I'd better take you to the magistrate."

"With respect, sir, the trouble isn't being made by me," Hsi-wei pointed out.

"No matter. You're the *occasion* of it," said Ying, pleased with his own perspicacity.

And so Hsi-wei took down his sign and up his bundle and was conducted by Constable Ying to the office of Magistrate Peng.

"What is it this time, Ying?" said the magistrate impatiently from behind his desk. Peng was a substantial man in middle age with sharp eyes and a rather pleasing face, despite the frown he had turned on his officious constable.

"A vagrant, Your Honor. A sandal-maker, or so he claims. Showed up from nowhere in the marketplace and made trouble with those two men you fined and cautioned last month."

"And so," snapped Peng, "you concluded it's the man I *didn't* fine or caution who created the disturbance?"

Ying didn't know what to say to this and so said nothing.

The magistrate addressed Hsi-wei. "Your name, please."

"Chen Hsi-wei, Your Honor."

Magistrate Peng's eyebrows went up, then he rose from his desk. "And you travel about making sandals?"

"That's true, Your Honor. Good sandals at a good price."

"No doubt a better one than those two louts charge."

"I couldn't say, sir."

"Do you by any chance also make something else? Poems, for instance?"

Hsi-wei, to whom this was not yet a common experience, expressed his surprise.

"Go away, Ying," ordered the magistrate and watched the constable do so. Then he called for a servant and ordered her to bring tea.

"Chen Hsi-wei, please put down your bundle. Have a seat."

Hsi-wei laid down his things and sat on the pillows indicated by the magistrate.

"'Yellow Moon at Lake Weishan.' My younger daughter sings it, you know, and rather well, if I say so myself. Our town is a bit out of the way, Mr. Chen, but we are not such provincials that we don't know of your poems. We even know your story, at least the part about your head being shaved and inscribed with the message to General Fu. That *was* you, wasn't it?"

"Yes, sir."

"Well, it's an honor to have you here in Hongchun," said Peng warmly. "Have you just arrived?"

"This morning, Your Honor."

"You haven't yet found a place to say?"

"No."

The magistrate clapped his hands. "Excellent. If you will be so kind as to accept, you shall be my guest. My family will be thrilled. Please do accept my inadequate hospitality, Mr. Chen."

"You are very gracious, sir. A corner of the stable will do for me. But I must first find a few customers."

Peng laughed. "Oh, we can do better than the stable. As for money," Peng waved his hand, "never mind about that. I'll happily make good your loss by buying sandals for my whole family—that's five pairs—and we can avoid any more incidents in the marketplace. Will that do?"

And so Hsi-wei became the guest of Magistrate Peng. While he left to buy straw, Peng sent an order to his villa that a storage room be cleared for him, the room well swept, a bed moved in and a small desk. It was quite cozy.

Chu-hua, the magistrate's wife was a plump, sympathetic woman neither too humble nor too proud. The elder daughter, Hua, was twenty, round-faced, cheerful, and soon to be married. The younger daughter was almost eighteen, more delicate than her sister, with a refined, pensive face. Hsi-wei guessed the magistrate and his wife kept trying for a boy and were rewarded. Their son, Hu-lin, the youngest child, was a vigorous, restless boy of thirteen.

The conversation at dinner was brisk. Everybody had questions for Hsi-wei. Peng wanted to hear about conditions in the provinces through which he had trekked. Were all of them doing as well under Wen's rule as Chiennan? Chu-hua asked about Hsi-wei's way of life—didn't he find it lonely, traveling by himself? The elder daughter, Hua, asked about what sort of clothing women wore in the larger cities—was silk as popular as ever and was its price dropping? Hu-lin bubbled with questions about Hsi-wei's adventures, particularly his trip to the south. "Were you my age or older? Did you have any narrow escapes? Was General Fu astonished to see you? Do you know what the precious secret message was? Did you carry a sword or a dagger? Did you ever steal a horse?"

All these questions Hsi-wei did his best to answer clearly and with the minimum of fuss. They were easy questions. Yenay, who could sing "Yellow Moon at Lake Weishan," being the youngest daughter, spoke last. She asked only one question and it was not easy to answer. As she posed it she looked straight at the poet, addressing him as "Master Hsi-wei," then cast her eyes down shyly, as if she were a little awed at meeting him.

"Master Hsi-wei, you have endured many hardships and seen so much of the empire. You've been to the south, lived in the capital, have walked through all varieties of landscapes and met all sorts of people. Your admirable poems—writing them must have been a glorious experience as well. Please tell me, if you would, of all your experiences which was the most beautiful?"

Hsi-wei was quiet for a few moments then spoke directly to the girl.

"My Lady, I suppose it's true that in an outward sense a man on the move sees more than one who stays put. Still, it's easy to overestimate such thing. You're right to say that there have been hardships and I am touched that you include among my experiences the writing of poems. That has been a sort of an adventure too, an inward one. But as to the most beautiful of my experiences—it would be like choosing the best verses from the Chuci masters or deciding who was the finest poet from among the three Caos."

"Then I apologize for asking such a silly question," said Yenay, flushing.

"No, no. The question isn't silly at all, just one I've never asked myself before."

Hsi-wei paused and considered.

"I will tell you about one experience I had. It stands out in my memory the way the most beautiful experiences do, I mean outside of normal time, though this one occurred the winter before last in the Hong Mountains of Luncyu."

Hu-lin mumbled that he would prefer a battle story. Hua said she hoped it was going to be a tale of love.

"I'm afraid this is about neither war nor romance. It may not even seem to you beautiful. In fact, it was only the Lady Yenay's question that made me think it so."

"Please tell the story," said Yenay in a soft voice.

"Yes, do," said her mother more imperatively.

"It will take some time," cautioned Hsi-wei.

"Then we'll make ourselves comfortable," said Magistrate Peng and looked at his fidgeting son. "Hu-lin, you can go if you wish." The boy didn't wait to be told twice.

Hsi-wei began.

I was on my way to Shan. I had heard many fine things about

the young duke and wanted to see his capital. To get to Shan I had to cross the Hong Mountains. I thought little of it as a shepherd had shown me the track I should follow; the sun was bright and the air bracing. I was well up on the mountainside when the weather suddenly turned, as can happen in high country. The sky seemed to fall on my head, the wind blew up, and snow began to fall like sheets of frozen milk. I could hardly see and the track was soon covered. As I picked my way across the side of the mountain I saw a dark indistinct globe to my right and made for it. It was an old man struggling under a huge bundle of sticks. He was thin and bent; I was astonished that he could even dream of bearing such a load and on such a narrow track, too. As I drew near, he fell on his side and the wood tumbled from his back. I hurried toward him and grabbed his arm fearing he might roll down the mountain. He did not seem surprised to see me. He merely pointed upwards and grunted, "There." I hefted his bundle of fire wood and, holding fast to his arm, dragged him as gently as I could up the mountain. It was hard going but at last we came to a hut, tiny and very old but stoutly built. I kicked the snow away from the door and we were safe. The hut was sparsely furnished, just what you would imagine of a hermitage.

"Tea," gasped the old man and pointed to a kettle, a jar of water, and a box of tea leaves.

After he got some tea into him, the old man told me his name was Bao Sying. He said gruffly that he was unused to speaking and did not enjoy it. In fact, he spoke in short bursts, returning to silence with evident relief. Bao Sying expressed no curiosity about me but during the night I managed to satisfy mine about him. I learned he had been born into a household that was not poor but overcrowded. His father had two wives and nine children. He was the youngest.

"We are all stuffed in these bags of skin but at the same time our species is a social one. So each of us seeks his own balance between solitude and society. It's because of that crowded childhood that I have always yearned to be alone, I suppose. As I was a third son, my father didn't object when I begged permission to become a monk. You see, I felt out of balance in my family home and imagined I'd find a better in the monastery. And so I did, for a while."

He showed me a half dozen precious Buddhist texts.

"They gave these to me when I left. Three acolytes were given the task of copying them out for me and they resented it. The young scoundrels knew I didn't like them so they put in little messages to me."

He asked if I could read and when I assured him I could, he opened *The Consecration of the Lamp* and pointed to where one of the copyists had written *Honorable Bao Sying, I send you this in my own voice which I hope you will find as annoying as ever.*

"They also put in foolish jokes. Look here."

In the middle of a commentary on the Eightfold Way the acolyte had interpolated a story: *The Emperor summons a famous holy man from the monastery of Keishan. When the monk arrives and bows before him, the Emperor asks what he would do if he were Emperor and the Emperor a monk. The monk replies 'I would summon you and ask what you would do if you were the Emperor and I only a humble monk.'*

"Exactly the sort of silly tale Chiang used to tell."

Even though Bao did not want to talk any more, neither was he able to go to sleep. I expect my presence in his hut disturbed him and prompted him to return to his fixed idea about the balance between solitude and companionship.

"At first, I desired the good opinion of my fellow monks, all of whom were older than I was. I behaved punctiliously in fulfilling my duties and was submissive to all. I studied the texts in our library and twice was trusted to go to the west to buy more. In the course of time I was tasked with instructing the acolytes. But as I became older the balance shifted. I found my students lazy and the habits of the older monks exasperating. All I could see were their faults, which I knew inside and out. I began to find the monastery as overpopulated as my family home, full of rascals like these copyists. It's not possible to be a hermit in a monastery."

"You've certainly found a remote spot," I couldn't help pointing out. "The view must be magnificent, and empty of people."

"This mountain has always been a place for hermits. When the last tenant of this hut died the villagers down below were out of sorts. They were so pleased when I showed up. Evidently, the peasants hereabout have their own notion of balance and it includes hermits on their mountain."

I sympathized and admitted that I too sought a balance that leaned toward solitude. "But I could never be a hermit," I confessed, "because people interest me more than vistas. Still, my vagabond life leaves me mostly to myself. Traveling from place to place I'm often among people yet never belong with any of them."

"You need people," the hermit said, "but you also need to leave them. It's a ghost's life."

"I'm not a ghost."

"What then?"

"A sandal-maker."

"And nothing else?"

"A poet."

"Ah, a *poet*." The old man smiled. "Put some more wood on the fire, recite a poem for me, and then we can both go to sleep. On second thought, forget about the poem."

Hua asked to be excused. Magistrate Peng and his lady wife did not chide their daughter; they sat with frozen smiles. Yenay alone seemed still attentive, but then it was her question that had set Hsi-wei off.

"The beautiful part comes next," he promised, "and it is brief to tell."

In the morning the storm had passed leaving a heavy load of snow on the mountain. I was therefore surprised to hear a knock at the door. It was another old man, all wrapped up in furs. He was not so old as Bao Sying, who still lay in bed, all covered up with rags, but almost.

The man was surprised to see me.

"Luo Nianzu," he said with just the hint of a bow.

"Luo," Bao grunted from his pallet.

Luo Bao nodded toward Bao.

I hoped Bao Sying could stand the crush; there wasn't room to turn around.

And so the mountain could boast of two hermits. The villagers down below must have felt good about that.

I made tea. The two sages said not one more word. No, not a single word passed between them and yet—this is what I found beautiful—they said everything needful. Luo had come to see if Bao had made it through the storm and Bao was touched. He rose from his bed. Luo seemed to accept my presence as natural. I handed them cups of tea and the two old men took up positions knee to knee in that overcrowded little hut. They looked at one another. With me, Bao had spoken and now I felt somehow ashamed of that. With Luo, who had given me only the three syllables of his name, talk was unnecessary. I kept the fire going and my mouth shut. After about an hour Luo Nianzu rose and left. It is difficult to explain but that hour of silence seemed loud, full of unheard music, banging tanggu and sweet sanxian.

"A poet who finds silence more beautiful than words, that's unusual," declared Magistrate Peng and ended the evening with a yawn.

The household retired. The next day Hsi-wei spent making five pairs of sandals and that night, commanded by her father, Yenay shyly sang "Yellow Moon at Lake Weishan." The next morning, Hsi-wei thanked the family for their hospitality and presented them with their sandals. As he departed he handed Yenay a rolled up piece of paper. On it he had written the poem which has become known as "The Silence of Hermits."

One winter morning I watched two hermits sitting together.
Luo Nianzu had come to pay a visit to Bao Sying.
I prepared tea. For a serene hour they faced each other
on the cold dirt floor, sipping tea, saying not one word.
I recall it as a beautiful hour, lovely, full and
still as Lake Weishan when the dawn mist lifts.

I learned how much can be said by saying nothing.
Silence may be noisy with gossip, jokes, endearments
when the silent are in perfect accord. That's how it is
with lovers, likewise those whose lives have brought them
to the same wisdom—lovers linked by feeling, sages by thought.
Such silences surpass even the verses of Qu Yuan.

Yellow Moon at Lake Weishan

When he was about thirty years old, Yang Wu-cho, a minor poet remembered chiefly as the compiler of the eighth-century Tang collection known as *The Celestial Casket*, had to travel north on business. He made a point of going to see the elderly Chen Hsi-wei, whom he ranked above all the poets of his generation.

After a vagabond life, Hsi-wei had settled in a house given him by the Governor of Chiangling. Yang wrote of his visit in a letter which has recently come to light. Most of the missive is taken up with complaints about the hardships of travel, gossipy questions about court life, slights aimed at rival poets, and an unflattering account of the city of Chiangling. Of Hsi-wei's house he reports, "It is deplorably tiny and rude, hardly better than the meanest peasant's hut. Its situation, far from the city, between a flooded paddy and waste land, is isolated and unhealthful. Such a gift does no honor to the Governor but takes none from Hsi-wei, who expresses only affection for the place and nothing but gratitude to his benefactor. With a warm smile, the old poet welcomed me to what he was pleased to call 'my last home and also my first.'"

Yang goes on to say that, after greeting his guest, Hsi-wei excused himself, went into the house and brought out a stool and an old box. "He said it would be more pleasant to sit in the courtyard, which was really just a bit of mud and weeds. With reason, I think he feared that there would not be sufficient room inside the tiny house for two poets. He offered me tea and pickles, which I turned down as I was afraid it might be all he had to eat."

Once they were seated, Hsi-wei inquired politely about Yang's family, his travels, and why he had become a poet.

"I told the old master that I had been inspired by his work, which I had first come across ten years before. 'Is that so,' he said. Hsi-wei's famous modesty is genuine; he appeared sincerely incredulous. I told him that my favorite of his poems was still the first I had read, 'The Yellow Moon at Lake Weishan.' On hearing this, Hsi-wei put his elbows on his knees and his head in his hands. I determined to remain silent until the master chose to speak.

"I should tell you that Hsi-wei spoke with me quite easily, as one does with a colleague, an equal. Eventually, he put a question. 'May I ask if, when you set out to be a poet, you met any older poets who told you to write about what you know?' I said that, yes, I had heard that pretty often from my elders. He nodded. 'I only came across one poet in my youth and that's what he told me too.' I asked Hsi-wei if he would advise me to do likewise. 'To write about what you know? Well, perhaps you should. But that old poet I met in my youth was a rascally humorist, and a second minister. It was natural that he should look down on an upstart peasant like me. After saying I should write what I know about he added, "That should leave you with plenty of time for planting rice." When I expressed indignation, Hsi-wei explained the deeper meaning of his story. 'Anybody with senses can grasp the look, the smell, the texture of things, of a clay pot, a ripe persimmon. But how can we know a thing apart from what our senses tell us about it, I mean the thing itself? After I wrote that poem you like, the one about Lake Weishan and the yellow moon, I understood better not only the moon, the water, the night, but also stillness and motion, timelessness and loss."

"I asked if the poem had to do with the wars in which he had so nearly perished.

"'There were always wars in the days before the Emperor of Sui united the two kingdoms. Back then war made the weather of people's lives. The roads were crowded with people fleeing, as if from earthquakes or floods. Crops were trampled by cavalry, stolen by foragers, storehouses burned. Would-be dynasties rose and fell like the tide; the mighty slew one another with regularity, with garrotes, daggers, and poison. Nothing felt safe or firm.'

"'Except for one moment at Lake Weishan?'" I dared to ask.

"He shook his head. 'A moment is inside time.'

"I thought I understood him. I asked, 'Then it is possible for a poet to transcend time?'

"'To my way of thinking, that is exactly what a poet yearns to do.'

"'And yet you disturbed the lake water,' I said, and quoted from memory: *The moon's light on the lake looks so precious and lovable, I reach out to touch . . .*

"The old man sighed, his lean face growing even longer. 'Yes. And that is what happens to perfection the moment we greedily try to catch hold of it.'"

Yang Wu-cho's letter concludes with more complaints about the trials of travel and a vulgar account of a dalliance with the daughter of an innkeeper.

While Hsi-wei and his poem have all but vanished into the teeming life of China, this letter shows that he and "The Yellow Moon at Lake Weishan" were once famous and spoke to the hearts of our people.

Yellow Moon at Lake Weishan

Weishan lies cool and still as a forgotten bowl of tea,
the moon immobile as a yellow disk embroidered
on a gown of black silk heavy with pearls.
As time is change, so these motionless bamboo leaves,
these reeds standing to attention like proud veterans,
yield a moment without war, decay, turmoil or age.

I too am still in this moment, captivated by
the moonlight on the enchanted lake, silver and gold.

The moon's light on the water looks so precious and lovable,
I reach out to touch it and so, with my foolish hand,
spoil eternal peace.

Alas! If only I had refrained.

Hsi-wei and the Good

It was high summer when Hsi-wei arrived in Bianzhou. He was footsore, thirsty, and troubled by the suffering he had observed in the counties through which he had passed on his way to the capital. In Qi, Tongxu, and Weishi, the peasants grumbled, both the poor and the well-off. In Lamkao, Hsi-wei agreed to take two apples in payment for a little pair of straw sandals. "They're for my grandson, Bo-jing. He's just learned to walk," said the old woman. Hsi-wei asked how things were. "Too much rain, then too little," she explained tersely. "We had some relief but now they've made these new taxes it's worse than ever." People were hungry and angry.

In accord with Emperor Wen's reorganization, the prefectural administration had recently been moved to Xingyanjun and it was here that his old schoolmate, Lu Guo-liang, lived. It had been nearly a year since Hsi-wei received, in a roundabout way, a surprising letter from him. He and Lu had not been close; in fact, though far from the worst, Lu had been among those who looked down on the upstart peasant who had refused gold for his service and had asked instead to be educated. Lu had enclosed his letter inside one to the painter Ko Qing-zhao, another former classmate but one with whom Hsi-wei had been good friends and with whom he intermittently corresponded. Lu's letter reached the vagabond poet enclosed in one from Ko. Lu wrote of his marriage and his appointment to an important administrative post in Bianzhou. He offered Hsi-wei a hospitable welcome, should he find himself in the vicinity, adding that he had heard of the growing reputation of the peasant-poet. "I well remember how Master Shen Kuo used to chide you for your calligraphy. If I recall correctly, he once compared your

73

brushwork to what a regiment of grass lizards would leave behind if they'd splashed through a puddle of ink then tramped across a sheet of paper. The old dragon probably brags about you now."

Hsi-wei noticed the contrast between the countryside and Xingyanjun at once. While the peasants were ill-fed, ill-clothed, and ill-tempered, here, though there were the usual beggars, most people looked nourished, decently dressed, and busy. When he accosted a robed official in a high hat and asked the way to the villa of the Secretary to the Deputy Governor, the fellow looked at him suspiciously. Should he deign to answer a dusty vagabond with a pack on his back?

"And why would the likes of you be looking for Secretary Lu?"

"To pay the visit he requested me to make, Sir."

The official scoffed and made to move off, but Hsi-wei stopped him.

"Perhaps you would care to see his letter?"

"You expect me to believe a peasant receives letters from a First Secretary?"

"One who can read them as well, Your Honor," replied Hsi-wei tartly and handed over the scroll. The official took it reluctantly then unrolled and skimmed it.

"Who's this Master Shen Kuo?"

"The teacher of the First Secretary."

"And of *you*?"

Hsi-wei wearied of this tedious conversation. "Sir, can you tell me the way or not?"

The official drew himself up. "Very well," he said. His directions were complicated, perhaps even more than necessary. "And you can tell Secretary Lu that Under-Assessor Hsieh showed you the way."

Night was falling when Hsi-wei found Lu's villa. It was an old-fashioned place, not notably large but sturdy and dignified, with weathered walls, thick beams, two wide windows and a red door, at which Hsi-wei knocked.

The door was partially opened by a stout female servant who looked Hsi-wei over in a way that was not unfriendly but cautious.

"I'm here to pay my respects to Secretary Lu, at his invitation."

"Secretary Lu is not yet home."

A young woman came up behind the servant. She was pregnant. The wife. Looking anxiously over her shoulder was a thin old woman. Lu's mother. "Go away," she said. "Send that man away."

Lu's wife replied calmly, "Mother, he says he was invited. If we send him away, Guo-liang might be angry."

"Invited? An obvious lie. Guo-liang wouldn't invite a peasant here, not ever, and certainly not as things are now."

"Mei, please let him in," said the pregnant wife.

The servant smiled at Hsi-wei and opened the door.

The mother gave a little yelp of frustration and Hsi-wei could see this was a small skirmish in a long struggle between the women of Lu's household. Such wars are a tradition; not for nothing is the character for strife two women beneath one roof.

"My husband is expected at any minute," said the wife. She spoke graciously, perhaps to spite her mother-in-law; but Hsi-wei could see that, taking in his rough, soiled clothes, the woman was perplexed and a little concerned.

In the background, the old woman growled. "Close the door. Can't you see he's a robber? He'll slit our throats," growled the old woman.

Hsi-wei bowed deeply and addressed the wife. "My name is Chen Hsi-wei. Your husband and I knew each other ten years ago in Daxing."

"In Daxing?"

"As students."

"Chen Hsi-wei?" the wife repeated then broke into a smile. "Oh, the poet. My husband spoke about you. He said he'd sent you a letter, but that was long ago."

"The letter took a while to reach me, and then I was not close by. If you like, I can return tomorrow."

The woman hesitated then said. "Please, Sir. Come in. Mei, fetch us some tea."

The old woman raised her voice. "Daughter, what can you be thinking? He's a stranger, a peasant. Just look at him."

"Enough, Mother," said the wife evenly. With a cry of protest, the old woman retreated inside the house, clutching her robe tightly. Hsi-wei never saw her again, not even at dinner which was served shortly after Lu came home.

With apparent delight and a bit of irony, the silk-robed Lu greeted Hsi-wei effusively. "Chen Hsi-wei. Is it really you? Yes, of course. Same face, same weight, too, I notice. So, you got my letter? Well, it's a pleasure to see you. I hope you'll be able to grace us with your presence for a day or two? I'd like to introduce you to my superior." Then, to his wife, he said, "Wouldn't you say our peasant-poet looks the part? Order Mei to prepare the spare room."

As soon as they sat down to eat Lu began to reminisce about their days in Daxing, speaking as if they'd been the best of friends, telling his wife how badly Master Shen had dealt with Hsi-wei and claiming that he had been treated with the same brutality.

"Congratulations on your position," Hsi-wei said to Lu, then, to his wife, "and on the child. I hope you are well?"

"Perfectly well, thank you."

"Yes," said Lu with satisfaction. "I think I can say that I'm a fortunate man."

"You enjoy your work?"

"Very much indeed," said Lu. "My superior, Deputy Governor Du, an excellent man, is not only wise but decisive. And we've a great deal to do, now that he's become Acting Governor."

"The peasants I saw on the way are suffering."

"Yes. That's regrettable, but there's a crisis."

Lu didn't inquire about Hsi-wei's departure from the capital, his ten years on the road, or his poems; however, he spoke with relish about the emergency with which he was assisting his superior who was now Acting Governor. He went on at length, taking pleasure in the details.

"Of course, the source of our difficulties is the weather. Floods in early spring gave way to drought in early summer. Crops failed. But the problem was compounded by the mistaken policy of our soft-hearted Governor, Hou Bo-qin."

"I've heard about the weather, but not Governor Hou's policy, nor why he's been replaced by your superior."

"The latter's simply explained. When the governors of all the prefectures were summoned to the capital to be informed about the new administrative arrangements, of course Governor Hou, though in frail health, undertook the journey. But, on the way back, he fell ill and was taken to Chiangling where he's been ever since, hovering between life and death. Before he left, though, Governor Hou took an unfortunate measure. He declared that, in view of the hard times, the tax on grain, the *zu*, would be cut in half. He went still further and suspended the tax on textiles as well, the *diao*. The consequence for our city has been catastrophic."

"But," said Hsi-wei, "the people in the city look well-fed and they're not wanting for clothes either. It's the peasants who are famished and in rags."

Lu smiled condescendingly and raised his forefinger, a gesture Hsi-wei recognized, as it was often used by Master Shen.

"That's so, but only because of our store houses. To give him his due, Governor Hou kept them full. However, the populace has been eating through the stores for months and now they're nearly exhausted. You see the problem?"

Hsi-wei did. He also foresaw what Secretary Lu and his admired superior would be likely to do about it. He reviewed what he knew of the Empire's method of taxation, the so-called Equal Field System. The word *equal* seemed to suggest something equitable but, in Hsi-wei's view, that is just what it was not. The officials he knew at Daxing and those he had encountered during his travels all approved of this system and believed it was good for the Emperor's military needs and his vast civil projects. Hsi-wei, however, assessed it with the soul of a peasant.

Under the prevailing system, the unit of taxation was the household. All peasant households—no matter how prosperous or poor—had to pay the same tax. Nobles and high officials were exempt. Those peasants who had no household, a considerable portion, paid no tax in grain or textiles. They subsisted by working for the rich landowners as servants, laborers, or tenant farmers. But there was a third tax in addition to the *zu* and *diao*, a tax all had to pay, the *yong*. Every peasant owed the Emperor twenty days out of the year to be paid in either military service or labor on the Grand Canal. More returned from the former than the latter.

"And what does Acting Governor Du propose?"

"As I told you, he's wise and decisive. The moment he received word of Governor Hou's incapacity, he revoked the ruinous tax remissions; and, in consideration of the impending crisis in the city, he increased the grain tax by half. To this urgent measure, he added a long overdue innovation, which shows his genius. It's aimed at the fat landlords. They're all to pay a head tax."

"A head tax?"

"That's right. So much for every servant, worker, and tenant farmer."

Hsi-wei, controlling himself with some difficulty, said sharply, "But doesn't he realize that the well-off landowners will simply dismiss their landless dependents."

Lu rubbed his belly. "Oh, don't believe it. They can't do without their servants and the others. They'll pay up. Anyway, they all have secret storehouses of their own, no doubt crammed with rice and millet—yes, and good cloth, apples, and root vegetables, too."

Hsi-wei was indignant. "So, the plan is to rob the peasants to feed the city?"

Lu frowned. "You put the matter in the worst way, Hsi-wei. There's no robbery. As Acting Governing Du has explained, it's the social and economic function of the peasantry to support the higher culture of the cities. In the same way, the country supports the Court and the Emperor himself. It's regrettable that peasants suffer when the weather goes against them and the harvest is wanting. But it's in the natural order, as is the precedence of the city over the countryside."

Hsi-wei forced himself stay still for a few moments, though he would have liked to shake his complacent host.

"You said Acting Governor Du is a good man?"

"It's a privilege to serve him."

"And his motives are virtuous?"

"Certainly. He always acts out of duty."

"Only that?"

"What do you mean?"

"Consider our old Master Shen Kuo."

"What's he got to do with it?"

"When Master Shen ridiculed, us, when he beat me, don't you suppose he too believed he was doing his duty?"

"Very likely. So what?"

"You didn't observe the pleasure he took in tyrannizing over us? You never noticed the old man's lust for power?"

Lu gaped at Hsi-wei.

"You've heard the saying that we love the good?"

"Something from one of the sages, I suppose. I can't recall which."

"Do you think that sage was blind to all the evil done in the world?"

Lu's face darkened. The two men faced each other alone. Lu's wife had excused herself long before and her mother-in-law had never come out of hiding.

"You mean to impugn our Acting Governor?"

"No. Merely to understand him. When I arrived, you said I hadn't changed. Neither have you, Guo-liang. You flatter your superior and are indifferent to the suffering he imposes on the peasants. It was just the same in Daxing."

With that Lu struck the table.

Hsi-wei got to his feet. "Thank you for this meal, which I regret eating and will have a hard time digesting."

Then the poet took up his pack and went out into the dark city.

Hsi-wei spent the rest of the evening walking the city's streets. He slept a little on the grounds of a small Buddhist temple. When dawn broke, he headed into the countryside. In Tongxu he paid a peasant family for lodging in their shed by making them all straw sandals. Po Ling-xi, the father, was a good man and took to the sympathetic sandal-maker. He confided that, when they learned of the new taxes, the people had gathered what grain they had left and filled clay jars which they buried on the wooded hillsides. They also chose representatives to carry an appeal to the new governor. The wealthiest landlords put themselves forward. Hsi-wei was still in Tongxu when these suppliants were beaten and thrown in prison. Du then ordered troops into the rural areas to confiscate the grain he was certain the peasants had in abundance. When his troops returned empty-handed, he was infuriated and declared that he would burn villages until the grain was forthcoming.

Those convinced of their own virtue are always the hardest to dissuade. In fact, it is rare that foolish self-righteousness is corrected or its bad deeds forestalled. But that is what happened in Bianzhou. Hsi-wei had been on the road south for a week when the news from Xingyanjun reached him.

Governor Hou had recovered and arrived from Chiangling before the troops fired the first village and before the desperate peasants grabbed their rakes and scythes to resist. The first thing the Governor did was to rescind the new taxes. The second was to have his deputy transferred to the far west. The third was to reinstate his lenient tax policy, except now he eliminated the grain tax altogether. These things were easily accomplished. But the problems of famine and the taxes owed the state remained and called for real ingenuity. What Governor Hou did was add ten days to the labor tax. He then used this measure to barter for grain from Jingzhou, which had a surplus, as he had learned in the capital. In return, the labor tax there was cut by the ten days added in Bianzhou. The Emperor was not cheated.

"Hardly perfect," mused Hsi-wei, "but not bad either."

Being a modest poet, Hsi-wei would probably not have rendered a better judgment on the verses inspired by his visit to Bianzhou. The poem has become popularly known as "We Love the Good."

Even sober, Heng thought it good to revenge himself
by murdering Lin who'd insulted him right in the tavern.
Didn't everybody detest that troublesome braggart, that sot?
Didn't everyone know Lin beat his wife and cheated at weiqi?

Captain Fu was sure it would be good not to wait for
the reinforcements promised by General Shao
but rather to attack at the hour just before dawn.
The enemy would still be asleep, their pickets drowsing.

The Emperor's nephew resolved it would good to remove
the Son of Heaven. He could rule far more wisely.
He would economize, take fewer concubines, win wars,
appoint less corrupt ministers. The peasants would adore him.

Bai-du was certain it would be good to leave the garlic
frying in her wok a little longer, just one more minute
so the cloves would soften and turn a deeper brown.
Then the dish would taste sweet rather than harsh.

Heng was dragged weeping to his execution. The would-be
usurper was stripped and beheaded, his wives and lands seized.

Before the sun was up, Fu led his men into a lethal trap.
Bai-du scorched the garlic and ruined her husband's dinner.

We love the good, says the sage, meaning all, no exceptions.
He didn't need to add that most of us are sleepwalkers
all-too-certain of our crooked ways, or that, should we wake,
each of us would swear that next time we'll know better.

Hsi-wei Cured

In the month when autumn changes to winter, the weather in Yangzhou turns cold and damp. Storms blow in from the sea; dark clouds overspread the plain and burst against the Southern Hills. Chen Hsi-wei was making his way down the eastern side of these highlands when, five *li* from the village of Wuzheng, he was drenched by a downpour.

He could not get dry. A stiff eastern wind blew his soaked clothing against his body. By the time he reached Wuzheng he was shaking with cold. Even though it was already growing dark, Hsi-wei, with some effort, set up his sign advertising straw sandals in the village's tiny marketplace.

A heavyset fishwife left her stall and walked right up to Hsi-wei. "Where are you from?"

Hsi-wei tried to reply but was convulsed by coughing.

"Just listen to you," she said in the angry tone some women use to express sympathy.

Hsi-wei managed to apologize for the coughing.

"You're shaking all over. Come here, sandal-maker. Let me feel your face."

Hsi-wei did as she asked. The woman laid the back of her left hand on his cheek, then his forehead.

"Hot! Very hot," said the fishmonger and motioned to another woman, a purveyor of stew, who was packing up her pot and grate. This second woman could have been the first's younger, thinner sister.

"The young man's sick," said the first. "His face is burning."

The second woman looked Hsi-wei up and down then told him to sit before he fell. The fish-seller fetched the poet a cup of tea from a pot under her stall. Meanwhile, the stew-seller

83

called to a passing group, an elderly peasant, his wife, and a woman of about thirty who looked at bit like them both. "Mr. Li, this stranger's just come to town and he's ill," she said. "He'll need a place for the night. You've got that empty shed, right?"

Hsi-wei put his head between his knees. He felt weak and dizzy. The shaking had become worse as well.

Li grunted and bent over to examine Hsi-wei. "Yes," he said with some reluctance, "we can put him in our shed." He turned to the young woman. "Mi-tzu, go fix up a pallet and get out the spare blankets."

"Poor young man. I'll get some broth," said his wife.

"Good, then we'll put him up in your shed," said the fish-monger, who seemed to relish ordering people around. "Just as well. He may be contagious. Still, he's young and looks sinewy enough. Could be a good night's sleep will set him up."

"Thank you," Hsi-wei managed to say between coughs and shivers. "You're very kind."

He was helped to his feet and surrounded as they made a little procession. Despite the fear of contagion, he was taken into the house and seated by the hearth while the young woman readied the shed. Mrs. Li heated some broth. Everyone kept at a discreet distance from the sick man but in a way that seemed more polite than fearful.

The young woman, Mi-tzu, came in and nodded. With the two market women holding his elbows, Hsi-wei staggered out to a shed made of loosely fitted planks. The place looked near to collapse. But the vagabond had stayed in worse accommodations, and he had slept on humbler pallets.

Mi-tzu had started a fire in a brazier and the shed already felt warm. Coughing and trembling all the while, Hsi-wei collapsed on to the pallet. The market women left with expressions of in-dignant, motherly concern. After covering him with two heavy blankets, Mi-tzu ran to the house and returned with a cup of tea made sweet and thick with honey. Hsi-wei took a sip gratefully and asked her about herself.

Mi-tzu spoke simply and without complaint. "My husband Huiliang is in General Hu's corps. He was promoted last year. They made him an officer and right away sent him to the southern frontier. We have no children and Huiliang's mother and father are dead. So I've returned here to look after my parents."

"And to look after me as well, it seems," said Hsi-wei with a wan smile. His words came out ragged and frog-like. His eyes were already closing.

Mi-tzu touched his forehead then quickly pulled her hand back.

"You should sleep," she said unnecessarily and left.

In the morning, Hsi-wei was not better but worse. His teeth chattered, and he was sweating.

"How do you feel?" asked Mrs. Li, frowning from the doorway. "Mi-tzu is busy."

"As if the bandit Feng and his thousand horsemen had ridden all over me," croaked Hsi-wei.

Mrs. Li left at once, saying nothing further. She's probably never heard of the bandit Feng thought Hsi-wei as he fell back into unconsciousness.

When he came to he found the fishmonger and a group of four men had crowded into the shed.

"We're taking you to our healer," the woman declared.

"Healer?"

"Yes. To Wu. Up the mountain. If you can be cured, she'll do it. The Hungs' son had a fever like yours, and so did Mr. Chang's wife Baiyu. No, don't try to get up. We've got a litter waiting."

Hsi-wei would have liked to resist; he would have also liked to find a proper doctor—*wu* being the word for sorceress. But he was too weak to protest. Two of the men hoisted him by his arms and legs and carried him outside to the litter, a frame on which the fishmonger laid two of the blankets from his pallet. She spread a third over Hsi-wei and tucked it around him closely. At once the litter was raised by the four men, the market woman warning them to be gentle.

The path was steep but smooth. Hsi-wei dozed intermittently. When he was conscious, he looked up at a gray sky pierced by the misty tops of pines. The trees reminded him of Ko Qing-zhao's landscapes. His friend Ko was fond of painting pine trees wreathed in fog.

The men were strong and the bossy fishmonger urged them to keep up the pace, occasionally murmuring comforting things to Hsi-wei in her usual cross tone.

"Nasty fever you brought to our village, stranger. New straw sandals would have been more welcome. I could use a pair myself. Don't worry. Wu will fix you up. Wu settles fevers and arguments. She settles disputes and sets broken arms. Never fear. Our Wu's a wonder."

Hsi-wei realized they had arrived when he saw no more tree-tops. The party stopped and the woman said, "Here we are. Wu, shall we bring him in?"

"Yes, please. At once," said a new voice, lower and softer than the fishwife's. A face with fine wrinkles and kindly eyes hovered over him. A palm was pressed against both his cheeks.

Wu's cottage was surprisingly spacious and exceptionally clean. Not so much as a single pine needle marred the floor. Hsi-wei saw shelves crowded with jars that he supposed held all sorts of leaves, roots, flowers, moss, lichens, and fungi. There were also bottles with colored liquids. He counted three cupboards and four brass lamps. The stone hearth was well made and, with surprise, Hsi-wei saw an indoor pump. A narrow bed was in one corner and a second sat under the windows on a low platform. A wide table took up most of the middle of the room. There were three stools and a padded chair. The tall windows on two sides looked out at the forest.

Hsi-wei was laid on the bed in the corner. It turned out to be soft and softer still was the blue goose-down coverlet laid over him. He was weak and felt as if the pull of the earth on his body had grown stronger. Hsi-wei noted that the four men and the fishwife showed no fear of the woman, the sorceress, the *wu*. On the contrary, they cheerfully told her the news of the village and answered her questions about the health of some children. Before they left, she predicted a mild, dry winter, once the storms at sea abated, and advised them to put by some extra measures of water against a summer drought.

Once the villagers departed, the woman subjected Hsi-wei to a thorough going over. She looked into his eyes and nostrils, felt all over his feet and hands, taking each toe and finger in turn. Excusing herself, she drew the coverlet aside and poked at his abdomen and then his groin. Hsi-wei said nothing.

The woman covering him up pulled one of the stools next to the bed.

"You have heat-flu. Heat-flu can be caused by cold which disrupts *chi*. It's not good to attack a heat-flu fever. The fever's there for a reason. It shows that your body is battling for you, struggling to restore the warm and cold balance. It's best to let it fight its war. What you need is rest and warmth and also chrysanthemum and peppermint tea. Twice a day. The tea will lessen the symptoms without disrupting the fight. I expect you haven't much appetite?'

"None," rasped the patient.

Wu nodded. "All the same, I'll feed you later. A light soup with bok choy leaves and a little chicken. It'll fortify you. We can talk then. Now sleep."

When Hsi-wei woke, it was dark. Only one of the lamps was lit yet the cottage felt cozy and safe. He was neither shivering nor sweating and had enough energy to sit up and drink his soup.

"Is your name really Wu?" he asked the old woman who sat beside him.

She smiled. "It's what I'm called. I once had another name, but I can't recall what it was. I was too young when I lost it."

Hsi-wei handed over the empty bowl and fell back into the soft bed. "How's that? Tell me your story."

"If you were strong enough, I'd make you go first."

"If I were strong enough," Hsi-wei retorted, "I wouldn't be your guest."

The woman laughed an almost girlish laugh. "That remark shows you're feeling better. Very well, then. Here's my story, Wu's story."

"Nothing better than to lie in bed and hear a story."

"I wasn't born here, not in Wuzheng, but in some place nearer to the coast. I never learned its name. I was a first child. My birth didn't go well. My mother was terribly ill and it was thought she'd die. My father must have been desperate. I'm sure he tried all the local doctors and healers. I can picture them shaking their heads, holding out their hands, and saying they were sorry. At last he came here, to this very place. He had heard of a healer who could work wonders with bark, with herbs, and the she lived on a mountain above Wuzheng. The villagers were afraid of the old woman and probably tried to discourage him. But he insisted so they showed him the way up the mountain. They called the woman a *wu* and then simply Wu, and they feared her all the more because her cures worked. But her manner was harsh. She cured without caring. Now, the woman had grown lonely and so she made a deal with my father. She would do her best to cure his wife but, if she succeeded, he must turn his daughter over to her the same week she was weaned. If he failed to do so, she promised his wife, my mother, would certainly die. My father must have been superstitious as well as desperate—perhaps one because of the other. And, after all, he loved my mother dearly but scarcely knew me at all. He agreed. I've been here ever since the week I was weaned. Eventually I inherited the old woman's cottage, her knowledge, and also her name. Wu."

As Hsi-wei listened to this strange story he took note of the calm with which it was related. "The people don't fear *you*," he said.

"Why should they?"

"They feared your predecessor."

"That was because she was so rough with them. It was her nature. Wu never told me her own story but I imagine it must have been a bitter one, another tale of suffering from the wars. With me, she was strict, yes; but, sometimes, nearly loving. She could even be indulgent. When I was little, she'd take me down to the village so I could play with other children. No one came near her. She sat by herself and watched me at play and making friends. But we always had to return before dark. She taught me all she knew of the woods, the weather, the stars, of healing. She never said it outright but I knew she wanted me to preserve her knowledge and carry on her work. She wanted to leave something behind. And that was to be me."

"Then you aren't...harsh? Rough?"

"With the villagers? Certainly not." She smiled. "They're my friends, and they adopted me too."

"But what of your own family?"

"I didn't learn of them until I was grown. When the old woman knew she hadn't long to live, she told me my story. I made inquiries but couldn't find my parents. I didn't know their names, let alone that of their village. Perhaps they died in the wars."

"How did you feel about what the old woman did, and what your father did?"

"At first, I was angry. Then resentful. I resigned myself. But, when the old woman's strength and eyesight began to fail, I realized that I loved her and that I was glad to have been given to her, glad that she taught me. In the end, I decided it was for the best."

Hsi-wei pressed her. "But the love you'd have had for your family—that was denied you."

"Yes. I suppose that's true, in a sense."

"Why in a sense"

"My family was lost to me, but not the love. The love that I might have given to my parents, to a husband, children and in-laws didn't vanish. It just seemed to spread out, like they say the Yang-tse does when it floods."

"It's no wonder," said Hsi-wei respectfully, "the people revere you."

To this, the old woman only shrugged.

The following day, Hsi-wei told Wu his own story—about his native village and its famous ducks, who taught him to make straw sandals, his dangerous journey carrying a secret message to the south, his education, why he left the capital, many of the places he had visited since taking to the road. He related some of his adventures as well. The one thing he didn't mention was that he had become a poet.

Hsi-wei stayed with the woman for two more nights before going back down to Wuzheng where he made straw sandals for everyone who had helped him and paid the Li family for the use of their shed. Two days after that, his health restored, he prepared for the road. But, before leaving, he made his way up the mountain.

Wu greeted him warmly and insisted he have one more cup of chrysanthemum tea with peppermint. Hsi-wei thanked her over and over. Before taking his leave, he removed from his pack a fine pair of sandals specially decorated with brass fittings and the poem that is popularly known as "So Much Goes on in the World":

So much goes on in the world every day.
A mantis swallows an ant, thieves steal, rice steams.
Liu launches his new skiff as friends cheer while
spreading out their nets. Not far from Lake Weishan,
Shin fights with Meiling over twelve yuan
while, close by, the just-wed Yangs make a son.
Wendi's mint stamps out a hundred jin of copper coins;
Zhou, the liuqin player, dreams up a melancholy melody.
Each day so many things happen in the world
That even the gods cannot record them all.
Hens lay, oxen pull, sheep bleat, silkworms chew.
In the cavalry barracks of Qingzhou, the young

officers laugh when a new stallion throws their captain.
In Yanghai, the Huangs slaughter their sow
because Han-shi has come safely home at last.
Who can tally up the goings-on of just one day?
In Daxing, the Emperor decides who's to
govern Ji and who Xu. On a bridge in Liangtse
a child drops her doll into the brook and wails
until her father picks her up and strokes her hair.
So many notable happenings, yet almost nothing's noted.
On the Grand Canal, three hundred laborers collapse an
hour before five hundred bewildered conscripts show up.
Who can say all that happens in even a single hour?
Though much will go unacknowledged, unremembered,
in Jing, in Sung and Shun unforgettable things occur.
In Wuzheng, for example, a traveling sandal-maker
falls ill. Strangers give him broth and a pallet; they carry
him from their village up a steep mountain path to the
cottage of their wise Wu who believes herself an
orphan and imagines the peasants have adopted her,
though the truth is it's she who has adopted them,
sorting out their wounds, their children and disputes.
She's solitary among the pine trees yet seldom alone.
The woodland path is wide and beaten flat.
She welcomes all, not excluding the helpless vagabond
who, on any ordinary day, might turn out six decent
sandals and, on a good day, one modest poem, writ in air.
So much goes on in the world every day, good and bad.
Chen Hsi-wei is grateful and humbly offers these gifts.
Though his poem is weak, the sandals are sound; yet
his memory of Wu and Wuzheng will outlast both.

Hsi-wei, the Monk, and the Landlord

The Tang minister Fang Xuan-ling, who visited Master Hsi-wei in his retirement and recorded their conversations in his memoirs, relates the following story about the origin of the Master's gnomic poem popularly called "Teacher Window".

While he was making his way through Jizhou, it happened that Hsi-wei was invited to rest for a few days in a hillside monastery. The monks were of the Ch'an sect, therefore exceptionally neat, disciplined, and, when not silent, economical in their communications.

The abbot, Du Bai-an, was an admirer of poetry. When he heard from a peasant that a stranger calling himself Chen Hsi-wei was selling straw sandals in the village, Du walked down to the marketplace to investigate. He was eager to find out if this stranger could be the author of "Yellow Moon at Lake Weishan," a poem he had more than once recited to acolytes.

Warm spring sunlight fell on the village where Master Du was rarely seen. Low bows greeted the tall, lean man on all sides. Several market women knelt, and he asked one of these, a seller of vegetables, if she had seen the stranger who made sandals. She pointed to the stone wall that marked the east end of the square where Hsi-wei squatted beside his sign.

As the monk approached, the poet got to his feet and bowed, more in greeting than reverence.

"You require sandals, Master?"

The abbot ignored this question and put his own, almost angrily. "Was it you who ruffled the surface?"

Hsi-wei was taken aback. "Pardon me, sir?"

"Weishan," brusquely demanded the monk.

The poet blushed. "Ah, I see. Lake Weishan. Yes, I caused those ripples, and I still regret it."

At this the stern monk broke into a genial grin.

"The author of that poem is surely a follower of the Enlightened One," he said.

"An admirer, certainly. But not a follower. I hope that doesn't disappoint you."

"Is it so? I'm surprised."

"Then we're in the same condition. It surprises me that you should know the poem and even like it."

"Fame means being known by those you don't know," said the monk sententiously.

"And it sometimes means being known by those you'd prefer *not* to know," Hsi-wei replied with a wry smile.

So far from being offended, Abbot Du laughed aloud.

"Master Hsi-wei, you must be tired. Accept our hospitality for a few days. You may like what you see. At least you can rest. We'll feed you. Perhaps we can talk."

A Ch'an monk who wishes to chat, thought Hsi-wei, is rare as a dragon's egg.

"I've taken three orders so far. May I work?"

"Of course." The abbot raised a finger. "Without work the day lacks a body, without prayer a spirit."

Hsi-wei thanked the monk and promised to climb up to the monastery at sundown.

Abbot Du nodded, turned sharply, and headed back across the square. Though no longer young, the way the monk walked reminded Hsi-wei of a youthful dancer. Again, everybody bowed or kneeled.

Hsi-wei was introduced to the monks very simply. "The author of 'Yellow Moon at Lake Weishan,'" said the Abbot.

"Ah," the monks sighed unanimously. They put their hands together and bowed to the poet.

The meal of rice, bok choy, and bing cakes was eaten in silence but, afterwards, the abbot invited Hsi-wei to his small, private chamber. The furniture consisted of a tiny desk, a three-legged stool, both of cheap, unpainted pine wood, and a thin, rolled blanket.

Master Du sat on the floor but offered Hsi-wei a choice of the stool or a cushion, "in view of your travels," he said.

Hsi-wei thanked him and chose the cushion.

As soon as the poet was settled, the abbot began. "Is it true that as a boy you carried a message to the South for the Emperor?"

"Yes, Master."

"On your scalp?"

"That's true." Hsi-wei ruffled his thick hair. "It must still be underneath all this."

"And your reward was an education?"

"Yes. That's so, too."

"So, you might have been an official with a high hat and a silk robe yet chose instead to become a poet and a vagabond?"

"You're astonishingly well informed."

The abbot nodded.

"I noticed," said Hsi-wei, "that the villagers show you great respect. I regret to say that this isn't always what I've observed. I've often heard people express resentment, even enmity, toward the monasteries."

"And why is that?" asked the abbot, though it was clear from his smile that he knew.

"They dislike that the Emperor shows favor to the monks; even some Buddhists resent the taking of land to build new monasteries. But the people here obviously revere you."

"Gratitude is often mistaken for reverence."

"The peasants are grateful to you?"

"Not to me, to my predecessor, to the monastery." Abbot Du grinned. "Would you care to hear the story? I fear you'll think it too comical and that it shows my illustrious instructor in a dubious light. Yet, I assure you, Master Huang was a great teacher. The story itself is about teaching and you too may find it instructive."

All the Ch'an monks Hsi-wei had encountered before were as tight-fisted with words as misers with copper coins. This abbot, however, seemed starved for speech and the poet was happy to indulge him.

"I'd very much like to hear the story."

Du straightened his back and began.

"When Master Huang-kai established the monastery with only six followers, the local people were, as you say, neither welcoming nor eager to learn. The few who had heard of the Enlightened One imagined all sorts of nonsense; for instance, that the Buddha was a bloodthirsty giant who lived in a fortress beyond the western mountains. The place was backward, poor, and miserable. The wise Master Huang quickly discovered that the people were oppressed by the local landlord who kept them in a state of anxiety and destitution. Li Zhang-hu charged exorbitant rents and had armed men to collect them. Those unable to pay up were whipped, their possessions confiscated, and turned out with their families. As our own land had been his before the Emperor allotted it to us, he was even more hostile to the monastery than the peasants. Li was not only cruel and greedy, but ignorant and therefore superstitious.

"So, Master Huang conceived a plan. He sent one of his monks to invite Li to the monastery, saying the abbot knew of a serious matter than concerned him personally. Li arrived late in the day and in a foul mood, accompanied by two of his men. He demanded to know what the serious business was. Master Huang calmly told Li that the Buddha was a prophet who was able to see into the future. His youngest monk, he said, by following a secret ritual, was able to communicate with the spirit of the Enlightened One. The night before, he said, the Buddha had told the young monk that one of Li's outbuildings would catch fire. Li scoffed at this but, impressed by Master Huang's dignified bearing and solemn tone, he was fearful too. Two nights later,

Master Huang sent a pair of monks to set fire to the thatched roof of one of Li's pigsties, after first releasing the pigs. As soon as the roof was consumed, they extinguished the fire.

"The following week, Master Huang again summoned Li. The landlord came more quickly this time. Master Huang said that he didn't know if the Buddha were angry with Li or, out of compassion, meant to warn him. However, through the young monk, he had said that two trees in the landlord's apple orchard would be uprooted. The following week, during a night storm, Master Huang dispatched his monks to tear up a pair of saplings."

"Master Huang deceived the landlord?" Hsi-wei couldn't help saying.

"Deceived? Don't you think that one can be deceived into the truth?"

"How?"

"As I said, Master Huang was a great teacher. He followed our doctrine of *pu shuo p'o*—never speak too clearly. I owe everything to him because he never explained anything plainly. Of course, he could easily have done so if he wished, but instead he set us problems and riddles that he claimed he himself could not solve. Was that deception?"

Hsi-wei was surprised and a little troubled but asked to hear the rest of the story.

"A week after the uprooting of the apple saplings, Master Huang summoned the landlord yet again, on 'a matter of the utmost urgency.' This time, Li came running and without his armed men. In his gravest voice, Master Huang asked the youngest monk to report what he had heard from the Buddha the night before. Looking sorrowful, the young monk told Li that he regretted to say the Enlightened One predicted that he would die within the month.

"Trembling, Li grabbed the young monk's hands. 'What am I to do? Can the future be changed?'

"Master Huang made the man sit and explained to him that

nothing in this life exists on its own, that all things are connected, that all opposites make a whole—night and day, male and
female, drought and flood. He made the terrified man listen to
a sermon on the unity and mutual dependence of life. Without the wind, he said, the apple saplings would not have come
down; without lightning the sty wouldn't have caught fire. All
things are one; good fits into evil. Then he explained *karma*. A
person's actions can be in accord with a good unity or at odds
with it. He said the first will lead inevitably to rewards, the latter
to inexorable punishment.

"'It would appear that you, Li Zhang-hui, are up against the
good force of the world,' he said harshly.

"'But what can I do?' begged the shaken and confused landlord.

"Master Huang turned to the young monk. 'Tell him.'

"In a firm voice, the young monk looked down at Li's pale
face. 'You can increase your years by a quarter, the Buddha said,
by quartering your rents. You can double your years by reducing
them by half.'"

"I see," said Hsi-wei. "And did Master Huang let the peasants
know what he had done to get their rents reduced?"

"No."

"And have you?"

The abbot smiled. "The people understand that we had something to do with their rents being reduced, that's all."

Hsi-wei thought of the bowing and the kneeling he had witnessed. "And have you told them?"

The abbot simply smiled.

Hsi-wei thought for a while. The story disturbed him.

"You said the tale was comical and I can see why. It's about a
deception that led to a happy ending. You believe that Master
Huang's deception was justified because fooling one guilty man
made many innocent ones happy. Pardon me, but is that per-
missible? Is the practice of deception in the hope of bringing
about desirable outcomes a good principle?"

The abbot took a deep breath. "I notice that you've fixed on the word deception, Master Hsi-wei, and that is why you disapprove. Yet who is more deceptive than a poet?"

"A good poet tells the truth."

"Agreed. But often you do so by duplicity, saying one thing and meaning another, as my teacher's pretense of ignorance was the proof of his wisdom."

"It's not the same. Unlike Master Huang's, a poet's motive is not to deceive."

"Nor was Master Huang's. What he practiced wasn't deceit but pedagogy. He taught Li to act decently. And the proof is that, after halving his rents, he became a better man and therefore a wiser one. He got on well with his neighbors, and his cruelty ceased with his greed. He did many people good turns and, existing in harmony rather than discord, he's lived not only happily but long. Li Zhang-hu is still alive and over eighty."

"And does he know by what means he was enlightened?"

"You use that sacred word ironically. But the truth is that Master Li really is enlightened. He's become a devout Buddhist and often comes to sit with us and to learn."

"I grant the happy ending and the landlord's piety too. But would he be a devout Buddhist and your attentive pupil if he knew he was tricked into enlightenment?"

"Tricked into enlightenment—that's good, Master Hsi-wei, almost a little poem. But, in this case, you're mistaken. It was only after I told Li the story I've just told you that he became a Buddhist."

Hsi-wei stayed two days at the monastery, made six pairs of sandals. He admired the monks' dedication to their spare way of life, and enjoyed two long conversations with the abbot. They talked late into the night, chiefly about poetry, the old masters. At the end of the last of their conversations, aware that Hsi-wei had not set aside his misgivings about his predecessor, Master Du quoted these lines:

House-Builder, you're seen!
You will not build a house again.
All your rafters broken,
The ridge pole destroyed,
Gone to the unformed,
The mind has come to the end of craving.

"Would you call that duplicity too, Master Hsi-wei? The Buddha describes ruinous destruction to extol the building of enlightenment, the end of many births."

Hsi-wei wished the abbot a good night.

The following morning, the poet prepared to depart. Along with many expressions of gratitude to the monks, Hsi-wei presented the abbot with a pair of straw sandals and these verses:

Enlightenment springs from benightedness.
Without diseases there would be no cures.

Those most in need of a lesson—the cruel,
The indifferent—never beg for sermons.

Learning is meant for those who learn,
Not the tutor who already knows.

To dupe the ignorant into looking
Is better than telling them what to see.

The best teacher is a pane of glass
through which clean light streams.

Hsi-wei and the Exile

The Tang minister Fang Xuan-ling devotes a lengthy section of his memoirs to a visit he paid the poet Chen Hsi-wei. This was near the end of Hsi-wei's life, after he had given up his vagabond existence and settled in the tiny cottage given him by the Governor of Chiangling, two rooms with a mean patio and a small vegetable garden. The place was in the middle of farmland three li outside the city gates.

In the following excerpt, Fang gives an account of how Chen Hsi-wei came to write the poem popularly known as "Exile."

The heat of the day was letting up at last. As we sat drinking tea on the wretched patio that Hsi-wei called his courtyard, I commented that he must sometimes miss the capital. He agreed this was so. It was then that I asked him why poets so often write about exile and reminded him that he also had done so.

"You're right, my lord. It does seem that sooner or later all poets write about exile. As you've pointed out, even I've done so, though I can't claim to be an exile. No one banished me from the capital all those years ago; I left of my own accord and for my own reasons. That poem of mine you mention didn't originate in my own experience."

"Whose then?"

"Master Liu Deyu."

"You knew Liu Deyu?"

"I met him, yes. It was a piece of great good fortune to run into the author of that sublime collection on the seasons. Do you know *The Four Jade Pillars?*"

"Certainly."

"Of course you would. Well, since I left the capital, I had met no poets at all, let alone one as eminent as Master Liu. We had a single night of conversation, and I consider it one of the great experiences of my life. I remember it well."

"How did you meet?"

"I was making my way through Ch'ienchung and stayed briefly at an inn in the town of Zhuhai. It is on the highway leading to Chiangnun Tung, which is where Master Liu was headed. We had to put up in the same inn, as Zhuhai had only the one. When I discovered the identity of my fellow guest, I was quite speechless, but he was patient with me."

I asked Hsi-wei if he had heard the stories about Liu Deyu's eccentricities. He said he had known nothing of the Master except for his poems until Liu himself told him about his life.

"So, he talked to you about himself?"

"When I met him, Master Liu was a humble and unusually candid man. I can't say if he'd been different before his misfortune, but I know that he was completely open with me and that he treated me with more respect than I deserved, graciously overlooking my background. I wonder if you can imagine, my lord, how I felt when I found he had heard my name and knew the story of my mission to the South during the wars, that he had actually read some of my verses. It was a year since I had slipped out of the capital, and I believed myself unknown to the world. Master Liu was the first to tell me that my poems were circulating everywhere, adding that he was pleased to meet the famous peasant-poet. As you can imagine, I was quite overcome with amazement and gratitude."

"He called you a peasant-poet?"

"That is what I am, my lord, and in that order."

"So you spent one night together with him?"

"Yes, only the one night, but we stayed up almost the whole of it talking. Perhaps it was our shared love of poetry and the awareness that we would most likely never see one another again that made Master Liu speak so frankly. Maybe, having been on the road, he was just as hungry for someone to talk to as I. We were like two men cast adrift who find one another in the open ocean. Whatever the reason, Master Liu was even more eager to talk than I was."

According to what I was told, the Duke of Shan had for years considered Liu Deyu to be the chief ornament of his court and treated him well, appointing him to the dignified and undemanding post of Marshall of the Horse Gate. Liu was also said to have carried out diplomatic missions for the Duke and to have offered useful advice about the building of a new canal. But Liu's reputation was rather complicated. He was described to me as prideful, absentminded, and remarkably ugly. There was also a story that he was given to somewhat ambiguous acts of charity. Apparently he had his servants look out for women in distress—widows, orphans, and abandoned concubines. When he heard of such a woman, he would send her money, always anonymously but in such a way that she would discover the name of her benefactor. When a woman came to thank him for his generosity, Liu would protest ignorance. Something about this scenario pleased him, and he was said to have played it over and over again.

I asked Hsi-wei if he were familiar with this activity of Liu.

"Yes, he told me about it. He blamed it on lust and vanity and the particular pleasure he felt in the gratitude of women. He declared that he didn't always take advantage of them—only the young ones and, he said, only if they insisted. My impression is that even before his exile Master Liu was a man critical if not of his own nature, then of his actions."

I told Hsi-wei that I had heard of another of Liu's oddities, that he dressed as a poor peasant once a week.

"Master Liu told me about that was well. It was a ritual he carried out every Friday. He would dress as you said for the whole day, even if he had to attend the Duke. In the evening, he would order the lowest of his servants—a girl from the kitchens—to whip him with a willow stick. He said it was his penance for all the things he had done wrong since the previous Friday. Master

Liu admitted these whippings never amounted to much, as the girl was weak and terrified of him; it was more like brushing than lashing. He also confessed that his disguise enabled him to enjoy mingling with the common people, especially in low taverns, where he would go after the penance was completed."

"Yes. Liu had a reputation as a drinker. It's said a servant followed him everywhere with a flask of wine at the ready."

Hsi-wei excused himself to go inside his hovel and refill our teacups. When he returned, he went on speaking about Liu.

"Master Liu told me he had been changed by exile, but I like to think his misfortune only purified inclinations that seemed equivocal when he was riding high in Shan— impulses toward decency, generosity, concern for the poor. Like you, he spoke about the theme of exile as a preoccupation of poets and accounted for it through his own experience. He said exile is a punishment more merciful than most, one reserved for the privileged; poor people who offend their lords are simply executed. Poets who have achieved any worthy position are frequently exiled, because they have trouble avoiding the truth and write words that don't evaporate. Court poets in particular find it hard to pass up a good epigram, he said, no matter how impolitic it may be. He explained that, to remain popular, a court poet must sometimes play the part of jester. Because they are surrounded by material for satire, it isn't surprising that at some point a poet will overstep a boundary and give more offense than mirth. Then, too, poets tend to be independent-minded and terribly vain. Against their own interests, they will suddenly refuse to knuckle under even over trifles. Then their affronted lords think they have forgotten their place, whereas the truth is that they had never entirely accepted it."

I told Hsi-wei that all I knew of Liu's fate was that he was banished by the Duke, gave up writing poems, and disappeared, but I had never heard the reason.

"If you're interested, I can tell you."

I said I would very much like to hear.

Hsi-wei stretched himself and began the tale in a reflective tone. "Very well, my lord. To be exiled makes some people more selfish. They believe nobody's troubles are as bad as their own; they become resentful, grumble of injustice, and fall into the worst kind of nostalgia. Others, however, are made more compassionate by exile; their travels broaden their experience, and because of their own misfortune, they feel more keenly the misfortunes of others. Master Liu was of this latter sort. After his banishment, having no place else to go, he took refuge with his sister and brother-in-law, a wealthy landlord. 'I became their useless dependent,' he said. Master Liu admitted that his brother-in-law treated his tenants neither better nor worse than others of his class. Nevertheless, Liu found it impossible to refrain from speaking up whenever he saw the man acting cruelly, and he often chided him for a lack of charity. Not surprisingly, this rankled his brother-in-law. Caught between the two men, the Master's poor sister begged her brother to keep his mouth shut for her sake. When she was compelled to take a side, she tried to argue that both were right to a certain extent. Her equivocation hardly pleased her brother, and it infuriated her husband, so she ended by refusing to say anything at all. What she really wanted, the Master observed with regret, was both reasonable and impossible, which was simply that there be an end to their disputes or at least that she be left out of them. The crisis was reached when news came that one of the tenants had died with his rent unpaid. Over dinner that evening, the brother-in-law announced his intention to confiscate the harvest, evict the dead man's widow, mother, and children, and install a new tenant who could pay up. This was too much for Master Liu, and he began a terrible argument with his brother-in-law. Their voices rose higher and higher until the Master's sister ran from the room in tears with her hands over her ears. They went on shouting at each other until the Master bellowed, 'I pay no rent either, so I suppose you'd like to kick me out as well!' The brother-in-law didn't let this opportunity pass. He thundered his enthusiastic agreement with the proposition, and so, saying farewell to his weeping sister, Master Liu went on the road the following morning. It was two weeks later that I met him."

"Where was he going?"

"He had heard that one of his former subordinates, a young man he'd helped back in Shan, had secured a good post in Ch'uanchow. The Master hoped he would take him in."

"Poor man."

"But a fine poet."

I asked Hsi-wei the cause of Liu Deyu's banishment from Shan.

"Master Liu was eager to tell me the whole story. You remember what he said about court poets and their satires? Well, his misfortune came about because of a few silly verses he impetuously composed to entertain a lady friend. The lady promised to keep the poem to herself, but trusting her discretion proved a capital error. I'm sure you've noticed how often people give in to the perverse desire to do the very thing they know they shouldn't? Well, Master Liu knew he shouldn't have written those verses, and, I suppose, the lady knew that she shouldn't have shared them with anybody else. But they both did."

"What were the verses about?"

"The Duke of Shan had just taken a new wife, a girl who was beautiful but spoiled and terribly vain. She doted on her looks so much that when her new apartment was being fitted out, she begged the Duke to have the reception room covered with mirrors—all four walls, the ceiling, and even the floor. Unhappy though he was, Master Liu couldn't help laughing as he told me about it. He said five of the six mirrors might be tolerable, but the sixth was one too many. He wrote me out a copy of his fateful poem about the young wife and her hall of mirrors, swearing it was the last he would ever write. Wait just a moment; I'll show it to you."

Hsi-wei went inside and came back with a small scroll tied with red string. He permitted me to make a copy for myself.

From the north, hair smooth and bright as a lacquered lamp;
From the east, a profile lovelier than the proudest filly's;
From the west, a back straighter than the Imperial Highway;
But O, from the south, the reflection of something altogether common.

Once shared, these verses quickly made the rounds, and when word of them reached the new wife, she was beside herself with vindictive fury. Neither Liu's *Four Jade Pillars* nor his many poems in praise of his lord mattered now, neither his successful embassies nor his engineering, for the Duke was still infatuated with the girl, and she would give him neither peace nor pleasure until the Master had been sent away.

"There's more dignity in being exiled for politics," Hsi-wei mused. "I mean, to be banished for preserving one's integrity like Qu Huan or Xie Lingyun. Perhaps it was owing to the silliness of his case that Master Liu was so ashamed that he renounced writing altogether. In any event, I'm sure exile was no less bitter to him than to Qu Huan, and that his sorrow was no less painful than Xie Lingyun's."

The poem inspired by Hsi-wei's encounter with Liu Deyu is neither frivolous nor limited to the fate of poets. It is typical of him to have made out of Liu's sorrows something that might touch anyone, a poem both speculative and humane—in short, something in his own style.

An exile is broken in half, a man living in two places at once.
He is the bereft wanderer before you, and also
one who was never banished at all but still smells
the polish on his worn teak desk, feels the faded cover
of his favorite cushion, and tastes the crisp skin of
the roasted duck, hot from the Duke's kitchens.

Could it be we are all exiles? Our lives in this world half a life?
Perhaps in the other world another self is strolling through
the heavenly gardens, his felicity marred by incompleteness
as he awaits the moment when the I who is here
surrenders all desire and is at last united with him.

Hsi-wei and The Magistrate

Note: In the course of their conversations, Minister Fang Xuan-ling told Chen Hsi-wei that his poem, popularly known as "Good to Protect the Good," was presumed to have been written for children, to inculcate virtue. Hsi-wei replied that he was pleased children liked his verses, even though they were not written for children. Fang then asked Hsi-wei to explain the origin of the poem and its puzzling title.

The village of Heping Linguy lay in Hebei province. During Hsi-wei's time about fifty families lived there, on good soil watered by the River Huang. This land was adjacent to the Shan family estate which extended over the ten thousand *mu* to which the great families were restricted by the Equal Field System. Emperor Xiaowen had introduced this popular and effective plan more than two centuries earlier and subsequent rulers wisely retained it. They had to do so against continuous efforts by the aristocracy who employed bribery, influence, legal actions and illegal seizures to destroy it. The System allotted land under a fixed formula: so many *mu* for able-bodied men, so many for women, so many per ox. Though the land was held and worked by the peasants it belonged to the Emperor. After death or advanced age made land available, the government would reassign it. There were exceptions for some *mu* to be retained within a family, especially those requiring development and tending, such as fruit orchards and mulberry plantations. The peasants paid their taxes in kind directly to the central government, ensuring the state a reliable source of income collected on a wide base. While great families owned their land and it was exempt from taxes, the size of their holdings was limited and therefore their power. This system fortified the peasants' loyalty to the Emperor; for they understood that, if he did not maintain this system, they would quickly be reduced to the condition of tenant farmers, serfs under the heels of landlords.

Hsi-wei's travels brought him to Heping Linguy village at the height of summer. He took note of the well-tended cottages and admirable fields, green with many sorts of crops. Here he found a ready market for his straw sandals and people eager to talk. Had he arrived a year earlier, the people of Heping Linguy would have been more gratified by his praise for their village and their work; like peasants everywhere, they were proud of their village and of their success. However, the people of Heping Linguy were in a foul temper. The young were angry, the middle-aged indignant, and the old fearful.

Injustice makes the timid fall silent, the proud protest.

"Your village is thriving," said Hsi-wei after taking orders from his first two customers, both strong young men. "It's one of the finest I've seen in Hebei."

"Yet it's growing smaller," said one bitterly.

"And may be swallowed up altogether," added the other.

"Why is that?" asked Hsi-wei.

"Six months ago, Chu was killed when some roof tiles, loosened by a storm, fell on his head. The same week a wasting disease took old Fung. As it happens, their eighty *mu* abut the Shans' land."

"The Shans?"

On hearing this name, a crowd began to gather. They wanted to vent their feelings and make sure the story was related correctly.

"A haughty family, wealthy and powerful. One of them got himself appointed a third minister in Daxing." The young man pointed east. "Their land lies over there, right up to the horizon."

The crowd couldn't hold themselves back.

"A greedy bunch."

"Arrogant."

"And devious."

"Devils!"

"They've been casting a jealous eye on our land for generations."

"And they'll stop at nothing."

A woman of about thirty, heavy and dignified, quieted everyone by holding up her hand and grunting loudly. "Don't all speak at once. I'll tell the stranger what happened. Who knows? Perhaps he can do something."

"What? A sandal-maker?"

She ignored this scoffing.

"Please," said Hsi-wei, who was feeling overwhelmed and bewildered. "I would like to hear the story."

"Well then, here's the truth of it," declared the woman. "You've heard about Chu and Fung dying the same week. Well, their land had to be reassigned. But before that could happen the Shans seized it and claimed it as their own. When we objected, they posted armed men."

"Those bloody-minded retainers of theirs."

"Brutes!"

The woman turned from Hsi-wei to those who had spoken up. "Be quiet," she said.

"Well then, get on with it, Hualing."

"Gladly," the woman said and turned back to Hsi-wei. "So we sent young Li and his friend Ping off to the capital, to Shiyi, to appeal to the governor himself. After overcoming many difficulties, they managed to get an audience with a deputy. Li said he was a good man and Ping thought he seemed suspicious of the Shans. The deputy promised the boys to take the matter up with the governor. And the deputy was as good as his word. Ten days later a magistrate arrived from Shiyi to sort things out."

"Unlucky job for him."

Hualing raised a hand then went on. "This magistrate was very young, hardly older than Lin and Ping. He must have just passed his examination when the governor sent him here on his first mission. He made a good impression. JunTi-an was an upright and respectful man. He carried himself with more dignity than his years would suggest."

Hsi-wei said it was clear that something bad had happened.

"You're right, sandal-maker. Something very bad."

"I regret to hear it."

"Of course when he arrived the Shans invited him at once to stay in their villa but he refused. He lodged with Mrs. Xiong who sometimes rents out rooms to travelers. She's a good cook too. Perhaps you'll stay with her yourself?"

"Enough drumming up business for your crony," somebody complained.

The woman frowned. "You'll be comfortable there," she whispered to Hsi-wei.

"I'm sure," he said with a smile.

"Go on, Hualing. Just tell him," somebody said.

"Very well. A place was set up for the hearing right here in the square, a little stage with a chair for the magistrate. He invited us to speak first. So we told him for how many generations the land had been worked by us, the names of all the families who had worked it, and what crops they produced. We gave him the names of two young men who could marry if the land were assigned to them. We reminded him that it was the government's duty to protect the peasants and to divide the land among us."

"Yes, among *us!*"

"As for the Shans, they came in numbers, and all dressed up as if it were the Emperor's birthday. None of them deigned to speak. Instead, they produced a scholar in a yellow robe and one of those high hats they wear. Skinny fellow with a long nose. This scholar had a lot to say but the long and the short of it was the false claim that the land—*and more besides*—had belonged to the Shan family from before the time of Emperor Gao Heng."

"And more besides!"

"Magistrate Jun let the fellow talk, then politely observed that, according to the records, the Shan family already controlled their allotted ten thousand *mu* of untaxed land. At that the scholar, knowing the law, ought to have blushed, but he didn't. Not a bit of it. Instead he brazenly claimed the land had been *stolen* from the Shans—stolen by *us*, mind you—and that the loyal and generous Shan family had suffered the injustice long enough."

"Stolen!"

"And by us!"

"Magistrate Jun listened patiently to this nonsense. When the scholar finally finished, he asked us if what the Shans' spokesman said was true. Had the land been wrongly taken? Any of it? Of course we told him it was all a pack of lies. Then the young magistrate said he would take an hour to eat and consider his decision."

Here a market woman stepped forward. "He bought four dumplings from me," she said. "And, when I turned to fetch them, the Shans thought I couldn't see. But I watched them out of the corner of my eye and I could tell what was up. One of them tried to bribe the young magistrate. He pushed back his sleeve like this and opened his palm and whispered in the young man's ear."

"Of *course* they tried to bribe him."

"And did he take the bribe?" Hsi-wei asked hesitantly.

The dumpling seller stamped her foot. "The young magistrate? Not him!"

Hualing took up the story. "We all gathered in the afternoon to hear the magistrate's decision. He wasn't longwinded, like that lying scholar. He said the land would be allocated among us, in accord with the law."

"Then it ended well?" said Hsi-wei hopefully.

"No, sir. Magistrate Jun went on to say that he would be leaving for the capital in the morning and when he arrived would see at once that the proper papers were prepared and recorded. But then he did something unwise. He added that he would also be making a report on the conduct of the Shans."

Hsi-wei suspected what was coming. "Did he reach Shiyi?"

"He did not. The honest magistrate Jun Ti-an was murdered

111

on the road. The Shans claimed to have found his body—stripped naked by robbers, that's what they said."

"The Shans are the only robbers here!"

"The government was informed?" asked Hsi-wei.

"Certainly. But you remember that third minister the Shans have in Daxing? He must have fixed things. The governor has issued an edict. He declared that Magistrate Jun had unfortunately been killed by unknown robbers and that the land he had been sent here to dispose of would be added to the Shans' estate."

Hsi-wei understood that the peasants of Heping Linguy did not rehearse this sad tale to satisfy the curiosity of a traveling sandal-maker but to vent their collective exasperation, to voice their anger and grief.

Not even Hualing could have taken seriously the notion that a vagabond like him would be able to do anything about the injustice. Yet they were wrong. Hsi-wei wrote a poem and enclosed a copy in a letter which he sent to an admirer in the capital city. It is impossible to be certain that Hsi-wei's letter and poem were brought to the attention of the court in Daxing; however, the record shows that Third Minister Shan was relieved of his position, the eldest Shan son exiled, and the size of the Shan family estate in Hebei reduced by five thousand *mu*.

Though it is now considered simply an instructive children's poem and called "Good to Protect the Good," the title given the poem by Hsi-wei is "In Praise of Magistrate Jun Ti-an."

The children were let into the orchard.
Fa quickly stuffed his sack with apples.
Though his stomach was full he wanted more.
Young Guo picked only two apples.
Then he saw Ai, who was too little
to climb trees. She poked among
the fallen apples but all were

rotten or thick with stinging wasps.
Guo gave Ai one of his apples
and they enjoyed them together.

It is sweet to share what is sweet.

In Chiangling, schoolboys, fed up
With being chided for their laziness,
Tied their master up and stuck him in a cart.
They called him bad names, pointed, laughed.
In mocking him they made fools of themselves.
Just then four monks happened by.
While one gently freed the sage the
Others beat some sense into his pupils.

It is wise to defend what is wise.

Should the fields be neglected weeds
Will seize the entire plot for themselves,
Strangling the young shoots. Though weeds
Never lack for land yet they are voracious.
When they invade good soil it's
Best to tear them up by the root.

It is good to protect the good.

Hsi-wei and Mai Ling's Good Idea

Among the many details recorded by the Tang minister Fang Xuanling in his account of his visit to the poet is an explanation of the origin of Chen Hsi-wei's most popular poem for children. Despite its fanciful and mythic qualities, the poem originated in one of the adventures Hsi-wei had after leaving the capital and taking to the road. In this case, the road was the one that ran the length of Lungyu province from Shan to Tunhuang. In this portion of his account, Fang tries to reproduce his conversation with the aging poet.

"Is there a story behind that poem of yours, the one children love so much? I mean the one people call 'Mai Ling's Idea'?"

"Have you ever visited the province of Lungyu, my lord?"

"No. I haven't had that pleasure."

"There's little pleasure to be had there. It's a narrow province, hardly wealthy, squeezed between fierce Tibetans to the south and the even less hospitable desert to the north. A land of mountains and gorges. The people lead narrow lives in narrow valleys where they have to cultivate every *mu*. And yet it would be unfair to say that the people themselves are more narrow-minded than those elsewhere. They are, in fact, much the same."

"I suppose you mean that the peasants are poor and the gentry rich."

"In Lungyu even the gentry aren't all that well off. In fact, the story behind the poem you asked about turns on a decision made by one of them. I never met the man but gathered he was a kindly landowner, but lonely and childless, a widower too shy or perhaps too inward to marry twice. The village of Zhaide belonged to him."

114

"What happened?"

"Excuse me, my lord. I've been digressing before starting."

"Then please begin again, Master."

"I was still young then. I had been on the road barely a year. I lived by selling my straw sandals and comforting myself by writing poems from time to time."

"Where did you learn the craft of sandal-making, Master Hsi-wei?"

"From my uncle. Uncle was highly respected for his sandals. He wove the straw so tight that none failed to last out a whole year. Sandal-making is the most useful thing I've ever learned."

"Do you mean that what you learned from Master Shen Kuo—reading and writing—was not useful?"

"To me, useful and beyond price. But to others, not at all."

"There are many who would disagree."

"You are pleased to offer me a graceful compliment, my lord. Well, I confess I'm pleased to receive it. All the same, it really is good to be able to make something with one's hands, something others need and will pay for. I often think with some pride of all those feet I've shod."

"I believe I understand. When I was a boy I loved fashioning pens from goose feathers, sometimes duck as well. I gave them away though. I doubt anyone would have paid me."

Here Fang records that Hsi-wei laughed as sweetly as a girl before resuming.

"Well, for no particular reason I had decided to make my way to Tunhuang. It wasn't hard to find the villages as the road ran through mountain passes from valley to valley and each valley had its own village, large or small. The approach to Zhaide was particularly arduous. The pass was high up and the lowlands at the head of the valley were heavily wooded; then there was swampland too, not easy to cross. When I finally arrived in the village I could tell something was wrong. The women at the well kept their backs to each other; the men passed one another by in cold silence. Even the children played in a strangely subdued fashion, and in groups of only two or three. Hostility fouled the air of that little village the way acrid smoke does after a house fire.

"I set my sign up by the well and announced that I would take orders for straw sandals. One peasant came up and wanted to know where I would be buying the straw for the sandals. 'Does it matter?' I asked. 'We all have straw,' he said, 'but if you're going to make sandals for me and my family then I don't want you buying straw from anybody else. Understand?' Oh, it was an unhappy village indeed."

"And did you discover the cause?"

"Oh, yes. I found lodging with an old widow and she told me all that had happened. Once, she said, the village was happy; that is, no more unhappy than any other. People looked out for one another and shared when times were hard. Then one afternoon a pair of monks from the monastery on Lan Shan showed up. As night was just falling, the landlord Mr. Fu, who happened to be near the well and who had plenty of extra room in his villa, offered them beds. 'It must have been quite a night,' the widow told me. 'By morning, Mr. Fu had made up his mind that he would also become a monk on Blue Mountain. He called us all together, recited some of that Buddhist twaddle—I couldn't make head or tail of it—and said he was renouncing the world which meant the land was now ours. Then, just like that, the three of them went off and we've never laid eyes on Mr. Fu since.'

"Apparently the first dispute arose over who was to occupy Fu's villa. The Wongs claimed that, because of their fine pigs, they were the best off family in the village and ought by rights to move into the villa. This was disputed by both the Changs and the Tsengs, the former because of the wife's golden bracelet, the latter because of their ducks. But that was nothing compared to what came next. As no proper boundaries had ever been drawn between one holding and another, greedy families began to claim land others were sure belonged to them. Even the humblest, those with the least, were forced to assert dubious claims as a defense against losing the little they had. By the time I arrived, there had been fights. A man named Chui had been injured in the leg. Zhaide had become a town feuding with itself and Mr. Fu's villa still stood empty.

"I thought of leaving this unfortunate place at once. There certainly wasn't much business to be done. But then I was possessed by an idea—a wild one. But perhaps you know how such things can take possession of one, just because they are so improbable. I asked my landlady to let it be known that the stranger had something to say to the people and would say it the following day at sunset, by the well."

"Did you really think the peasants would come together to listen to you?"

"No, and neither did the old widow. Nevertheless, she did as I asked and spread the word. And, to my surprise, most of the people did show up. This showed that, beneath all their hatreds, jealousies, and mistrust, the villagers knew something had to be done and were willing to listen even to an itinerant sandal-maker.

"I began by bowing low and admitting that, as a stranger, I was ignorant of the complex history of their village. Then I dared to offer a proposition. I spoke of the swamp and woodland at the foot of the mountain. I said that, if this land could be cleared, drained, and carefully terraced, it would add several hundred productive *mu*. But such a task would, of course, be a huge undertaking. It could only be accomplished if everybody pitched in. Once the work was done, I said, you could draw up proper boundaries for the new land and the old as well. You'd have plenty of wood for fences, if that's what you want."

"I see. You were hoping that, if they took up your proposal and worked together, they'd return to the old ways, weren't you?"

"I thought it was unlikely; but I confess I did muse about how, if such a thing came to pass, it would please Mr. Fu, should he get to hear of it up on Blue Mountain. Still, I knew such a happy ending was unlikely. The people of Zhaide had become intoxicated with the idea ownership, with property, and would not readily give it up. Yet, even if joint labor didn't bring the villagers to renounce their greed entirely, I hoped that the new land might at least help to launch negotiations over boundaries."

"And did the people of Zhaide agree to your idea?"

"They argued over it, of course. Some said that, if the swamp could be drained, the forest cleared, and the land terraced, their ancestors would have done it long ago. Others retorted that their honorable ancestors had never been more than serfs and so had no reason to undertake work from which the profit would go to the landowner. They broke into two factions. The larger favored the project and, so out of fear of losing out, the smaller felt compelled to go along."

"And did the peasants of Zhaide manage to reclaim that land? Did you restore peace to the village, Master?"

"All I can say is that, when I went back on the road, a dozen peasants had new straw sandals and the work of draining the swamp was underway. Yet there was one project, much more modest, that did come to completion. You asked, my lord, about that old poem of mine, the one children like. It was written on the road from Zhaide to Tunhuang."

Mai Ling's Idea

Long ago, between Night and Day there was war.
They taunted and insulted one another. Spite and spleen.
Like a woolen curtain, Night sought to black out Day
while Day, like a huge bonfire, labored to outshine moon and stars.
From these mighty battles, people and animals suffered,
enjoying a little respite only at noon and midnight.

With Winter and Summer it was much the same.
They detested each other and all the more
for being evenly matched. Midsummer and Midwinter

were calm, but, in between, the seasons' wrestled ceaselessly;
tempests and earthquakes afflicted the world.

One day, as her parents were complaining,
Mai Ling, a little girl of eight years, spoke up.
"Nobody can tell me what time is or how much there is of it.
Why not just make more? Then Uncle Winter can have
his time and Auntie Summer hers; then Day can be day
all day and Night can be night the whole night through."

Mai Ling's parents laughed indulgently, as parents will.
But her old granny reproached them. "Listen to the child.
New eyes see better than old ones." And so
the people convened a parley with Day and Night,
with Winter and Summer, and let Mai Ling explain.

"Uncle Day, when you get sleepy you shouldn't struggle.
Auntie Night, when you're worn out, you ought to go to bed.
You shouldn't rub your eyes and spite each other.
Neighbors need boundaries, little walls, not too high.
We can make new time if only you'll agree.
We'll set fences between you: Dusk and Dawn.

"And as for you, Uncle Winter and Auntie Summer,
you should do the same and not rub up against each other
ruining our rice with mistimed warmth and blasts of cold,
hail and sleet, too much rain or parching heat.
Let's set new seasons between you, just little ones, low walls.
As Winter tires, we'll have Spring, and as Summer fades, Fall.
That is my idea. In the night people and animals shall
sleep and during the day we'll work and play.
In Spring we'll sow and in the Fall harvest.
Then you can stop this nasty wrangling and enjoy yourselves.
Then we shall all be grateful to you, blessing
each day and each night, every season and every year."

The Bronze Lantern

After he united the Northern and Southern Kingdoms, Yang Jian took the title Emperor Wen of Sui. His memory is revered for the peace and prosperity of his reign; China had seen nothing like it for three centuries. The Emperor is said to have had only two concubines, the fewest of any of China's emperors. Wen cherished and respected his wife; he took on the concubines, says one historian, only on her death and chiefly for form's sake. In any case, Wen's energies were focused elsewhere. Though he united the country by force and stratagem, his greatest talent was not for war but administration. According to tradition, nothing was beneath the Emperor's notice. One credulous writer insists that Wen knew exactly how many grains of rice were harvested each year in every province. Aiming to bring order out of conflict, the Emperor issued many rules: he fixed the price of each grade of jade, prescribed the ingredients of ink and how many bristles should go into each writing brush, standardized measures of weight and distance and struck a single currency for North and South. Wen set limits on the power of landlords and organized a professional police force. He personally reviewed the decisions of provincial magistrates and ordered the most corrupt beheaded until only honest ones were left.

To diminish the long-established tensions between North and South, Emperor Wen adopted a policy of homogenization. His encouragement of the spread of Buddhism may have owed less to the doctrine's appeal to him personally than to its effectiveness in unifying and pacifying his subjects. He built temples in a new style that resembled the traditional architecture of both North and South, yet was identical to neither. For the same reason, he introduced Northern cuisine into the South and

120

vice versa, promoted new fashions, furniture, roof ornaments, shoes, and landscape painting.

The Tang minister Fang Xuan-ling's memoirs record several conversations with Chen Hsi-wei, the Sui peasant-poet. Fang includes what the poet told him about the origins of *The Bronze Lantern*. According to Hsi-wei the Emperor's policy of transmuting discord into harmony is what lies behind the collection of poems. Its author, Ban Juyi, has always been identified as Wen's chief court poet. As such, his primary job would have been to extol the Emperor and his reign and, indeed, there is plenty of that sort of thing in the *Lantern*. A good example, is "The First Hour and the Last," the brief prelude that opens the collection:

The sun leaps up each morning
To drink the still mists.
Each night the pale moon floats
Over the still lakes.

The verses' political significance is obvious: the sun and moon are Emperor Wen; day and night, mists and lakes, stand for North and South. The reiterated word *still* suggests the happy unity and serenity of the Emperor's reign.

The new documents also suggest the real identity of the supposed court poet Ban Juyi and the origin of his book. Here is a reconstruction of the story.

Shortly after his victory over the South, Emperor Wen summoned the two foremost poets of each kingdom, Chu Juyi and Ban Zhouyi. When the two men, youthful Ban and aged Chu, had come into his presence and had made the customary gestures of submission, he politely invited them to get to their feet. He held out his hand to the elder poet, the one from the South, and addressed him first.

"Chu Juyi, it is an honor to meet you. I have long admired your work. The poetry you write in the South is eloquent, smooth, and subtle. You may well boast of its purity. However, to be frank, the verses of you Southerners tend to be rather languorous and the subjects you choose are often frivolous, even, if you will pardon such a harsh word, decadent."

It may be imagined that Chu was not well pleased to hear this.

To the Northern poet, his friend Ban, the Emperor said, "Our Northern poetry is vigorous, its language plain and earthy. It has weight and seriousness. However, to be candid, it is also rather austere and unrefined; it suffers, alas, from a lack of elegance."

The two poets, conscious of representing two distinct and hostile traditions, must have had to work hard not to frown.

But the Emperor at once mollified them by quoting their own verses to them from memory.

"Chu Juyi, I am particularly touched by your famous poem about the dead wife's tortoise-shell comb:

Any darker and I would have missed the one hair left.
As the sun set, I plucked it from the tortoise-shell teeth.
Graceful as the stroke of Po Chu-i's brush
Your still-warm hair curled up in my palm."

Chu smiled.

"Ban Zhouyi, you know well how I love both you and your poems, especially those about the terrible wars we have at last brought to an end. I must say none is better than your most recent effort, the one about Kunnei:

Just here one army made camp around General Fung's pavilion,
The other hard by the Duke of Shizu's scarlet tents.
Here in the fields of Kunnei, once known for cabbages
and millet,
Just here, the plows now turn up more bones than dirt,
What remains of Fung's archers and all Shizu's spearmen,
Of the cowards and brave men."

Ban was flattered to think that the busy Emperor had made time to read his poem, quite overwhelmed that he had memorized it.

Wen fell silent for a while, as if to do justice to the verses he had recited. Then he went over to an inlaid table and idly picked up a dagger lying on it. As if musing aloud, he said, "Bronze, as you know, is made by mixing copper with tin. If the smith measures correctly, then the result is something brighter and stronger than either."

After these words, the Emperor dismissed the poets, confident that their sensitive minds would understand him.

Hsi-wei and the Funeral

Chen Hsi-wei had been wandering through the interior for three years, making poems and straw sandals, when he decided it was time that he saw the ocean. Even his dangerous mission to the South had never brought him near the sea. And so he set out for the province of Yangzhou.

For several reasons Hsi-wei made his destination the city of Jiangdu. First, as the capital and largest city in the province, all roads led to it. Second, while the city did not lie on the coast, it was only a few days from it, less if Hsi-wei could persuade a bargeman to give him passage down the Yangtse. These were reasonable, disinterested considerations, but there was another, a more personal reason.

When, as a peasant lad, he returned from his successful mission to the Emperor's army in the South, Hsi-wei had been offered rewards of money and land by the First Minister himself. These he had turned down, instead asking to be educated. This request astonished everyone, but the Minister the same day had agreed and placed him under the authority of Shen Kuo. Master Shen resented being told to teach a peasant lad and made no secret of it; however, he was hardly in a position to refuse an order from the First Minister, no matter how absurd or disagreeable. There was, however, no accompanying command to treat the boy with any kindness, respect, or to encourage his efforts. Shen Kuo was proud of being the second son of a provincial governor and of the esteem he enjoyed at court; he had tutored many high officials and more of their sons. In his opinion, a peasant like Hsi-wei could not be educated at all, or if, by dint of great pains and superhuman patience such a boy could be made semi-literate, he would never accomplish anything of note.

"Your head's as dense as a granite tombstone; it's no wonder they chose to chisel that message on it," he often said to Hsi-wei. Another of his favorite sayings was this: "Trying to make you understand poetry is like teaching astrology to a dog." To improve Hsi-wei's calligraphy—which, to tell the truth, never rose much above bare legibility—Master Shen delivered one blow of his thick rod for each inelegant stroke of the brush. Every stage of Hsi-wei's progress was thus accompanied by discouragement, insults, and whacks; yet progress there was, even if Shen Kuo declined to acknowledge it. When Hsi-wei dared to show Shen his first efforts at writing verse, the teacher was perplexed. On the one hand, he was unable to conceal that Hsi-wei's compositions had shaken his prejudice. On the other hand, he thought the poems poor and explained why in detail. But Hsi-wei went on studying the classics and gradually his writing improved to such a degree that Master Shen, without praising a single line, began to circulate them at court. He did not hide from Hsi-wei that he did this and explained it was not to show off the boy's talent—according to him, Hsi-wei had no talent—but to advertise his own skill.

In Chingchi Province, Hsi-wei crossed paths with a young under-magistrate on his way from the capital to take up his first post in Kunnei. He had heard the story of the peasant boy who became a vagabond poet. He was delighted to meet Hsi-wei and politely asked if he might see some of his recent poems. As for Hsi-wei, he was eager for news about matters in the capital. It was then that he learned Master Shen had fallen out of favor. According to the under-magistrate, he had struck one of his pupils, a spoiled, lazy, and insolent boy. But this boy happened to be the nephew of the Second Minister and Lord of the Imperial Stables. He had run straight to his aunt to complain, and the aunt had taken it up with the uncle. So, it was arranged that Shen Kuo, who was far from young, would be permitted to retire to his native town. He was said to have a fine villa there where he housed his first wife. This was in Jiangdu. Under the circumstances, Hsi-wei considered that his old master might welcome a visit. He even imagined the old man asking to read some of the poems his pupil had written since they had last seen each other, three years before.

In those days Jiangdu was a peaceful town, without soldiers on the streets or camps in the squares. This was in the time of Wendi, long before his willful son became the wicked Emperor Yang and fled there seeking the protection of the Xiaoguo Army, whose generals promptly had him assassinated. In those days there were beautiful pavilions on the lake shore and fine villas in the hills; business flourished along the riverfront, lined with docks and crammed with barges. But when he arrived Hsi-wei took note that there was no shortage of poverty in Jiangdu. There were many beggars, swarms of famished urchins, and an extraordinary number of stray dogs, packs of them.

Hsi-wei found a tavern by the river that had what the keeper grandly called an inn behind it. This was just a weathered shack divided into three tiny rooms. But the rooms were cheap and Hsi-wei took one of them. He then saw to his own business, putting up his sign by a warehouse, and quickly had six orders from dock men for themselves, plus three more for children's sandals. Then he set about inquiring after the villa of Shen Kuo. The poor could tell him nothing but a man in a silk gown whom Hsi-wei accosted as he was coming out of a temple shocked him with the news that, just two days before, the esteemed Shen Kuo had passed away. Hsi-wei asked about the villa but the gentleman, being in a hurry, merely pointed in the direction of a hill and rushed off. Feeling deeper grief than he had expected, Hsi-wei climbed the hill. He had to ask directions three more times before he found the villa where he arrived just as the sun was setting. The wake was already in its second day.

The house was pretty, not excessively large but well proportioned, with ornamental trees surrounding the front courtyard where Hsi-wei saw a group of men gambling. These would be family members serving as guardians of the deceased. As they had to hold their vigil through every night of the wake, the tradition of gambling was adopted to keep them alert.

The men, intent on their game, took no notice of Hsi-wei as he strode up to the doorway, across which hung a white cloth. Because Shen Kuo had died at home, the coffin would be placed inside the house. Had he died in Chang'an or elsewhere then the coffin would be set outside the house. A brass gong had been hung to the left of the entrance to signify that the deceased was male. As Hsi-wei drew back the cloth and entered the house, Hsi-wei saw that the statues of the household gods had been wrapped in red paper and there were no mirrors to be seen. Clearly, the funeral rites were being carried out punctiliously, which would have pleased Shen Kuo.

The vestibule led straight into a large room where the three-humped coffin had been set on a stand a foot above the floor. An old woman in a white robe—the first wife—sat by the corpse's right shoulder. At the left sat a man of about Hsi-wei's age dressed in black with a sackcloth hood hanging from his neck. His expression made a contrast with his mother's. The widow looked stricken by her loss, but the son appeared bored and fed up, as if he would much prefer to be outside with the gamblers. Shen Kuo had never mentioned a son.

The room was anything but quiet. A mechanical wailing rose from a gaggle of women gathered behind the widow while children clad in blue tumbled around the room, squealing and shouting at one another. Perhaps yesterday their mothers had tried to control them, but now nobody bothered. At the foot of the coffin lay three bowls of food, dried out now, two fading wreaths, and a painting of the deceased. This portrait was painted on rough wood and poor in quality. Hsi-wei had the impression it had been hurriedly executed after the death.

Seeing that the wake was being conducted so strictly according to custom, Hsi-wei did what late-comers were supposed to.

He got down on his knees and crawled up to the coffin then peered in. There lay his master in his formal court robe over which a light blue cloth had been spread. His face was covered by a yellow one. Hsi-wei imagined it as stern and, notwithstanding the propriety of the rites and the cost of the extended wake, disapproving.

An altar had been set up against the far wall. On it, sticks of incense smoked beside a white candle. Between these sat a large porcelain platter full of ashes, the remains of joss paper and prayer money. At the end of the altar sat the heavily carved donation box. Hsi-wei got to his feet, fished for some coins in his leather pouch, then made his way carefully around the boisterous children to the altar.

The son glanced once at Hsi-wei's rough clothing and turned away contemptuously. The widow examined Hsi-wei more quizzically, then, seeing him deposit coins in the donation box, nodded with surprising energy. She motioned him to her. "You're a stranger. You knew Shen Kuo in Chang'an?"

"Yes, in the capital. I was his pupil."

Her face brightened. "What a tribute to Shen Kuo that you've come so far and so quickly to pay him respect. And how fitting. I can see that in your haste to arrive you've lacked the time to change out of your traveling clothes." This was intended as a reproach, though couched as an excuse. Hsi-wei thought it best to allow her to believe what she wanted. "It was two weeks ago," she said with a sigh. Then, frowning, she nodded toward the wailing women. "My daughter-in-law over there confessed to me that she had dreamt of snow."

"Of snow?

The widow dropped her eyes. "But surely you know that to dream of teeth or snow foretells a death in the family?"

Not only the splendor but the duration of funeral rites depends on the wealth of the deceased. Shen Kuo's widow proudly informed Hsi-wei that her husband, the second son of a provincial governor, did not die a poor man.

"This morning a courier arrived, sent by the Second Minister himself." She turned to indicate the donation box on the altar behind her and told Hsi-wei exactly how much money was in it, not counting his own few coins.

"Please stay in the city if you can. The burial will be in three days."

Hsi-wei realized that of all those boys Shen Kuo had taught, now men of position and accomplishment, he alone had shown up and that was more or less by accident. "Of course," he said.

"And perhaps," the widow added in a whisper that failed to soften her words, "you'll take the time to dress more decorously."

After it grew dark a monk came into the house. Behind him were three men, one holding a gong, another a flute, the third a trumpet. The son handed money to each after which the monk went to the altar and began to chant sutras, accompanied by the musicians. Hsi-wei recalled this ritual from his childhood when he was taken to the wake of Mr. Wu, the wealthiest man in his village. In that case, there had been only a one-day wake and only a gong. After death, his father had explained to him, a soul faces many obstacles, even torture for the sins committed in life. The wealthy help their deceased by paying for the chanting of holy texts which can smooth the soul's passage into heaven. Everything is easier for those with money, even being dead.

Hsi-wei spent the following days making sandals, for which he received three more orders. On the day of the funeral he cleaned himself up as best he could.

The graveyard of Jiangdu lay on another of the hills outside the city. Hsi-wei arrived just in time to see two gravediggers chasing a couple of dogs away after which the burial rites got under way. A cut stone had been set up at the gravesite. Though only a temporary marker, it was imposingly large. The extended family was assembled but there were at least twenty other mourners he had not seen at the villa—Hsi-wei wondered if these had perhaps been hired. It was a noisy group. As three monks in full regalia began chanting texts from *The Book of the Three Officials*, the women started their ritual wailing. The children, pulling at their starched clothing, were herded up to the grave where they bowed and were ordered to mumble the phrases they had been told to memorize.

It is improper for the old to pay respect to the young. How often had Hsi-wei heard it? Now he thought of what that rule meant for death rites and realized that, if he should die a young bachelor, then his body would not be brought into his parents' house, nor could they offer prayers for him. Childless and un-married, there would be nobody at all to perform funeral rites for him. That was what tradition dictated. Silence.

At the far end of the graveyard, in the marshy land where the small stones of the poor were crowded together, Hsi-wei spot-ted three people standing before a small pile of dirt. A gravedig-ger stood nearby impatiently leaning on his spade. Leaving Shen Kuo's grave, Hsi-wei wandered closer.

The grave was tiny and shallow, the coffin was so small. The father, mother, and a little girl he guessed was about eight years old, must have dressed in their best clothes, but these were nei-ther good nor clean. All three stood silently. The older cannot show respect for the younger.

Moved by a rebellious impulse, Hsi-wei stepped up to the edge of the little grave and, in a clear voice, recited *The Embryo Breath Scripture of the Jade Emperor*. He had memorized it for his grandfather's funeral, when the words meant nothing; but now it came back to him. The little girl stared at him blankly, the father with something like terror; but the mother, in tears but still silent, looked at Hsi-wei with gratitude.

The Embryo is formed by the concretion of concealed Breath; and the

Embryo being brought into existence, the Breath begins to move in Respiration.

The entrance of Breath into the body is Life; the departure

of the Spirit from
the external form is Death.

He who understands the Spirit and the Breath may live for ever; he who
rigorously maintains the Empty and Non-existent may thereby nourish
the Spirit and the Breath.

When the Spirit moves the Breath moves; when Spirit is still the Breath is still.

If you desire to attain immortality, your Spirit and Breath must be
diffused through one another.

If your Heart is perfectly devoid of thoughts—neither going nor coming,
issuing nor entering—it will dwell permanently within of its own accord.

Be diligent in pursuing this course; for it is the true road to take.
So says the Heavenly Lord Jade Emperor.

Hsi-wei gave up his idea of seeing the ocean. He felt an urge to return to the interior, to the rough roads, ramshackle villages and hard-working peasants.

On the road out of Jiangdu, he composed a poem, the one popularly known as "Two Bones."

Quon drops his scruffy head on his filthy paws
and lays both on the sweet-smelling soil of the grave.
How often had Master beaten him to make him good?
Quon is hungry. His imagination summons two bones.
The one he wouldn't touch says, "He beat you," but
the other, the one he yearns to gnaw, says,
"He was your master." Soon Quon will have to go

131

*masterless into the world's lanes and fields, armed
only with what he has learned and what he is.*

Hsi-wei's Letter to Ko Qing-zhao

*Note: This letter by the Sui period poet Chen Hsi-wei begins as a whimsi-
cal yet conventional letter-poem but continues in prose and at length.*

A biting wind blows through Tafang, gusts from
the direction of Hsuan where we drank
till the moon set and you let me see your
elegant landscapes. Could it be these blasts
are sent by you, old friend, reproaches
for my silence? If so, please relent and
instead of snowscapes paint green mountains behind
bamboo sprays. A-tremble are the walls of
Qiong Inn; Tafang's curs are shivering.

Last autumn, I spent three days in Daxing, my first visit to the
capital in many years. The city is thriving, orderly, cleaner than it
was in our day. Officials and couriers rush down the boulevards,
for the new government has a great deal to do in planning the
Emperor's construction projects and prosecuting his wars. To
be candid, these ambitious enterprises make me fear for the
peasants. Emperor Wen is doing much to spread Buddhism
and, as you know, he reinstated the Confucian examinations so
that his ministries are staffed with cultured men. Now that the
empire has been united, quite a few southerners are to be seen
in the city, elegant figures in their bright yellow robes and exotic
headgear. Their conceited wives and still haughtier concubines
are borne about in sedan chairs, an intimidating sight.

Among the poor I could discern no change.

I went to Daxing uninvited. Even had somebody conceived
the wish to summon me, where could they have sent an invitation when even I don't know where I'll be from one week to
the next? Why did I want to go to the city in which I had so

seldom been happy? Well, you too must know the longing that sometimes squeezes one in its gentle fist; I mean the yearning to see again the scenes of one's youth and how even the memory of long-ago miseries can be dear.

By a stroke of fortune, I was well received. Wu Da-quan, who in the old days was also a pupil of my late Master Shen Kuo, recognized me in the street. Wu's family is well-connected; and, after passing his examinations with distinction, he was appointed to the Ministry of Revenue. Now he is among those charged with carrying out the Emperor's currency reform. He invited me to dine. He shouted my name, took my hand and, as he had to rush off, told me where he lived and insisted that I dine with him that very evening.

Wu's villa is painted the green of a spring forest and furnished for comfort rather than display. You would like it. His wife Nuan greeted me herself at the door and in a charming fashion. Taking my hand, she said she had heard much of me from her husband then recited, without a single error, "Yellow Moon at Lake Weishan."

The dinner was delicious, the dishes simple and fresh. There were two other guests and they were well chosen. The oldest of us was Mr. Luo yet he has the open enthusiasm of a child. He works in Wu's department but his passion is the study of old chronicles which he seeks out and collects at his own expense. The other guest was Master Shao, a maker of string instruments—indeed, Wu assured me, the very best in the capital.

This company could not have been more congenial nor the conversation more pleasant. No one said a word about my cotton robe or that I am a peasant. Wu and I reminisced, of course, telling the others tales of our Master's ferocity, stories of terror that now made us laugh. Master Shao and I felt an immediate sympathy, perhaps he fashions pipas and ruans as I do poems and sandals. Unlike the others, we both know making and trade and spoke almost as colleagues. But, much as Wu, Shao, and I enjoyed our conversation, we fell quiet and attended to the story

Luo said he was bursting to tell. His eagerness was so insistent that he felt the need to apologize for it.

"You must pardon me. Two days ago I received an ancient scroll from my agent in Kaifeng and I've only just read it this afternoon. It contains a remarkable story."

"I understand," said our host affably. "Good stories, like good jokes, demand to be shared. I'm sure we'd all like to hear the story."

Luo's scroll purported to relate events from the reign of Gaozu. After a career as a foot soldier, prison guard, and bandit, Liu Bang became the strongest of the rebel chieftains who rebelled against the Qin and so the first Han emperor, known by his temple name of Gaozu. The story Luo was so eager to tell us dated from late in the Emperor's reign, during his war with Xiang Lu. Two of the Emperor's generals came to him and accused a cavalry officer named Chang Jian of handing military information over to Xiang's forces. They impressed on the Emperor that this Chang was particularly dangerous because he was popular with his troops and might, at any moment, take them over to the other side, which would be a disaster. The Emperor asked to examine their evidence against Chang. They produced two documents critical of Chang and a secret dispatch they claimed was from a loyalist among Chang's men; it was this report that accused the cavalry officer of treason. The Emperor observed that the evidence was slim. "But damning," insisted one general. "Lord of a Thousand Years," seconded the other, "the man must be executed at once, and, given his popularity, in secret." Trusting his generals, Gaozu set his seal on the warrant and three officers of the guard, accompanied by the Imperial executioner, sped to the front. But somehow an error was made and they seized a different Chang Jian, one of the officers in charge of supplies. Almost before he could protest, the man was beheaded by the executioner with a single stroke.

That night the Emperor had a dream in which an owl flew into his room and perched on his bed, an ill omen. When he received word that his order had been carried out, he was uneasy. The two generals returned and in exasperated fury explained that some fool had made a mistake, that the wrong man had been seized. Again they insisted that cavalry officer Chang Jian must be executed and the sooner the better. But now the Emperor grew suspicious.

"You may have the man arrested," he said sternly, "but he must be brought here for a trial."

The prospect of a trial frightened the generals. It might reveal that their evidence was false, the documents forged and the secret dispatch suborned. The truth was that they were jealous of this brave and loyal officer, envied the devotion of his troops and his spectacular success in the field. Anxious that he might replace one, or even both, of them, they had conspired to get rid of him.

One of the generals had a bad night and the following day begged an audience with the Emperor. Even as he kowtowed he began babbling. "Lord of a Thousand Years! I've only just learned that my colleague, envious of Chang, forged the evidence against him. I am greatly to blame that, in my zeal for your cause, I was taken in."

Gaozu ordered the man to be placed in an inner chamber, under guard, then had the other general summoned. When the second general was brought in, the Emperor had the other fetched.

"Say what this man did," thundered Gaozu. Confronted by his colleague's denunciation, the second general lost no time blaming the first.

Sickened by the treachery of his generals and remorseful over the unjust death of Quartermaster Chang, the Emperor was reluctant to execute anyone else.

"I shall show you a mercy you do not deserve," he said. "Exile." He then ordered the generals' property confiscated and had them escorted by armed guards to the border with Goguryeo. Their wealth he divided between the widow of the Chang who was beheaded and the one who wasn't. The latter he promoted to command of all the imperial forces arrayed against Xiang. All records of these events were suppressed and an official story concocted by Gaozu's First Minister. The beheading of Quartermaster Chang Jian was explained by a charge of embezzlement. As to the two generals, the official account was that one had begged to be allowed to retire due to ill-health, the other owing to age.

"And so," said our host, "the poor quartermaster was killed twice. First his life was taken and then his reputation."

"That's so," said Luo with a sad shake of his head, but he at once regained his good humor. "I'd like to think the blood money amounted to a considerable fortune. Perhaps the widow Chang and her family were satisfied."

"They had to be," observed Shao with acerbity. "It's a well known fact that emperors never make mistakes—not until they're overthrown."

Soon after, the party broke up, but neither Shao nor I was eager to return home. We two bachelors walked as far as the Cloud Gate Pavilion, chatting of things at random, just as if we were old friends, as I would with you. Before we parted Master Shao invited me to visit his shop the following day.

"Just don't come too early, Master Chen," he said, laughing. "I drank more than you did so I'll be sleeping later."

I waited until noon then followed Shao's directions to his shop. He welcomed me with a smile.

"I slept and slept," he said. "And you?"

"Oh, I was up with my landlord's rooster, I'm afraid."

"Your host keeps a rooster? Too bad. Well, you might as well look around."

The instrument-maker had secured an excellent location for his shop, across from a tidy park enclosed by closely trimmed elm hedges. Shao told me later that the park had been designed and dedicated by Emperor Wen himself. During my visit, I saw monks coming and going through the red gates. I went to look at it later in the day. At its center a statue of the Buddha sits under a maidenhair tree with pruned lower branches.

Master Shao's shop was nothing like one finds in the provinces. I admired the fine appointments, the teak cases and paneled walls. I praised the pipas and sanxians on display, beautiful objects, inlaid with ivory and so highly polished that they seemed to emit rather than reflect the midday light. I complimented Master Shao on his workmanship.

"My workmanship," he scoffed. "Come. I'll show you something."

We went behind his counter and, opening a narrow door, Shao extended his arm. "My workshop," he said.

The contrast with what I had just seen could not have been more complete. Here all was dirt and disorder, shards of wood on the floor, broken liuqins and smashed ruans pushed in corners, dried puddles of spilt varnish, tangled skeins of broken strings, animal guts, gritty bowls, and a heap of stinking rags.

"Well?" he said crossing his arms over his chest. "What do you think?"

I hesitated before replying, "Last week I had to abandon a *fu* about a peasant woman I met in Fangshu, a widow, once the local beauty. I started the poem over fifteen times and still couldn't make it come out right. The words fell apart like cheap sandals."

Shao nodded his sympathy and pointed to my feet. "Well, at least your straw sandals are well made."

"You never let anyone at all in here?"

"Certainly not. Neither customer nor competitor. Would you pass around that botched fu about your Fangshu widow?" Shao pounded on his workbench. "Like Gaozu, we know our mistakes but prefer others not to."

[Note: Hsi-wei concludes his letter with the poem that has become known as "The Broken Fence."]

That broken fence will delight the fox but
not the chickens nor Tung's new father-in-law,
come to see where his Mei-ling now dwells. And so,
drenched by unrelenting rain, Tung ties up
loose palings and replaces the cracked ones.

The bungled fu, the botched portrait, these we
shove into our workshop's corners like
Shao's spoiled liuqins and sanxians.
We'd rather display what has been polished
and made smooth, though truth is never seamless.

Hsi-wei's Visit to Ko Qing-zhao

The poet Chen Hsi-wei and the landscape painter Ko Qing-zhao had not seen one another in two years. During that time, three letters from Hsi-wei had reached Ko; but, owing to the poet's nomadic life, the painter had nowhere he could address a reply. The one he tried to send through a mutual friend in Daxing chased the poet around Emperor Wen's dominions in vain.

The two men had one of those friendships that are struck up in an hour and outlast even long separations. As is usual when two people instantly take to one another, their liking was initially physical. Hsi-wei and Ko detected in one another's faces intelligence, sensibility, and honesty. Their immediate sympathy was deepened by the esteem in which each held the other's art. As they tilled different fields, their friendship was free of any taint of competition or jealousy. They were perceptive about one another's work, understood their aims, rejoiced in their achievements and growing reputations. Whenever one heard the other's name mentioned approvingly, he felt gratification.

While the vagabond Hsi-wei was always in motion and his livelihood insecure, Ko was settled quietly in Hsuan where he held a minor sinecure in the office of the magistrate. His income was not handsome but adequate for a bachelor whose major expenses were for artist's materials. Moreover, his job was not demanding and left Ko plenty of time for his real work, though less than he would have liked. Gradually, collectors began to seek him out and, when the peers of the great Zhan Ziqian were listed, Ko's name was frequently mentioned. As a young man, Ko saw Zhan's *Spring Excursion* and dedicated himself to the art of *Shan Shui*, mountain/water landscapes. This kind of painting does not aim at realistic representation but conveying the feelings aroused in the artist by the scenery. In Ko's landscapes, Nature is always still; even his waterfalls appear motionless. Movement is confined to the few human figures—tiny sages climbing with staffs, minuscule fisherman pulling up nets, drovers with miniature oxen. The busyness of these humans is too small to affect the tranquility of mountains and rivers. In this way, *Shan Shui* painting sets the colossal extent of the cosmos and the immeasurable length of history against the paltry exertions of humans.

Ko had labored hard to become a *Shan Shui* master. Had he been more ambitious and less attached to Hsuan, he might have aspired to and secured a position at court.

Hsi-wei's journey took him by slow-flowing rivers, through the forests and mountain passes of Huangshan. It was natural to think of himself as one of those little figures in his friend's landscapes, coming from nowhere, passing into oblivion. Yet the poet's spirits were high; the splendor of the scenery and the crispness of the air exhilarated him, honing the edge of his eagerness to see his friend.

Hsi-wei arrived in Hsuan at mid-morning, earlier than he had expected thanks to a peasant's offer of a ride on his oxcart. Hsi-wei took his ease atop fragrant radishes, carrots, and spring onions. As they descended toward the town, the air grew sultry, shapes dissolved, and there were clouds of insects. Hsi-wei began to miss the sweet air of the mountains, the noise of flowing rivers.

When they reached the market square, the poet helped the peasant set his crops out for sale. Bowing deeply, he thanked the good man for his kindness. Across the road, he spied a passing official in a high hat and ran up to ask the way to the magistrate's office.

The youthful official, who was trying to grow a beard without much success, took in Hsi-wei's dusty clothes and pack. He pointed and answered curtly. "Go that way and look for a red roof."

A guard lounged in the gateway of a low building with a steep red-tiled roof.

"You have business?" asked the guard in a tone both bored and surly.

Hsi-wei knew how to deal with such people.

"Yes, Your Honor," he said with a medium-sized bow. "I have business with Master Ko Qing-zhao."

The guard made a face. "You're in luck. He happens to be here, which he often isn't." He escorted Hsi-wei through the gate and pointed him down one of four corridors.

At the end of the hallway Hsi-wei came to a small, windowless chamber. Here he found Ko Qing-zhao crouched at a low desk, brush in hand, a scroll open before him. There were scrolls everywhere, both big and little.

His old friend looked up, shouted, got to his feet. The two embraced. Bubbling over with pleasure, both spoke greetings at once, then burst out laughing.

"You inconsiderate peasant! Not a word of warning. Ah, what a wonderful surprise!"

"Well, I missed you. And I want to see what you're up to. Your work."

"I've seen three of your poems. People copy them, you know, and they make the rounds."

"Still unmarried?"

"Still making straw sandals?"

Hsi-wei shrugged. "We both have to eat," he said, gesturing toward the low desk, the inkpot, the scrolls.

"Just so. But I'll have you know I sold two pictures last month." It was a proof of their friendship that Ko did not try to conceal his pride.

"I'm not surprised. I've heard your name mentioned in the same sentence as Master Zhan Ziqian's. More than once."

Ko blushed. "Truly? Famous, am I? Like you?"

Hsi-wei scoffed, blushed, and again the two laughed.

"You must be starved," said Ko. "Let's get some rice and

dumplings in the market then go to my place and talk and talk."

"What of all this?"

"What? This copying? It'll keep. Come, let's eat and then I'll show you my real work."

As they strolled to the marketplace, the friends summed up their lives since they had last met. At first, each felt there was far too much to tell but then found there was not. Ko said he copied documents, took down the testimony of witnesses, and painted his pictures. Hsi-wei said he traveled, met all sorts of people, made sandals out of straw and poems out of words. Though one was always on the move and the other planted fast in Hsuan, it seemed to them both that their outer lives had settled into routines. As for their inner lives, these could hardly be described quickly in the marketplace over dumplings and rice.

"Now," said Ko as they finished their meal, "we'll go to my place. It's not quite finished, but I want you to see my new picture."

"Is it a big one?"

"Huge, like its subject. *Autumn in the Yellow Mountains*. I'm putting everything into it."

As they walked toward the western edge of Hsuan, Ko fell silent. When Hsi-wei inquired if something were disturbing him, Ko replied that a troubling case was to come before the magistrate that week. Though it would involve personal risk, he said he felt compelled to intervene.

"And that would be dangerous for you?"

"The contestants are wealthy landlords with few scruples."

"I see."

"More to the point, as an official in the magistrate's office, I have no standing to participate. Even asking to do so would be deemed improper. I could lose my post."

"And yet you see a likely injustice?"

"That's it exactly."

"I want to hear all about the case. But only after I've seen your autumn painting."

Ko lived in a rambling old farmhouse. Ko explained that it had once been at the center of wide fields but had been overtaken by the town's expansion. Yet the building stood on what was still a considerable plot of land, some of which was cultivated. There were five fruit trees and a small but attractive stand of white pines. Ko had a lease on two rooms and also a long, narrow outbuilding by the pines which served as his studio.

Ko's painting was indeed large. It leaned against the shed's wall, matching its length and nearly its height. If Hsi-wei had seen Zhan's *Spring Excursion*, he would have recognized the work as both an homage and a sequel. The composition closely echoed Zhan's. A broad stretch of river runs diagonally from the top left to lower right. The stillness of the river is magically emphasized by many fine black lines. A white sampan with a standing boatman floats in the middle of the river at the very center of the picture. To the left juts a triangle of riverbank on which sit two female figures almost hidden by elms and pines. Where it is free of fallen leaves and pine straw, the ground is invitingly mossy. On the right of the picture, the opposite bank rises steeply to rocky hills behind which the Yellow Mountains extend in ever more misty waves to an empty background. Nothing of the sky to be seen, as in a map.

Hsi-wei was immediately attracted by the size and beauty of the picture. After taking in the whole, he stood close to examine its details. He felt he could hear the sound of the river in the delicate pattern of water lines. He took note of Ko's cleverness about the crookedness of the branches, was delighted to make out the nearly invisible pair of red footbridges below the water falling from the sheer rock faces. A minuscule peasant on his donkey and a brace of doves high in the branches of a pine were charming touches.

All the while, Ko was trying to look through his friend's eyes; he wanted to direct them to this or that patch of painting. But there was no need, as Hsi-wei missed nothing, nor did the poet have to pretend to praise the work. He was astonished by how far Ko had advanced in his technique and full of admiration for such a large work, one fit for an imperial palace. Yet he said nothing until Ko begged for his reaction.

"It gives me two feelings."

"Yes?"

"The gladness and also the melancholy of—"

Ko finished the sentence with pleasure. "Of autumn," he said.

"Yes, autumn's just like this, or it ought to be. You've chosen the perfect moment, with the leaves in color and the air clear of humidity, bracing rather than cold." Hsi-wei stood back, looking from right to left, up to down. "It's splendid. But. . ."

"But?"

"But how will you ever outdo it?"

Ko laughed with gratification and relief.

The afternoon being fine, the two men took tea outside. Hsi-wei told Ko about a few of his adventures and showed him the poems they had provoked. Ko was bound to praise them, of course; but he did so sincerely and with insight. Yet Hsi-wei grew impatient and said he was eager to hear about the case that was troubling his friend.

"What's it about?"

"It has to do a large piece of land ten *li* to the west. Chin, the landlord, was an exceedingly good but unfortunate man. He took his wife and son to see the work on the Grand Canal. They hired a boat. A sudden storm overturned the boat, and only Chin survived. He was a broken man but still a good one, perhaps even a better one.

"Chin died unexpectedly two months ago. The two neighboring landowners, Cao and Lu, who are quite unlike the virtuous Chin, both filed claims saying that he had left his land to them. However, I heard a different story from a friend of mine. According to him, Shao-sing, Chin's oldest servant, visited the inn and drank too many toasts to his deceased master. In his cups, he said that, shortly before his death, Chin invited Cao and Lu to dinner and informed them that, when his time came, he meant to leave his land to his tenants. Evidently, he died before drawing up a will to that effect. At least none has been found."

"I see."

"It gets more complicated. In fact, there are *two* wills. Cao and Lu both submitted wills in their favor, claiming they were written by Mr. Chin. Both have also produced witnesses, former servants in the Chin household. I believe the witnesses were bribed and both wills forged."

"Well, at least one must be. Why do you say both?"

"Because I think I know who forged them."

"And can this forger be produced in court?"

"Well," said Ko slowly, "that's unlikely. You see, I'm almost certain the work was done by Ouyang Xun, a calligrapher. Though we were not close friends I knew him well enough. He's a learned young man, a good doctor as well as an exceptional calligrapher. He lacks connections and his parents left him nothing. He was unhappy here in Hsuan, desperate to get away to the provincial capital where his talents would be better appreciated and rewarded. Shortly before the false wills were submitted, he paid me a farewell visit. He said that he'd come into some funds and would be leaving for the capital the next day. If I'm right, the last thing Xun would want is to return here."

Hsi-wei made up a proverb. "Liars don't always lie, just as honest men don't always tell the truth. Do you think this Xun would lie about the forgeries?"

"What can you mean? Forgeries *are* lies."

"Quite true, but not quite *his* lies."

"Ah, I see what you mean."

"Might a sworn statement from Xun be secured, perhaps by someone he knows and respects?"

"It's not impossible. He is not really a bad man."

"Could you yourself go to the capital and try to obtain such a statement?"

"Even if I succeeded, it would take a week and the hearing is in two days."

"Can the hearing be delayed?"

"Someone would have to come forward with a good reason for such a request."

"The old servant?"

"Shao-sing? He's frail and his position is insecure. He is likely to be dependent on either Cao or Lu. I think he'd be too frightened to speak up. Besides, even if he's suspicious of Cao and Lu, our good but prudent magistrate is unlikely to take the word of a servant over that of two powerful landowners."

Hsi-wei slapped his thigh. "Very well. I understand. You can't argue the case and the old servant won't request a delay. However, I can think of one person who is willing to do both."

Ko smiled. "You mean yourself?"

Hsi-wei, the peasant who was also a poet, the poet who was also a peasant, grinned.

"Are you willing to try?" he asked Ko.

"Without you, no. With you, yes."

When Ko asked how he planned to identify himself to the magistrate, Hsi-wei insisted he would say nothing that was untrue. "I'll say I'm a traveler who has heard of the perplexing Chin case and may be able to produce evidence that would resolve it. Then I'll say that this will require a week's delay. I suspect your magistrate will be eager to grant it."

"In that case," said Ko, "we'll have to dress you properly, in an official's robe. I can borrow one. Our magistrate is a decent and fair man, but he's insecure and has an irrational fear of other officials."

Ko arranged for Hsi-wei to meet with the magistrate who greeted the poet courteously. Just as Hsi-wei had guessed, the man was only too willing to have the case resolved in a way that would relieve him of a difficult decision, one that could make him a powerful enemy. He did not hesitate to grant the delay.

Ko requested leave to visit a sick uncle in the nearby village of Yagong but, before he left for the capital, the two friends paid a visit to Shao-sing, the old servant who had overheard what his master said at the dinner with Cao and Lu. The other Chin servants had returned to their families or found new jobs, but the faithful Shao-sing had appointed himself caretaker of the villa. He was still hale enough to sweep the rooms every day and see to the vegetable garden, which is where the two friends found him.

When Hsi-wei asked if he would be willing to testify, the old man shook his head.

"I wouldn't dare to do such a thing. I'm over sixty and I've never had to stand before a magistrate. Not once. I'd dissolve into a puddle. The law's a terror, your honors. Besides, I can't go against either liar since one of them is going to become my master—if I'm lucky enough to have one at all."

Ko wanted to argue with Shao-sing, but Hsi-wei stopped him.

"What do you say we all have some tea? Would that be possible?"

The old man said he had some freshly made and went inside the villa to fetch the pot and three cups.

When they were settled, Hsi-wei spoke to Shao-sing gently, with respect, but to the point. "I'm told your son, your daughter-in-law, and your two grandchildren were tenants of the honorable Mr. Chin."

"That's true. The kind master rented the land to them for my sake"

"Well then, what if they owned that land?"

"What?"

"If, as I have reason to hope, we can win our case against Cao and Lu—"

"I can see that you know little of the world, young man. They're big men, rich. The law's made for the likes of them."

"With respect, at least one of them must lose; however, I think both will lose, as both deserve to. And, if they do, then you'll be free of both. In fact, if you help with the case, there's no reason why you and your family shouldn't move in here, into

Mr. Chin's villa, as its new owners. Wouldn't that please you? Wouldn't that be worth the risk?"

The old man gawked at Hsi-wei, then turned to Ko.

"Who's more deserving?" said Ko. "And just think how your son will bless you, how your grandchildren will dote on you. Think how your daughter-in-law will wait on you!"

After Ko rushed off to the capital, Hsi-wei busied himself with making a few inquiries in the marketplace where he took orders for straw sandals and worked out how, if Ko succeeded with Xun, he would manage the hearing.

Six days later, a triumphant Ko returned with a sworn statement from Xun declaring that he had been hired first by Cao and then by Lu to prepare the two false wills. "I am a scribe," his statement concluded, "whose services are available to all."

The hearing was set to begin in the morning. Hsi-wei arrived in the borrowed official's gown. Cao and Lu entered the magistrate's court promptly, each accompanied by two witnesses, all former servants of Mr. Chin. Cao and Lu looked determined and angry; the four witnesses trembled and avoided looking at one another.

The bailiff pounded the butt of his pike on the floor three times and called the hearing to order. The magistrate entered through a high door and, with dignity, took his seat on the dais. He proceeded to take two scrolls from the wide sleeves of his yellow gown, the false wills. Speaking gravely, he reviewed the facts of the case. Looking first at Cao and then Lu, he reminded them that, as they had been informed, a delay had been granted when a stranger presented himself promising new evidence. With the authority granted by himself, that stranger, Mr. Chen Hsi-wei, would be serving the court as an examiner.

Hsi-wei stood before the dais and gave a low bow.

"Thank you, sir, for granting the delay and permitting me to pose some questions. It shouldn't take too long."

Hsi-wei turned around and asked which was Mr. Cao.

"Over here," Cao barked impatiently.

Hsi-wei strode over to the landlord. Cao, a man of about forty, had sharp eyes and a pointed gray beard.

"Good morning, Mr. Cao. A few questions, if you please. Do you believe the document submitted to the court by your neighbor Mr. Lu to be a forgery?"

"Most certainly."

"And that his two witnesses, lamentably now unemployed, were bribed?"

"That's obvious."

"Thank you, sir."

Hsi-wei approached Mr. Lu, a short, fat man of sixty with a wide face. He looked as if he'd just swallowed a cup of vinegar.

"Mr. Lu, good morning. Do you believe the document submitted by Mr. Cao to be a forgery?"

"Clearly. It's just what the greedy rascal would do."

"And his witnesses bought?"

"Naturally, and probably cheaply."

"But, as you've just heard, Mr. Cao says precisely the same of your document and your witnesses."

"The difference is plain. Cao's lying and I'm not."

"It's the other way around, you old scoundrel!" shouted Cao.

"Very well," said Hsi-wei calmly. "So, we have two irreconcilable versions of the truth. But there is a third."

"What do you mean?" roared Lu.

"What did he say?" growled Cao.

"Obviously, the third possibility is that each of you is telling only half the truth. Mr. Cao, you are correct in saying that your neighbor is lying, but so are you, Mr. Lu. Both documents are forgeries and all four witnesses have—in their desperation—succumbed to temptation and fear. In fact, you both agree with me about one another. I make that two votes for double fraud and only one for either of you."

"But that's preposterous!"

"And offensive!"

"It might be a preposterous offense if we didn't have this statement." Hsi-wei drew a small scroll from the sleeve of his official's robe. "This is a sworn declaration from the calligrapher Oyuang Xun, former resident of Hsuan. Please note that it is officially stamped by the prefect of police in the capital."

Hsi-wei handed Xun's affidavit to the magistrate, who read it and frowned. "This would appear to be conclusive."

"I agree, sir. But, that's not quite all," said Hsi-wei.

"What? There's more?"

"Yes, sir. We have now ascertained that Mr. Chin did not give his land to either of his neighbors. But we also know to whom he intended to give it. Indeed, so do these two honorable gentlemen."

"How's that?" asked the magistrate.

Hsi-wei nodded to Ko who left the chamber briefly and returned with their star witness. "Sir, this is Shao-sing, loyal senior servant to the late Mr. Chin. He has something to say."

The old man was shaking and wringing his hands. "It was a dinner, Your Honor," he mumbled.

"What's that?" said the magistrate. "Speak up."

Shao-sing shuddered but pressed bravely on.

"It was a dinner, Your Honor. A good one, with both pork and fish."

"Never mind the menu. What about this dinner pertains to the case?"

"Well, Your Honor, you see the girl was sick and that's why I was serving, which usually I wouldn't do. Mr. Chin had invited Mr. Cao and Mr. Lu. They talked a lot about crops and rents, and the weather too. And they drank a lot of yellow wine."

"Get to the point, man."

"Yes, Your Honor. Well, you see, since they were eating and drinking so much, I was always being called to bring in more of this or that, especially more wine. And, because I was in and out of the chamber the whole evening, I couldn't help overhearing what was said."

151

"And what was said that has a bearing on the matter before us?"

"Well, Your Honor, you see, it was at this dinner that Mr. Chin told his neighbors that—being childless—he was going to turn the land over to the peasants when he died. That is to say, his tenants. He said he thought they ought to know."

Cao and Lu, who had fumed and grumbled with feigned indignation at Hsi-wei's questioning, scowled at Shao-sing's testimony and looked at him with disdain and fury. Finally, neither could contain himself.

"He swore he would give it to *me!*" insisted the one.

"To *me!*" cried the other.

At this, Hsi-wei turned to the magistrate, smiled, and delivered an eloquent shrug. Shao-sing looked around in distress. Ko barely stifled a laugh.

The judgment was delivered the following morning. Deeds would be drawn up for the peasants and, in accord with a suggestion Hsi-wei made privately to the magistrate, ownership of the villa would now be assigned to the family of Shao-sing. As for Cao and Lu, both were soundly rebuked by the magistrate and required to pay substantial fines.

Ko and Hsi-wei celebrated that night with a large meal and plenty of yellow wine. They were pleased with what they had done and with one another.

After a pleasant week's stay, Hsi-wei prepared to depart.

"A most satisfactory visit," said Ko. "It's been fun. You're the ideal guest, Hsi-wei."

"And you, the perfect host. And we managed something good. You can believe the traveler who says that such justice is rare. And I'm excited about your work, the huge new piece in particular."

"Your praise is a great encouragement to me. And our collaboration on behalf of Chin's tenants really was a special pleasure."

"About collaboration."

"Yes?"

"I've had a thought about collaboration."

"What?"

"If there can be *Shan Shui* painting, why not *Shan Shui* verses as well?"

"Why not indeed. That's a splendid idea!"

"I'm glad you think so," said Hsi-wei and handed a small scroll to Ko Qing-zhao. On it he had written the poem that is known by the same title as the painting universally acknowledged as Ko Qing-zhao's masterpiece.

Autumn in the Yellow Mountains

Deep in a golden grove on the riverbank
a slender lady in a silken gown sits with her maid.
Both look out at a drifting sampan; the
inattentive boatman has dropped his oar.
The lady holds her hand to her mouth.
If I were that boatman I too would fail
to see the laughing lady and her maid
among the vivid leaves and twisting boughs.
My gaze too would be fixed higher, on the
waterfall like molten silver, the crooked
Huangshan pines, the rocks upholding all.
Leaves turn and fall. We laugh and drift
and soon are gone. Mountains endure.

Hsi-wei and the Witch of Wei Dung

Note: In the first years of the Tang Dynasty, the minister Fang Xuan-ling visited Chen Hsi-wei at the little house outside Chiangling to which the poet retired at the end of his life. Among Fang's several accounts of Hsi-wei's poems is the following narrative.

It was springtime and Master Hsi-wei, finding himself only twenty *li* from the city of Ch'engta, decided to visit his friend Lin Zhong-yong. He had heard that Lin had been appointed to a good position in the city, responsible for securing and maintaining cavalry horses and overseeing the district's livestock.

Hsi-wei arrived late in the day and found a boy who showed him to the Lin villa. By then it was dusk, just after the family had finished the evening meal. The women and children had already withdrawn but were summoned back by the overjoyed Lin to bow before their distinguished visitor. Hsi-wei's appearance was so rough, his clothing so lowly, that the children stared with big eyes and the two wives exchanged puzzled looks.

Lin quickly ordered more food to be brought for the hungry traveler. Lin had befriended the despised peasant-scholar during his student days in the capital and felt for him the affection one does toward those one has helped.

"Do you know how famous your poems have become?" he said, clapping Hsi-wei on the shoulder. "They're more popular than ever. Just the week before the one called 'Justice' reached me. It made me long to see you, and now here you are."

"It's a poor poem from a poor poet. But yes, here I am."

Lin looked his friend up and down and wagged his head. "Poor as any vagabond sandal-maker," Lin laughed, "but you're hardly a mean poet. You know, it's almost as if I called you."

"Well, they say that friendship is one soul in two bodies."

"Do they? That's well said, then. Oh, but I forget myself. I have another guest." Lin turned and held out his arm. "Here is Pei Duan, son of my colleague Pei Tsai-tung. I've known him from a pup."

The young man, who had been standing discreetly apart, came forward, blushing in a way that pleased Hsi-wei. "He's been in Daxing for two years, preparing for his examinations. He's just returned to us," said Lin.

"It is an honor to meet you, Master. Two of my favorite poems are yours," he said and bowed.

"I'm flattered," said Hsi-wei, returning the bow.

"But too modest to ask which two," Lin chimed in jovially.

"Tell me, Master Pei, do the literary men of Daxing, if they ever condescend to speak of me at all, still call me a freak?"

"They never use your name, Master. You are always just the Peasant-Poet. To me, that is a distinction rather than an insult."

"Why's that?"

"Because it shows you are unique."

"And yet I would rather not be."

"Never mind all that," said Lin. "Duan, tell Hsi-wei how your examination turned out."

Pei was silent but glowed with pleasure.

"Oh, so you are modest too? Well, he passed with highest honors. An imperial courier arrived yesterday with the news and also that, as a reward, he's received an important appointment. Yes, at only nineteen, our Duan will be a magistrate."

"Congratulations," said Hsi-wei warmly. "And where are you to carry out your new duties, Master Pei?"

"No place very special. It's a rural district up north, in Hotung. Very poor and lamentably backward, I'm told. Still, it's a start."

"I see," said Hsi-wei.

The evening passed pleasantly. Lin insisted that Hsi-wei stay at least two nights. They reminisced. Pei spoke enthusiastically of the new things he had learned in Daxing and his plans for his magistracy. He asked Hsi-wei why he didn't settle in some city but persisted leading his vagabond life. He did not ask anything about peasants.

At length and with some reluctance, the young man took his leave, saying his parents would begin to worry about him. "They didn't know my whereabouts for the last two years, but it's different when you're home."

"That's true," said Lin.

"It has been an honor to meet you, Master Chen."

Hsi-wei thanked Duan then asked if it would be possible to meet the next day. "It would be a pleasure to prolong our conversation," he said, "especially about your plans. Besides, Master Lin will be at work and I would welcome the company."

And so it was arranged that Pei would come to the villa at midday.

Before they retired, Lin explained to Hsi-wei that Pei's two years of study in the capital as well as his appointment were owing not only to the boy's merits but also to the influence of his wealthy and well-connected family. "I'm fond of the boy. He's been carefully raised but not spoiled. You didn't think he was spoiled, did you?"

"No, I hope not spoiled," said Hsi-wei.

When the young man arrived the following day, Hsi-wei suggested a stroll so that Pei could show him the sights of his native city.

"Very well. I can say my farewell to each of them."

They visited Kamba Fortress, climbing all the way up to the battlements, and then stopped for refreshment in the market square, after which, by special permission, Pei showed Hsi-wei the extraordinary water garden of the Mengs, family friends.

As they walked, Pei grew more voluble. "If the people of Hotung really are as backward as I'm told, then I regard it as my duty to elevate them. Apparently, the worst of it is that they are steeped in superstition. In Daxing they particularly warned about that."

"A noble goal," said Hsi-wei dryly. "To elevate the people."

As they made their way toward the Jade Dragon Pavilion, Hsi-wei noticed that Pei was skirting a poor quarter and asked if they might walk through it.

Pei was taken aback. "But there's nothing of interest, only open sewers, shabby buildings, and crowded lanes. The smell!"

"Nevertheless," said Hsi-wei.

Pei gave in with a good grace.

The quarter was indeed squalid and Hsi-wei pointed out its worst features. There were beggars and sleeping drunks. At the end of a crooked lane, they came on a family gathered around a small brazier. As they watched, the oldest boy handed his parents a pair of paper dolls. The grownups bowed to the child, then laid the dolls in the brazier, briefly mumbling something as the paper went up in flames.

"Master, do you know the meaning of this nonsense?"

"It's a *Zhi Ren* ceremony. The child has made two paper dolls, Golden Boy and Jade Girl. These are offerings to the recently deceased. People believe that when the dolls are burned, they pass into the next world where they have to do the bidding of the dead."

Pei frowned; he shook his head. "This is the sort of thing I expected to deal with in Hotung, but not here in my own city."

Hsi-wei let that statement stand a few seconds before responding. "The poor," he said softly, "are everywhere, Master Pei. This service they are doing for their dead is a consolation to them. You see, it's something for them to do."

"You don't mean to say you believe burning paper dolls furnishes the dead with servants in the afterlife?"

Hsi-wei shrugged. "I know nothing about the next world."

As they resumed their walk Hsi-wei said, "Last night you were gracious enough to ask about my experiences on the road. I'd like to tell you about one of them."

"Yes. Please do."

"About year ago I found myself in a tiny western village called

Wei Dung. As usual, I set up my sign in the marketplace advertising straw sandals. The place was very poor, even by the standards of that unfortunate district, and I had few customers. Late in the day, an old man, all bent over, shuffled up to me. He was dressed in tatters and was barefoot.

"He said to me, 'They say you make sandals.'

"I told him that was indeed my trade.

"He looked down at his swollen, dirty feet. 'But I have no money.'

"'Never mind, Uncle,' I said. 'I'll make you a good strong pair tonight. You can come back for them in the morning.'

"It was sad to see the stiff old fellow try to bow, but he did the best he could and then hobbled off. About ten minutes later he was back with a small bundle of fresh straw in his hands.

"In the morning I gave him his sandals. He was so pleased, he clapped his hands and put them on at once.

"A nearby woman selling cabbages and spring onions motioned me over and said, 'Stranger, this man to whom you've done a good turn is so old nobody here is even half his age. And yet I tell you his mother's still alive.'

"I expressed my astonishment and the woman came closer. She whispered in my ear as if afraid of being overheard, 'She is a *wu* and folk say she's as old as the rocks and river.'

"This interested me and I asked the old man if he would take me to see his mother. He hesitated but agreed, and I followed him to the outskirts of the hamlet.

"I've seldom seen a sorrier tumbledown hut. The houses around here are palaces by comparison. An old blanket full of holes served as a door. The old man pulled it aside for me. It was dark inside, and the air was as thick and fetid as mud in summer. The old woman lay against the wall on a sort of pallet made of straw and rags from which all the color had faded. Her body looked like a bundle of twigs, and her face was nothing but wrinkles. The old man bowed to her. To me he spoke peevishly, 'Mother has not moved for years, though she can pass through all the seven realms. She cannot see you; she's blind and sees only invisible things. The people here don't like me because they are afraid of her; yet,' he added with some pride, 'there's nobody in all Wei Dung who hasn't come to her. They sneak in at night, begging to be healed or for rain or to have a curse lifted.' I asked about his father, and he said he had no human father. Later, I learned the villagers believe she is a survivor from the evil days when spirits mingled with men. The ancient creature groaned with every breath. The son could see this distressed me. 'She's always being pestered,' he explained, 'by earthbound spirits and the hanging ghosts. They come to complain and threaten, many *Nu Gui*, *Shui Gui*, and *Yuan Gui*. But the worst of all,' he said, 'are the *Jian*.' I had never heard of these *Jian* and asked what sort of spirits they were. 'The ghosts of ghosts,' he said with a kind of horror. As I have learned not to despise what I cannot believe, I bowed to the old man and, being eager to get away, thanked him for the privilege of being allowed into his mother's presence. She had a haunting stare but it was never turned on me and didn't follow me as I left. Once out of the hut, I avidly gulped down fresh air and thought that, if there were such things as the *Jian*, then they would look like the Wu of Wei Dung.

"I took to the road at dawn the next day. It was refreshing to see the forested mountains and clear blue sky. I can hardly tell you how good it was to exchange the atmosphere of that destitute village for the open road. I felt I had escaped something and recalled the advice of Kong Qiu: 'Respect ghosts and gods, but keep away from them.'"

The young magistrate came to halt. "I can see you mean to tell me something, Master."

"Only a story, Master Pei. You may certainly think badly of the peasants' superstitions, but perhaps they deserve some respect. These beliefs run deep and far back, and we should bear in mind that what is new doesn't replace them so much as it is erected on them."

"A disturbing notion, Master."

"I do not wish to disturb you, let alone for you to question those good things you learned in Daxing. But as to your new post, the best thing you can do is to govern justly. Where there is more justice, there are fewer ghosts. Where the people are happy, there is less need for witches. Then someday, perhaps, things will happen as you wish."

"What do you suppose I wish?"

"For these beliefs to become the ghosts of ghosts."

As Hsi-wei took his leave of Lin and his household the following day, he thanked his host for his hospitality and handed him a scroll.

"Would you do me the favor of seeing this is delivered to young Master Pei before he leaves for Hotung?"

Lin smiled. "Certainly. If you will promise to visit us again."

This is the origin of the poem that has become known as "The Wu of Wei Dung."

The world has mysteries to spare yet the people desire more.
The sages in Daxing deplore the peasants' obstinacy.
They think what they don't know isn't worth the knowing.
Peasant lore is ignorance, they say, their wisdom folly.

The Middle Kingdom teems with the living.
Why overcrowd it with countless spirits of the dead?
Yet the people need ghost tales, though in the stories it is
the dead who are needy, begging to be fed, avenged, reborn.

The world overflows with injustices
that swell the throngs of restless ghosts.
The Nu gui, with their long tresses and white gowns,
abused in life, raped, dressed themselves
in red then hanged themselves or drowned.
Wrongfully killed, the Yuan gui drift though
the countryside seeking to clear their names,

crying accusations and leaving clues.
Stories of redress slake a peasant's thirst for justice,
if only in imagination and only for a night.

Belief, observed Gaozhi, is first cousin to need.
As bad, he warned, to believe nothing as everything.
Even the Enlightened One did not deny the existence of ghosts.
Show them compassion, he admonished, but do not worship them.

In Wei Dung lies a woman older than the eldest juniper.
She dwells in a world swarming with spirits through whom
she heals tumors and brings rain. So swear the villagers,
whose harvests nonetheless wither and whose children die young.

Hsi-wei and the Grand Canal

The following narrative is included in the Tang minister Fang Xuan-ling's record of his conversations with Chen Hsi-wei during the poet's retirement in Chiangling. At the head of the passage Fang wrote down a proverb, "Blessed is the grandson who knows all he owes to his grandfather."

For two years, the court poet Zhang Chu-po was exiled from Daxing. This was owing to some verses in *The Autumn Festival Banquet*, a work he intended to circulate discreetly among a few friends. Unfortunately for Chu-po, a copy fell into the hands of a high official, a member of the southern Shun clan, a man more wealthy and proud than competent or intelligent. The Emperor's chief officials in the South, General Tung and Governor Cheng, while noting his deficiencies, urged the prudence of shoring up the loyalty of the Shuns by appointing this man to a significant post in the capital. Emperor Wen reluctantly acceded and placed Shun in the Ministry of Fisheries. However, to limit the damage, he insisted the man be given the title of Deputy Minister. Shun accepted the post with a formal show of gratification but private resentment.

The new Deputy Minister for Fisheries was the sort of envious person who could not bear to hear others praised. Perhaps this is why he took against the celebrated Zhang Chu-po and went out of his way to insult him on several occasions. Chu-po knew better than to protest these slights in public. The trouble arose because he could not resist including these lines in his *Autumn Festival Banquet*:

As the wine passed around for the sixth time,
a certain deputy minister, already deep in drink,
thought to amuse the company by mocking me.

"Master Chu-po, you have a reputation for wit,
though I have heard many say it is not well deserved.
In fact, some tell me you are ignorant, others that you
are stupid. Perhaps then," he demanded, "you are
qualified to tell us the difference between stupidity
and ignorance." To this I replied, "That's easy,
Your Excellency. Only one of them is curable."

Shun was furious and exerted all his family's influence until the Emperor agreed to exile Chu-po from the capital. He was given a sum of money and sent to a fishing village on the shore of Lake Tai near Suzhou. When the Deputy Minister Shun died of an apoplectic fit two years later, the Emperor at once recalled Chu-po to the capital. With some reluctance, the old poet returned to the court. He was welcomed at first but never regained his old popularity. Chu-po's *fu* had turned humorless, a fault-finder who made unpleasant remarks at table. He was invited to few banquets.

Hsi-wei told me how he met Chu-po during his exile when his travels brought him to the town of Suzhou. The local captain of cavalry, a lover of poetry, had befriended Chu-po. He had also read and admired several of Hsi-wei's poems and had heard that the peasant-poet lived as a vagabond supporting himself by making straw sandals. One day, while walking through Suzhou's marketplace, this captain encountered a newly arrived itinerant advertising straw sandals made to order. He asked his name.

"Chen Hsi-wei, Your Honor."

"The poet?"

"Your Honor, it's true that I make poems, though most people prefer my sandals."

"Not everyone," said the delighted captain. "It's an honor to meet you. My men have been ordered to send me any poems of yours they come across."

"I'm most flattered that my humble scribblings have found favor with you, sir."

"Tell me, Master Hsi-wei, do you know the work of Zhang Chu-po?" asked the good captain.

"Certainly. Chu-po's poems are famous. Even within the strictures of the court forms, he manages verses that are entertaining and well made. Yet I especially like a poem of his that I was shown just two weeks ago in Huzhou. This poem surprised me because it is so different from his other work. It's called *On A Peasant's Wife Giving Birth Beside Her Sow.*"

The captain nodded. "I know it. Perhaps you aren't aware that Chu-po has been exiled to the shores of our lake?"

"No, I hadn't heard."

"We've become friends. It's my impression that his misfortune has changed him," said the captain.

"I expect it has. A court poet would have much to learn here. Sooner or later, I've noticed, all the best poets are exiled."

"Yes, I believe he's actually proud of it. Yes, the man's taken his adversity nobly. Instead of turning his eyes to the capital with resentment and longing, he takes an interest in what's around him. He's become quite sympathetic with the peasants. Almost, I sometimes fear, to excess."

"That's to his credit, surely. Nobility isn't always a quality of the happy. I think it rather lies in one's attitude toward unhappiness. Exile can make men bitter and has turned many poets into the authors of ceaseless complaints."

"Not Chu-po. When I met him he said cheerfully, 'The way I see things, it's the Emperor who's in exile from Chu-po.'"

Hsi-wei laughed. "Bravely said."

The captain was silent for a moment then broke into a grin and clapped his hands together. "Master Hsi-wei, a certain Mrs. Shin runs a small inn nearby. She serves well prepared fish, always fresh. Would you do me the honor of being my guest there tonight with my friend Chu-po?"

"That would be a great pleasure for me," said Hsi-wei then looked down at his dusty clothing.

The captain laughed. "Don't worry. Chu-po has put aside his

court robes. We're not in Daxing and Mrs. Shin is no imperial hostess." The captain told Hsi-wei where to find Mrs. Shin's establishment and when they would meet, then went off to find Chu-po.

The three men met at dusk and enjoyed both a fine dinner and a memorable evening. Mrs. Shin's inn was a narrow two-story wooden structure, unpainted and listing like a doomed junk. But the wine was good and the steamed fish still better. To Hsi-wei it was a banquet and he said so.

"A banquet without either the stupid or the ignorant," quipped the cordial captain. Chu-po had told him the story of his exile, which the captain eagerly related to Hsi-wei.

"The greatest of exile's compensations is freedom," observed Chu-po. "Here I can say what I like. At court, to tell the truth is perilous."

"And to do it elegantly even more so," added Hsi-wei.

Chu-po nodded, pleased with the compliment and quick to return it. "You were often mentioned in Daxing, Master Hsi-wei. The peasant who aspired to become a poet, my colleagues liked to call you. After I'd read a number of your poems I'd correct them. No, I said, this is a poet who used to be a peasant."

"A dog who can walk on his hind legs is nevertheless a dog. I'm a peasant still, Master Chu-po."

The elder poet slapped Hsi-wei on the back. "I say good for you, then. Peasant-poet or poet-peasant, either way you've reason to be proud. I've known enough poets to fill a garbage scow—a good place for many of them—but I've learned much about peasants of late. They endure. They're stubbornly loyal and complain so much less than they could. When I think of the scorn with which they are spoken of at court, I'm ashamed. And when I think of the injustices they suffer, I'm indignant."

Hsi-wei liked the older poet's appearance. He had the dignified look of a man who had gained stature by losing weight and a healthy color by being much in the open. He was past fifty but wore his age lightly. The skin over his high cheekbones was tight and his nose was narrow and straight. Though of middle height, Chu-po seemed taller. He held himself very erect, his back as rigid as their host's.

For a time, the men spoke of poetry, especially the ancient masters. Chu-po and Hsi-wei agreed that it was their youthful enthusiasm for these masters that had inspired them to write. Chu-po could quote them at will, which the captain urged him to do.

"Yes, for me it was reading the Masters that led to writing," remarked Chu-po. "It's common enough. People call it being in-spired. But, in my experience, many would-be poets are moved by vanity and envy rather than reverence."

When Hsi-wei complimented Chu-po's poem about the peas-ant woman giving birth beside her sow, the older man grinned. "Ah, that's one for which I have to thank Deputy Minister Shun. I'm particularly pleased you approve of it, you above all. It says things I could never have said in Daxing, wouldn't have been able to say—matters people at court wouldn't care to hear about." Here Chu-po gave a little nod or bow. "Things *you* would say, in fact. I've learned from you, Master."

Hsi-wei did not know what to say to this. He only blushed. The captain smiled and passed the wine around.

"Where are you staying tonight?" asked Chu-po, putting down his cup.

"I've found a place in a shed by the docks."

"I suspected something of the sort. I've heard how you live. But, though in exile, I'm not without resources for humble hos-pitality. I have a lease on a house by the lake. No one would call it spacious but it's comfortable and there's a room there for you. If you'll do me the honor to consent, you're welcome to be my guest for as long as you like."

Hsi-wei accepted gratefully. There were rats in the shed. "I received only six orders today. I'll finish the sandals tomorrow and you'll be free of me the day after."

"That's settled then. Let's drink on it."

After that, Chu-po made a disparaging remark about the new governor and a still more pointed one about the Emperor's First Minister. The captain squirmed then suggested that it was late, beyond time for him to return to his billet. He rose and went off to settle with Mrs. Shin.

"A splendid young officer. But even with him, even here," whispered Chu-po, "it's risky to say too much."

"You put me in mind of those Buddhist teachers who say their first principle is *pu shuo p'o*."

"Yes, never speak too plainly. They are experts in self-defense, those Ch'an masters."

When the captain returned, Chu-po and Hsi-wei thanked him warmly and bid him farewell. The captain said that he would always treasure the memory of the evening, then made his escape.

The two poets walked down to the docks to retrieve Hsi-wei's belongings, exchanging stories about their lives. As they strolled back along the shore of Lake Tai they took turns reciting poems. Chu-po chose ancient verses from the *Shijing* and *Chu Ci*, Hsi-wei lyrics by Tao Yuanming, the lover of hedges and chrysanthemums. Then the talk turned to genres and the elder poet delivered what amounted to an enthusiastic lecture on the form known as protest *fu*.

"Many—too many, I'll grant—are just whining raised to high art, but the form has great flexibility and potential. The best are like roses forged from sharp spearheads, delicate and indirect but making piercing points, and always about the powerful. The bad *fus* make you despise the poet; but the good ones make you sure that the Duke of this and the Minister of that deserve all they get."

Chu-po's house was a trim one-story abode with a tiled roof and red-painted portico. A middle-aged woman with wispy hair and an anxious face sat in the doorway. On seeing the two poets, she leapt to her feet and bowed low. Chu-po told her she was free to go home for the night. She bowed again, walking backwards.

"My housekeeper," Chu-po explained with a sigh. "I don't really require one, but there are so many widows."

They went inside. The central room, dimly lit by two shaded lamps, was sparsely furnished and immaculate, with a pair of matching chairs, low couch, and a teak desk with a stool. Chu-po showed Hsi-wei around. The main room was flanked by two small bedrooms. At the back a kitchen gave on to a patio and a little hedged garden that Hsi-wei said would have pleased Tao Yuanming.

"It's exile," retorted Chu-po with a shrug, "but, to tell the truth, it suits me. Shall we talk or are you too worn out?"

Hsi-wei really was drowsy, more from the wine than his travels, but appreciated that his host, accustomed to late nights and court gossip, longed to go on talking. So each took a chair and, rather abruptly, Chu-po asked what Hsi-wei thought of the Emperor.

"I revere Emperor Wen."

Chu-po scoffed. "*Revere?* Really? You who know the suffering of the peasants?"

"It's true the people suffer; the poor always do. But they suffer less under Wendi than they have for four centuries."

"Your tone suggests you think me wrong to be critical, or perhaps naïve."

"If so, I apologize, Master. That's not what I meant. For you the tribulations of the rural poor are a new discovery."

"While you've known these things all your life? And so you think my indignation is the zealotry of the disillusioned. You're indeed a peasant, Hsi-wei. You have a broad back, strong legs, practical skills, and readily accept things I cannot."

"The Emperor has done much good."

"Such as?"

"He unified North and South."

"At the cost of how many lives?"

"Ending the perpetual wars saved more."

"He's waged new wars."

"He's an emperor, Master, not a saint."

"That's a tautology, not an excuse."

"He promotes Buddhism, which is good."

"And neglects Confucianism, which is bad."

"The Empire's prosperous now. They say in Daxing there is enough food stored to last for fifty years."

"Full storehouses in the capital? No surprise there. How many bursting granaries did you see in Tafang and Hsuan?"

"He's defeated the four great enemies—in the north, the Ti-jue, to the west the Tibetans, in the east Goguryeo, and Champa to the south."

"As I said, more wars. The Emperor's appetites are insatiable."

"He has only two concubines and it's said he sleeps with neither."

"So he's uxorious. His wife and her greedy relatives hold too much sway."

"He built Daxing."

"Yes, and a magnificent parasite it is. The capital costs a lot, and who pays?"

"The Emperor reduced taxes, redistributed land, reformed the currency. He even refused to break his own laws for those nearest to him, as in the case of Princess Cui."

"And he's whelped a spoiled and unworthy successor."

"Who can say?"

"*I* say. I've seen the boy. A little viper. No, I say the Emperor is cruel not kind. He imposed the death penalty for theft."

"But soon rescinded that law."

"He executed the Dukes of Cheng, Qi, and Shu, his three oldest comrades."

"Because they plotted against him."

"The evidence was thin."

"I heard the documents were damning and, when they were shown to him, the Emperor wept."

"It's a good story, just the kind peasants would swallow."

"Well, as you say, I'm a peasant."

"Did you know he gave permission for supervisors to thrash their subordinates?"

"What do the sages say? Respect is a marriage of love and fear. The Emperor is strict but fair."

"He much prefers being strict to being fair. What else?"

"He's improved the land."

"Such as by building his madly gigantic canals?"

"Yuwen Kai, a competent engineer, advised the Emperor to dredge. The project has created work for many."

"Oh yes. Work for millions," said Chu-po caustically. "But for how much pay? The whole aim of digging that blood-soaked trench from Daxing to Tong Pass is to supply luxuries to his precious capital and its fat inhabitants."

"With respect, that seems unfair."

"No, Master Hsi-wei. I too can be strict but fair. Have you seen the canal?"

"No."

"Then you ought to. It isn't so far. When you leave here you should see the works. On the way you might stop at the village of Weizhuang; it's on the way, only a dozen *li* off."

"Very well."

"Good!" Chu-po slapped his thighs and got to his feet. "Now, I have to apologize for keeping you up so late. I can see you're losing the battle with sleep, poor fellow. Forgive the gluttony of an exile starved for intelligent company. Go now. Get some sleep. There are sandals to be made in the morning. Six pairs, wasn't it?"

Two days later, Hsi-wei took his leave of his host with many thanks for his hospitality, and headed in the direction of the canal. Chu-po shouted something after him. Hsi-wei wasn't sure if it was "I hope you'll return" or "None will return."

Weizhuang was in a deplorable state: fences falling down, fields untended, houses collapsing. Hsi-wei found only hungry children and starving grandparents, all barefoot and poorly dressed. He left them with what money he had—the Emperor's new currency—and a dozen pairs of sandals. "Thank you, sir," said one old man. "I hope you'll come this way again. When our children return from the canal, we'll be able to repay you."

It took Hsi-wei another week to get to the canal which had almost reached Bian Qu. From the top of the eastern embankment he looked down on an astonishing sight, hundreds of men and women struggling in thick mud like ants. Around him the exhausted and sick lay under lean-tos, wheezing in crude tents. On both embankments men and women strained under huge bags, heavy with mud and rocks.

He found an overseer, a powerfully built man with a cudgel in his fist.

"Sir," he said, "where can I find the people from Weizhuang."

"Weizhuang? Why are you interested in them?"

"I have messages, sir."

"There were rains last month," growled the overseer and began to turn away.

Hsi-wei stopped him. "Rains?"

"It's bound to happen. The embankments get undermined. Those useless weaklings from Weizhuang were supposed to be shoring them up."

"There were over two hundred men and women from that village."

"Two hundred?" scoffed the overseer. "We lost three times as many in one night. They're easily replaced. We have the Emperor's authority to conscript all the people we need."

"And their pay?"

The man laughed and, looking Hsi-wei up and down, said, "Interested in some work?"

Though the formal title of the following poem is "The Guangtong Canal in a Hundred Years," it is generally known simply as "The Grand Canal." Chen Hsi-wei confessed that he wrote it but he relished the irony that it has been attributed to Zhang Chu-po.

On some far off spring noon, a little girl
will sit quietly while at the tiller her father
guides their barge, broad bottomed and laden
with good things for the nobles of Daxing:
worked iron, brass bowls, lotus root,
lemongrass and lychees, dressed pork
and salted fish, rolls of paper, bolts of silk
and cords of the finest rosewood. How she will
delight to see the breeze in the tall shore reeds
and the carpet of new violets rising up the
embankments. Far above, she'll see white pines and
fragrant Yulan magnolias, homes for the
birds whose songs sound as bright to her ear
as their feathers look to her eye, and never suspect
the thousands of bones mingled with their roots.

Hsi-wei and the Rotating Pavilion

During his visit to Chen Hsi-wei, retired then to his little house outside Chiangling, the Tang minister Fang Xuan-ling inquired about several of the poet's works. His detailed record of their conversations has survived and done much to illuminate the origins of well-known poems like "Yellow Moon at Lake Weishan," "Exile," "Justice," and "The Silence of Hermits."

At one point, Minister Fang asked Hsi-wei about "The Rotating Pavilion," a less celebrated poem.

A thousand globes of orange, green, and blue floated on the summer night,
lighting lacquered pillars, glinting like will o' the wisps over the teak floor.
The lords and ladies of the court, ten score at least, reposing in their silk
robes, wondered at the pavilion's beauty, gleefully giggling
at its measured revolution. One by one, they took turns standing
at the still center, a merry game. Here they might truly feel
themselves at the very center of the Middle Kingdom.
Our Northern nobles behaved courteously to those
up from the South, made them welcome, as the Emperor
had sternly directed. As for the defeated princes of Chen,
they upheld their dignity without being standoffish or servile.
Men spoke approvingly of the new currency, tax laws, penal code,
the clever plan for militias. Women rejoiced at the peace,
admired the exotic fashions, greeted old friends, new rivals.
All breathed in the promise of the newly united empire,
looking out on Yuwen Kai's dream of a vast Daxing, its
gardens and temples, broad roads extending on every side to the
horizon, as if the capital of Sui were the whole world.
Emperor Wen arrived in state and all bowed low,
not with grudging submission but in tribute to what he had
already accomplished and the foreseen glories yet to come.

The gods themselves must have nodded, smiling as
the stately pavilion circled reverently about their Son.

"'The Rotating Pavilion' is not much like your other work, Master," I ventured to say. "I hope you'll pardon my saying so, but it's more a courtier's poem than a peasant's. I'm expressing myself poorly, but those long verses feel loose, weightless though at the same time heavy."

Hsi-wei nodded. "Like a river man's cable falling through thin air. Like the fulsome flattery of a hired woman."

His comparisons startled me, but they were, unlike the poem, in his mature style. "If you like," I said. "Am I wrong to think it's an early work?"

"Not wrong, my lord. And early enough to show all too clearly how early. 'Rotating Pavilion' is indeed a court poem, one written by a novice whose wretched calligraphy could hardly be read even by himself."

"I've heard of the rotating pavilion. Did you actually see it the evening it was unveiled?"

"Oh yes. The poem is accurate in an external sense. Master Shen Kuo dragged me along with him on that memorable occasion. As one of the official ornaments of the court he was invited to attend and received permission to bring one of his pupils."

"Dragged you, eh? Why was he keen for you to be there?"

"In order that I should write this poem. You see, Master Shen wished to make a gift of it to the Prime Minister. Remember, I began my career as a dancing dog. The object was to demonstrate the trainer's skill, not the dog's."

"So these verses were written under duress?"

"No. That would be unfair. Master Shen did not threaten to beat or behead me. But he had the ability to make himself quite clear. It was an assigned task, a duty. He wanted a court poem and explained the requirements of the form to me. His idea was that I should be dazzled and say so in respectable verse. I was to glorify the occasion and, of course, the master of my master, the Emperor."

"You had already done good service for Emperor Wen on that perilous trip to the south. As I understand things, you turned down the offer of money, land, and women asking to be educated instead."

"That's true." Hsi-wei laughed and grabbed at his knee. "Master Shen was not well pleased by the order to educate an illiterate peasant boy whose only virtues were fast-growing hair and an unaccountable knack for survival. He was strict with me and quick with barbed criticisms; but the more he insulted me, the more I learned. It was an effective method for us both."

"The poem, then, is an accurate account of that evening?"

"Yes, the evening that sealed the reconciliation with the nobles of Chen, the night the empire was truly unified for the first time in three centuries. I was overwhelmed by the experience, as my Master anticipated, and struggled to do what he asked of me. Still, he made many corrections."

"Was your heart in it?"

"My heart? An urchin who stares at a princess becomes tongue-tied. I come from a small village and had only glimpsed Daxing briefly before being sent off to the south, though even that glimpse awed me. By the time of my return, the Emperor had transformed and expanded the capital. He had made it magnificent."

"'Yuwen Kai's dream,' you called it. Who was he?"

"He was the Emperor's architect and engineer, one of the truly remarkable men of his generation. It was he who recommended that the Grand Canal be built and it was he who laid out the plan for the magnificent capital in only nine months. To create a final touch, a marvel for the city, he conceived the rotating pavilion. Has he been forgotten already?"

"He belongs to another time."

"That's true," sighed Hsi-wei.

By then, afternoon had turned into night. A waning moon was

on the rise. My host asked if I would care for some more tea.

"Rice wine would be more welcome," I said, "if you have any."

"I'm sorry, my lord. Only tea." The poet blushed and I regretted my words.

"Tea will be most welcome."

Hsi-wei went inside the little cottage. Perhaps our conversation stirred his memory. After he returned with the tea he spoke more freely of the past.

"When I was a child I believed Mr. Kwo's four-room villa must be the grandest building in the world. When I was told that Emperor Bei Zhou lived in a great palace in the capital, I imagined it as just a larger version of Mr. Kwo's place, with more rounded pillars and fresher paint."

I laughed.

"Well you may laugh, my lord, at the innocence of a poor peasant boy; but I think Mr. Kwo was a better landlord than Bei Zhou was an emperor. My village was poor; even Mr. Kwo just scraped by. Nevertheless, when Mrs. Ts'ao's husband died and she could not pay him the rent, he didn't turn her out. The laws of Bei Zhou, on the other hand, were hard benches without pillows."

Hsi-wei's image appealed to me. I replied, "And Emperor Wen put pillows on those benches so they would compromise with life's imperfections?"

"Just so. Wendi began all things afresh, just as he did with Daxing. At his direction, Yuwen Kai made space for large markets in both the east and the west. He got rid of the tangled lanes and laid the city out in good order, on a grid. To honor the Emperor and display his skill, he devised the rotating pavilion where two hundred guests could take tea together without once bumping elbows. The night it was unveiled the most sophisticated courtiers were as amazed as this peasant boy. Between them, the emperor and his architect rolled all Daxing out before us the way a merchant does a carpet."

"You think well of Emperor Wen?"

"I do."

"Yet he could be cruel. He is said to have executed fifty-nine princes of Zhou and to have emptied the state treasury."

"I've heard the tale of the fifty-nine princes. Even if it is true, it was one of the evil necessities of war time, not essentially different from the savage battle on the Yangtse or the razing of Jiankung. As for the treasury, if Emperor Wen emptied it at least he did so in good causes. He built granaries for the people and the empire's defenses. It was not empty flattery when the scholars he patronized nicknamed him the Cultured Emperor."

"And the Emperor Yang, his successor?"

Hsi-wei made a face, as if he had tasted something sour. "His son, executed, it's said, not by your master but by his own ministers, poured money and lives down his so-called Grand Canal. Lusting for dominion, but not leading his troops, he sent whole armies to be slaughtered in the mountains of Goguryeo. Yang would have done better if, like his father, he had economized on concubines and cruelties, paid attention to the grumbling of the nomads, taken into account the widows planting rice. He might have given a thought to men too old to dig or fight who wished only to be left in peace to recite the verses of the Shijing masters."

"So in your opinion Wen's son was in no way worthy of his father?"

"Yang may have been a fair poet, but he was a terrible emperor. In my last travels I saw the villages he had stripped of men and money, poorer than ever. While the people suffered he led a shameful life in Daxing, carelessly spilling lives and money as people say he did the strong yellow wine. To speak plainly, I'm glad that your master has replaced him."

Though it felt strange to hear such bitterness from Hsi-wei's mouth, I wasn't all that surprised. By the time of his overthrow, Yang had scarcely any defenders left and—if half of what was said of him is true—merited still fewer.

Before departing for the night, I asked if I might return in the morning to resume our conversation. The poet agreed with his usual courtesy, then excused himself and went inside again. He returned with a scroll tied up with the rough twine peasants use to stake climbing beans.

"You were right to criticize that early poem of mine. I never think of it without shame. When I heard of the overthrow of Emperor Yang I recalled it again. And so to get the bad taste out of my mouth, I've written a second part, a sequel. As you'll see if you honor me by reading it, it's not the naive effusion of a callow youth but something different."

This poem, in Hsi-wei's true style, is blunt, elegiac, and angry, an epitaph for the Sui. In the rotating pavilion of Daxing he finds a new significance, an emblem rather than a spectacle.

I was careful to keep the scroll dry and delivered personally it to Emperor Tang on my return to the capital.

So, the glorious Duke of Tang
has declared Daxing no more.
It is to be called Chang'an now.
I'm told it looks much the same.
Would I still recognize its alleyways,
its markets and villas? Perhaps not,
but I shall never forget that
evening of the rotating pavilion.
Our new emperor must be brave.
It's said even his daughter,
the Princess Pingyang, raised her
own troops and led them well, too.
And so ended the Sui dynasty.
Somewhere in Lungyu the news
will have reached the village of Zhaide.
At first the peasants would be impressed
that Heaven had stripped Yang of its
mandate and settled it on Tang.

But that is far-off news, business of the capital,
home of marvels, murders, intrigues, luxuries.
Perhaps they had once heard talk of a teak
pavilion that goes round and round.
Emperor Yang should have taken better note
of the moral of Yuwen Kai's masterpiece,
how nothing stays, not even dynasties
that look immovable as the Blue Mountains.
The pavilion rotated so slowly that one
enthroned in the middle might well think
himself secure. But still the pavilion turns.
Such an end from such a beginning,
the peasants in Zaide would say, then shrug.

Hsi-wei and the Liuqin Player

The marketplace was nearly as still as a painting of itself. The villagers drooped, just like the leaves on the medlar tree under which Hsi-wei had set up his sign. Anyone who stirred moved as if resenting the necessity. Two sweating workers shuffled lethargically up to the dumpling seller. A boy almost tottered from a dry goods shop to the well to get a drink. A woman holding a little girl by the hand approached Hsi-wei with small steps. What would new sandals for her daughter cost? Though Hsi-wei's price was low, when he saw the look on the woman's face, he made it still lower.

The summer had turned oppressively hot and dry. Up north there was drought, rumors of famine. This region, watered by the Yangtze, was better off, but still sweltering and dusty. Hsi-wei was making his way south to Chiangling. An invitation from an old friend had reached him. Zhu-li had been appointed to a high post in the city and promised Hsi-wei a gracious welcome if he would visit. When they were students together in the capital, Zhu-li had defended Hsi-wei against those who insulted the upstart peasant. In return, Hsi-wei helped Zhu-li prepare for his examination. Hsi-wei was making his way south from Daxing. He had stayed in the capital only long enough to pay his respects to the widow of his old teacher, Master Shen. It was she who handed him Zhu-li's letter.

At mid-afternoon a wagon with a faded green awning pulled into the marketplace. Hsi-wei could see the horses were suffering from the heat. The man at the reins jumped down quickly, unhitched the poor animals, and led them to a stone trough on the east side of the square.

Three people emerged from the big wagon: a young girl, then, more slowly, a fat man and a thin one. The men stretched and looked around them drowsily, while the girl wrestled a carpet from the wagon, rolled it out over the hot ground and called sharply to the two others. The men rubbed their eyes and ignored her. The girl struck Hsi-wei as unusually self-contained. Her narrow face was closed, giving her the squinting, severe look of an over-studious child.

The fat man waddled to the well, drew water, and gulped it down straight from the bucket. The thin one was right behind him and did the same. The girl shook her head at them, then jumped back on the wagon. Hsi-wei wondered why she hadn't drunk as well. She emerged carrying two musical instruments by their necks, like dead fowl. In her right hand she held a *pipa* almost as long as herself, in the left a small *liuqin*—goose and duckling. Across the marketplace, the fat man flopped down in the shade of the well, feet splayed out. The thin man wiped his mouth, grunted at his companion, then made his way back to the wagon and climbed inside. A moment later he emerged carrying the kind of flute known as a *chi*, also an *erhu* and its bow. These he laid on the carpet.

The fellow who had seen to the horses left them at the trough, strode over to the well to get a drink for himself, then went into a shop. Hsi-wei guessed it was to inquire about stabling the horses. Meanwhile, children gathered to look at the instruments laid on the rug. The thin man pointed and named each instrument for them but kept the curious from touching them. "You'll hear them soon," he said, then bellowed the same again, turning his head, broadcasting an invitation to the whole town.

Hsi-wei liked the look of the fellow who had driven the cart and seen to the horses. He was energetic, well built, around thirty-five, with a kind face. None of the musicians could be called finely dressed but he wore a leather jerkin over his shirt, a garment common in the northern village where Hsi-wei was born. When the man came back into the marketplace Hsi-wei accosted him.

"Pardon me, sir. You'll be performing?"

181

The man stopped and sized up Hsi-wei, with provisional approval. He inclined his head in a manner that conveyed both humility and dignity. "My name is Ping," he said. "And yes, we'll be playing around sunset. That's the best time. It will be cooler and people will be at leisure."

"So you're itinerant musicians?"

Ping laughed. "Well, at present, I suppose that's just what we are."

"At present?"

Ping glanced across the marketplace. "Excuse me. I can't let the horses drink too much."

"Of course."

Ping started toward the horses then turned back.

"You'll come listen to us, I hope. There's no charge. We ask people to give what they want. It's more for practice than money."

Hsi-wei pointed to his sign. "My own prices are low—but fixed."

"Fair enough. Sandals last longer than air."

"Not always. Straw wears away more quickly than a song whose melody's good and words are true. Even the best sandal won't last two years."

This thoughtful reply pleased Ping so much that he invited Hsi-wei to join his troupe for their evening meal. "After we play. Then perhaps we'll talk some more. I have a notion there's more to you than sandal-making."

Hsi-wei took three orders, bought some straw from a peasant, and negotiated with the tavern owner for a corner in which to sleep. The rest of the afternoon he spent making sandals but kept an eye on the musicians. Toward sunset they took stools from the cart and set them up by the well. Word of the performance had spread. About twenty people gathered and Hsi-wei joined them.

Ping, obviously the troupe's leader, announced each piece, folk dances and popular tunes, just the sort of music to please a rural audience. But there was nothing rustic about the playing. Ping was a master on the *pipa* and the two other men, thin and fat, played their instruments more than competently. But it was the girl Hsi-wei watched most closely. Her playing was unlike the others'. It wasn't that she played better or worse but that she played in a different spirit. It seemed to Hsi-wei that the men were performing for their listeners while she played for herself or for some higher, imagined audience. The men smiled, nodded to the people, and encouraged them to clap; the girl looked inward with an earnestness that was almost comic. She was not a pretty child; her face was too thin, her ears stuck out, and her hair was crudely cropped; yet Hsi-wei found it a pleasure to watch her. He felt she was sympathetic; he thought he understood her. He liked the intensity of her playing. He liked her bright eyes.

The crowd was pleased; there was much applause at the end. The musicians bowed and clapped for the audience. Ping collected some coins.

After the recital came the meal. During the afternoon Ping had bought a load of vegetables and some fresh pork. Now the girl brought a bag of rice out of the wagon while the fat man saw to the brazier. They even had a little table which the thin man and the girl set up, placing the four stools around it. The fat man was the cook. While the rice simmered, he chopped the vegetables and sliced the pork. Ping fetched a fifth stool from the wagon, then walked over to where Hsi-wei was working, made a formal bow, and courteously asked him if he would be pleased to join them.

Hsi-wei put away his work and gathered up his things. Ping introduced him as a traveling sandal-maker with whom he'd struck up a conversation earlier. That the others were not surprised and that there was a fifth stool suggested to Hsi-wei that Ping often invited guests and the others had to put up with it.

Ping himself was eager to talk. He sat himself beside Hsi-wei and began by explaining that they weren't really itinerant musicians. "We are—or were—retainers of the Duke of Shun. Our Master is a good man but young. I'm afraid he can be a little headstrong. Some months ago he sent a letter to the Emperor's First Minister complaining that too many of his people were being conscripted to work on the Grand Canal and too few were coming back. On top of that, he added some impolitic words about the wisdom of invading Goguryeo and doing it over and over again. The Emperor banned the Duke from the Court. We're part of the Duke's apology. Everybody knows Emperor Wen's fondness for music. It's said he keeps seven orchestras!"

"I've heard there are now nine," said Hsi-wei.

"You've been to Daxing?"

Hsi-wei nodded. "I'm coming from there."

Ping had dozens of questions about the capital and Hsi-wei answered all those he could. He described the famous rotating pavilion, the broad avenues, the new Buddhist temple, the palace and its grounds, the capital's full store houses. All the while he kept glancing across the table at the girl, who ate slowly. She had no questions. She did not appear to be listening and said nothing at all.

After they'd eaten everything down to the last grain of rice, Ping invited Hsi-wei to join him for a stroll around the marketplace. "Old people say a walk's good for the digestion."

As they headed toward the well, Ping looked over at Hsi-wei with a sly smile. "I've heard that a certain Chen Hsi-wei, the peasant/poet as people call him, walks the roads as a vagabond. I've also heard that he makes straw sandals."

"Is that so? And do people say which are better, his poems or his sandals?"

Ping laughed. "I've heard his poems last longer."

"Ah," said Hsi-wei.

"Am I plagiarizing?"

Hsi-wei came to a halt at the well and bowed to Ping. "The

Duke is sending a treasure to Daxing. You're a gifted artist. Your whole troupe is excellent."

"So then I'm not mistaken, am I? You're the poet Chen Hsi-wei?"

"The way I see it I'm only a poet when I'm writing a poem. A flute-player who never blows the flute is no flute-player."

"I have to disagree, Master. He may still be a flute-player because he *has* played the flute and may do so again. And you may write a new poem, maybe even one about us."

"If I do, *then* I'll be a poet."

They laughed at their own silliness, laughed like colleagues in different fields who like and respect each other and never have to compete.

"Look," said Ping, "I can see the girl intrigues you. Now, that one's a musician *all* the time."

"Is she your daughter?"

"My daughter? No, not that. Are you curious about her story?"

"I am."

"Very well, then. Yin's parents were well off, almost gentry. Her father and I grew up together. While I was studying music, Lu was learning the cloth trade and establishing a good business. He and his wife had two children. Yin came first and two years later her brother Gao-tzu who, of course, became the hope of the family. Lu's ambition was not for his son to go into trade but to become an official. So he hired a tutor for the boy. I often saw this young man when I visited, a lively fellow who loved the arts and cracking jokes. This tutor did not object to Yin sitting in on his lessons with her brother whenever she was free from chores. Yin learned to read and write so quickly that it was obvious she was far more gifted than her brother. She particularly loved the old poems her brother was assigned to copy; in fact, she confessed to me that she did far more copying than her brother. Everything that was a burden or a stumbling-block to him was a joy to her. The tutor and Yin got on well. It was a pleasure to watch them tease each other. The tutor was also an amateur. He had a *pipa* that Yin was always begging him to play."

"All this couldn't have pleased the parents."

"Well, no. But they didn't discourage her. They thought it wiser to urge the boy to be more like his sister, to outdo her."

"I see."

Ping paused and then sighed. "We're all dancing over an abyss that can swallow us up at any time. Everybody knows this but we seldom think about it because, if we did, how could we live?"

"That's true. A catastrophe, then?"

"My friend Lu often traveled on business. On one of these journeys he was set on by bandits. He had two guards with him but they fled. Lu was robbed and killed. His wife's health had always been delicate. The news destroyed it. She died a month later. The only relatives were the wife's brother and his wife who had always been jealous of Lu. They grudgingly agreed to take in Gao-tzu but not Yin."

"So that's how it was."

Ping pitched his voice high. "'*What use is she? She's so small. Besides, she'll marry and leave us, but the boy is strong. He can work now and when he marries his wife will serve us.*' That's what the aunt said. I know because she said it to me at the funeral. So I took the girl myself. I know, it was madness but what else could I do?"

"Then Yin's your ward?"

"Ward? Yes, I suppose that's the word. My ward, but also my pupil, my apprentice. The *pipa* was too large for her, so I got her a *liuqin*. You've heard the result."

Hsi-wei noted that the good man was more proud of the girl than of his own charity. But all he said was, "Yes, she's very good." He could tell that Ping had more to say.

"Yin was a favorite of the Duke. '*Such a big sound from such a little instrument, from such tiny fingers.*' That's what he said when we first played for him. I've always believed it was because of Yin that he took us on."

They were still standing by the well. The arid sky was as

crammed with stars as the capital's storehouses were with rice. A half-moon silvered the tiles.

"She's different, isn't she?"

Ping shrugged. "We make music the way tailors make clothes. Excellent tailors, mind you, and silk gowns, but yes, with Yin it's something else, something more."

"Higher?"

"A child whose life falls apart in a month, rejected, taken in but not by a family. For Yin, it's as though music is the path to enlightenment and she's condemned to be always marching down it. Can you imagine? The old tunes aren't enough for her. She makes new ones to sing her favorite poems. I'm always on the lookout for poems for Yin. She keeps a little library of them."

"So she likes poems as much as music?"

Again Ping smiled slyly. "Let's get back."

Two lanterns sat on the table, attracting moths. The fat man and the thin one were playing a game of *Xiangi*. Yin busied herself inside the wagon. "Wait," said Ping and went in after her. Hsi-wei couldn't help overhearing.

"You were rude to our guest at dinner. Now, come out and offer the man a proper greeting."

"Too late for greeting sandal-makers. Anyway, you can see I'm busy cleaning up."

"If you don't come out you'll be sorry. And if you do—"

"If I do?"

"Just come, Yin. Now."

The girl jumped down and stepped up to Hsi-wei. She looked up at him and in a flat voice said, "I hope you enjoyed your meal, Mr. Sandal-maker. Good night." Then she picked up some chopsticks that were still on the table and began to turn back to the wagon. But Ping, standing behind her, put his hands on her shoulders and held her still. Hsi-wei could see the man was almost bursting with anticipation, with mirth.

"Yin, our guest makes more than sandals. In fact, I believe you may have heard of him."

The girl swiveled her head, confused.

"His name, my dear, the name for which you neglected to ask, is Chen Hsi-wei."

Yin dropped the chopsticks. Her bright, black eyes widened. "Is it really?"

Then, knocking over a stool, she fell to her knees and bowed to the ground. Hsi-wei was horrified. He hurriedly helped her to her feet.

Some say he and the young liuqin player stayed up all that summer night talking about the making of poems and music, Yin overflowing with passion, Hsi-wei more measured but equally absorbed. It is to be regretted that there is no record of this conversation, if indeed it took place.

What we do have, however, is Hsi-wei's poem.

Tallow leaves hang low; grass is brittle underfoot.
Birds spiral lazily then flutter down in the shade.
Prickly lettuce and withered jasmine
lie flat, like bing cakes baking on the dirt.
Paving tiles burn right through straw sandals.

Her eyes are so alert, it's as if she just found them.
The heat barely touches her, this devotee of song.
She's not the sort to compromise, not yet.
She asks me about music, what I've heard and whom.
Did I hear the great Zhang Chu in the capital?

Her reverence for her art exalts them both. She's
sure a celestial melody floats just above her head;
if only she could tug it down and play it then
the world would certainly change for the good.
The sun wouldn't scorch, perhaps taxes would drop.

She is small, delicate, nearly a child, though
if you look closely, you'll see that's half true,
that she's a soft soul in a hard cocoon.

Her faith is as unspoiled as her smooth skin.
Who would dare to scoff? Not me.

When she's told my name, she leaps to her feet,
then kneels and calls me Master, says she
can scarcely believe it, tells me how much she
loves my old poem about Lake Weishan.
Her face is fervent as a praying monk's.

Taking up her liuqin, she begins to sing
and it's like running water by a dusty road.
I feel my old poem surfacing from
Lake Weishan transformed, summoned
by the sudden beauty of this butterfly.

Hsi-wei and the Twin Disasters

Note: The following is drawn from the Tang Minister Fang Xuan-ling's account of his extensive conversations with the peasant/poet Chen Hsi-wei, whom he visited in his retirement at his cottage near Chiangling. Minister Fang customarily relates Hsi-wei's stories about the sources of his poems. In this instance, however, he questioned Hsi-wei about a particular poem, not one celebrated at court, though it is said to have been popular with peasants. As Fang does not include the poem itself in his manuscript, it has been interpolated following his opening remarks.

The conclusion of Hsi-wei's poem called "Between Flood and Drought," a minor piece, has always puzzled me. I resolved to find out what was behind it.

It happens now and then that rain pours like
a judgment on Shannan Tung. Then Yangtze
laughs at its banks as if the greedy
dragon meant to seize all the land, anything
that's dry in the Empire, for its own.

It happens from time to time that rain sits tight
in heaven, enthralled by some celestial
tale or stunned by the heat of the sun, and
refuses to leave the clouds. Then crops
wither and gusts blow away the soil like smoke.

If the river wishes, it overwhelms even
the biggest oxen, turns wide fields to lakes,
and drowns those who bend their backs to plant.
If the rains won't fall, the brown land sprouts
only the dusty graves of hopeless harvesters.

Like rope-walkers in a gale, peasants stagger
between flood and drought. No matter
how careful of their balance or what pains
they take, they may be blown left or right.
No matter, as ruin lies on either side.

Think how patient a weaver Fortune is,
how two cradles can yield three fates.
Out of too much water came salvation
and from too little a shining act
that, in a dark time, lit up the land.

I arrived at the Master's cottage earlier than usual, well before noon. Hsi-wei welcomed me with fresh tea and a dish of
pickled radishes. As we made ourselves comfortable on his little
terrace the Master remarked on how fine the weather had been.
I seized on this to ask him about his floods and drought poem.

"It's straightforward," I said, "and does what your work does
better than anyone's; I mean to remind those who read it of the
peasants' harsh lives. But the last stanza, if you can recall it, is
obscure. It makes me think there must be some story behind it."

"Which stanza, My Lord?" he asked politely. "You must pardon my memory. These days it often gets up from the table
rudely, without excusing itself."

"*Think how two cradles can yield three fates?*" I prompted.

"Oh yes." The Master slapped his thigh and broke into a
smile. "I was young when I wrote that. It was shortly after I
left the capital. For no particular reason, I'd decided to head for
Shannan Tung province. Yes, I remember now. How could I
ever forget that dreadful time? The summer was relentless and
the sky almost cloudless. The great river had fallen so low that
in many places a ten-year-old could wade across. The tributar-
ies were dusty gullies, memories of brooks. All the ditches and
canals were bone-dry. The result was famine. Pitiless hunger.
No customers for straw sandals; in fact, there was a surplus,

so many pairs left behind by their owners. As always, the children and the old bore the brunt. I passed through harrowing scenes. Even some large towns were abandoned. Empty lanes and shallow graves. Though neither too young nor too old, I was soon in serious straits myself. Then I came to a district where, though water was strictly rationed, the cisterns and wells closely guarded, everyone was well fed. I passed through four such villages, the largest of which was Haidong where I stayed for a couple of days.

"I remember that everything there was unusually neat and clean. This was because there was no point in going to the fields so the people kept busy painting houses, fixing fences, sweeping the sand and dust from the lanes, seeing to their surviving chickens and pigs. I had several customers in Haidong and I asked one how it happened that the people of the region had managed to feed themselves while all around people were starving.

"'Wang Ling-jiang!' answered the man at once. 'Our landlord, may Shennong bless him and us all. He's the one who's been feeding us—and not only out of his storehouses either. He's paid Heaven knows how much to bring in supplies from the north. When this drought took hold, he made a vow right here in the market that no one on his land will go wanting.'

"I was astonished. Elsewhere, the rich landlords had not opened their stores but kept them locked and guarded. As for the poor landlords, they were as badly off as their tenants. Naturally, I was eager to meet this Wang Ling-jiang.

"'I will introduce you myself, stranger,' said the friendly fellow. 'Don't worry about your rough clothes. Mr. Wang won't mind; he's a friend to all travelers. And he visits us every day to see how we're faring.'

"Here the man pointed to a low hill to the west. At the top sprawled a red-painted, old-fashioned, one-floor house, squat and sturdy, and several outbuildings."

"Did you get to meet this marvelous landlord?"

"I did indeed and that very day, too. As promised, he came to the marketplace. I watched him walk down from the villa accompanied by one servant. Wang carried a pouch and I saw take from it treats for the children who ran to greet him."

"What did the man look like?"

"He was humbly dressed, not like the proud landlords in high hats I'd seen elsewhere. He was of medium height and as sturdily built as his villa. To tell the truth, he looked like a peasant. He had one of those broad faces that are common in the region; his eyes disappeared when he smiled. And he smiled easily, a cheerful man. When he came to the market where I was offering straw sandals, my friendly customer, true to his word, accosted him and brought him to me.

"'Welcome, stranger,' he said, and with almost the same breath asked, 'Are you in need?'

"I told him I wouldn't refuse some water and perhaps a little food, because it was the truth. No use pretending otherwise.

"'Then you shall have both,' said Wang Ling-jiang and ordered his servant to go to the guard at the well and fetch me back a cup of water, also two dumplings and a bowl of rice from the nearest home.

"I ate and drank greedily. Wang watched me with evident pleasure. And, after I'd refreshed myself, he inquired about me. I gave him a brief account of myself."

"Did you tell him about your poems?"

"No, I omitted any mention of them."

"Was that out of modesty?"

"Rather doubt of my ability. It was a long time before I felt entitled to call myself a poet. Even now, it makes me uncomfortable. But what I did say so interested him that he asked me to come to his villa at nightfall so we could talk more. 'We get little news here, and what we get is all bad. I'd like to hear about what you've seen on your travels and especially about the capital.'

"Of course I agreed."

"You were, I imagine, as eager to hear his story as he was to hear yours."

"I was. But I would have agreed to anything this virtuous man asked of me."

"You were poor, half his age, and a vagabond. How did he greet you?"

"Most graciously. He met me at the door himself. The interior of the villa was as old-fashioned as the outside. All the seats and cushions, the carved wood and couches were well cared for, though they must have dated from long before Emperor Wen's time.

"We shared a modest meal, rice and vegetables, no meat, served by the same man who'd accompanied Wang to the market. After we'd set the dishes aside I described Daxing and the Emperor's innovations after which I related the horrors I had seen in the province. I made special mention of how the gentry had locked themselves away and shared nothing with the peasants. Then I ventured to ask my host about his extraordinary generosity; for it was clear the good man was denying himself for the sake of his tenants, that, in fact, he was ruining himself.

"Wang Ling-jiang was about to speak when two women came into the room. One was my host's age and she was assisting the other, an aged lady dressed in faded silk, who moved painfully with a cane. They had apparently come to wish Wang a good night but perhaps also to see with whom he was conversing. The younger woman had Wang's round face and cheerful eyes. As I learned later, she was Wang's twin sister, Jiao-jiang, and she greeted me courteously. The other he introduced as their mother, Lady Wang Mingzhu. Her face was narrow and her eyes cold. She scowled, said good night to Wang but nothing to me. Then she turned to Jiao-jiang and said curtly, 'Take me to my bed.'"

"So, then you heard a story?"

"Yes, indeed. Wang told me a marvelous story about him and his sister, about his two fathers and two mothers. Later, in the village, I picked up more details."

"I'm all attention, Master."

Hsi-wei paused, got to his feet and stretched. "Yesterday I bought some dried fish and a friend brought some newly-picked bok choy. Will you stay for lunch? I think I might be able to finish telling Wang's tale by then."

"Thank you for your hospitality, Master," I replied, enticed less by dried fish and white vegetables than the promise of a tale to explain the ending of the Master's poem. Hsi-wei resumed his seat, and settled himself.

"Wang and his sister," he began, "were not the offspring of the rich landlord Wang Honghui and his proud wife Mingzhu. They were born to a desperately poor ferryman and his sickly wife, the Jiangs. Ling and his sister didn't learn this for years, not until Wang Honghui told them on his deathbed. Here's what happened.

"As you well know, the Yangtze has its bad moods, like any great dragon. At times it crouches low, as during that dreadful drought; but at others it rears up and behaves in the contrary fashion."

I nodded and quoted Hsi-wei's poem. "*Laughs at its banks.*"

Hsi-wei was pleased that I remembered the phrase. "Wang's story started with a flood as terrible for the people as the drought I witnessed. Worse yet, the flood came without warning. Not much rain had fallen on Haidong, but upstream a great deal had. As a result, people weren't prepared and the river rose so swiftly, during a single afternoon and night, that everyone was overwhelmed and many were lost. The water rushed through the villages and grew so deep that even the Wang house up on the hill was threatened.

"As it happened, two weeks earlier Mingzhu had given birth to twins and, on the same day, so did Mrs. Jiang. The peasants considered this wonderful coincidence must be a sign from the gods, but couldn't say of what.

"When the water rose through the town Wang and his wife grabbed as much money as they could, and put the infants into

195

a double cradle, a gift from Mingzhu's wealthy uncle. It was a fancy affair, that cradle, made of sandalwood decorated with heavy silver and inlaid jade. Wang took the cradle and the children's nurse and, over Mingzhu's objections, they fled toward, rather than away from, the river.

"The Jiangs had neither money nor sandalwood cradles. But they did have an old crate discarded by fishermen and into this they placed their swaddled babies. Then they made their way to the place where Jiang had moored his small ferry, rushing to get to the boat before it should be swept away. Just as they reached the boat, the Wangs arrived too. Honghui was desperate to get hold of anything that would hold his family and float. He offered Jiang a huge sum for his ferry. But the craft was small. Jiang pointed out that it couldn't hold all five adults and the infants too. If they all got in, the boat it was sure to be swamped. Honghui doubled his offer. Jiang, the poor man, was tempted. Perhaps he and his wife could survive without the boat? He agreed to take the money and give up his ferry but on one condition. The Wangs must take their children aboard. 'There's enough room for them and your nurse too. We'll take our chances,' said Jiang, 'but you must promise that, if my wife and I die, you'll raise our children as if they were your very own. If you want my boat, you must swear this by the gods.'

"By then water was already surging around their waists. So Wang took the oath, pressed the money into Jiang's hand, and hastened his wife into the boat, also the nurse, holding the cradle high. With her tears adding to the flood, Mrs. Jiang leaned into the ferry and gently placed the rough box holding her twins at the nurse's feet. Then she and her husband waded back towards the darkened town and were never seen again.

"The darkness grew nearly total as little craft bobbed and yawed in the flood. The wind blew hard and Wang was not skilled in using the oar. The women screamed as the ferry rose and fell. Then the bow struck an uprooted tree. They were lifted high then the boat crashed down on its side and nearly capsized.

The cradle was pitched into the water and so was the fisherman's crate. With a cry, the faithful nurse leaned halfway out of the boat to retrieve the sandalwood cradle with its jade and silver fittings, but it sank like a block of iron. The wooden box, however, floated long enough for her to grab hold of it. Then Honghui grabbed her sash and hauled her back into the boat.

"The Wangs were devastated. In her grief, Mingzhu tried to throw the two peasant twins overboard. 'Why should these insects live!' she cried. Honghui and the nurse had to struggle to restrain her.

"They rode out the flood; the night passed; the river calmed and withdrew to its course. The Wangs returned to their villa, and Honghui began the repairs on the old house. The village below, though, was ruined and many had perished. Honghui decided he must bear his misfortune and keep his vow. He adopted Ling and Jiao, gave them his name, hired tutors for them, dressed them well, and in every way treated them as he would his own lost twins. His wife, however, became even haughtier and far more bitter. The villagers assured me that was why she was never again able to conceive and that she was never kind to the twins, though both were good children who served her obediently and honored her as their mother. And they believed she really was their mother because Honghui ordered that Ling and Jiao should be kept ignorant of their true history. And so they were until, as he lay dying, Honghui told them all.

"Ling inherited his adopted father's wealth, lands, buildings, and all his goods. He never replaced a single stick of furniture but maintained everything as it had been. As for Jiao, she had many suitors not only because she was modest and good-looking, but because it was known that her brother would offer a large dowry. Yet Jiao declined all offers, saying that it was her duty to care for Mingzhu. That's the sort of woman she was.

"Ling, raised to be the greatest man in the district, the one to whom all must kowtow, thought long and hard about who he really was and how he ought to live. The peasants told me that it was then that he added the *jiang* to his and his sister's names, to honor their father and mother and as a token of their divided identity."

Here Hsi-wei stopped speaking.

"So that's why he took so much care for the peasants," I said. "Of course! *Two cradles and three fates.*"

"Yes."

"I see now. *Out of too much water came salvation.* Wang Ling-ji-ang was spared from the flood and saved his tenants from the drought. *From too little a shining act.*"

Hsi-wei nodded and sat back quietly for a while, looking into the distance, then he spoke in a soft voice. "I was young when I made my way through Shannan Tung. The horrors of the drought impressed me, but this tale moved me even more. Like Ling-jiang, I'm a peasant myself, one with a little education. I felt I had to write his story down in some way. I think many poems are written because poets can't help it."

Then the Master slapped his thigh, got to his feet, and said loudly, "But now let's see about that dried fish and bok choy."

Hsi-wei and the Southern War

Note: The Tang minister Fang Xuan-ling begins the record of his conversation with Chen Hsi-wei about the latter's poem known as "The War in the South" with a few comments of his own. It is hardly surprising that a minister of the new dynasty should have certain opinions concerning the recently ended one, the briefest in all of China's long history.

Hsi-wei does not willingly talk about politics and yet his poems are replete with veiled or indirect political statements, most often criticisms of the wealthy from the standpoint of the poor. One senses the poet's conflict: the peasant in him feels the unnecessary suffering of the people while the educated man has an understanding of the authorities. Hsi-wei believes Emperor Wen was a good man and a good ruler; one might even say he cherishes a romantic concept of the first Sui emperor. To Hsi-wei, Wen's mistakes were due to pride and ambition, never greed or malice. In his view, the Emperor's faults had their origin in his virtues, his failures in his triumphs. On the other hand, he is quite willing to attribute the worst motives to Wen's son, the late Emperor Yangdi. Dislike for the son seems to have reinforced Master Hsi-wei's sympathy for the father. Indeed, he sometimes speaks of Emperor Wen as if he knew him, would have liked to encourage the Son of Heaven when he did the good and to correct him when he chose foolishly. Now everybody knows Wen's errors which were made obvious by his son's augmenting them. Though Yangdi was a poet of some repute, Hsi-wei never mentions this; he sees Yangdi as a wicked and licentious man and is inclined to believe the rumor that he assassinated his father.

Everyone agrees it was their grandiose building projects and disastrous wars, costing millions of lives and emptying the treasury, that doomed the Sui. Yet it was by war that Wen reunited the North and the South, by war that he drove back the Turks. As for their colossal engineering projects, who would now dispense with the Grand Canal? Emperor Wen contributed a great deal: he reformed the currency, re-instituted the Confucian examinations and so raised the quality of the civil service. He was also the first emperor to promote Buddhism. Though Master Hsi-wei admits to being powerfully attracted by their teachings, he does not count himself among the Buddhists. Nevertheless, he told me that, for him, the high point of Emperor Wen's rule was his Buddha Edict which he called "the noblest sentence ever uttered by any emperor."

All the people within the four seas may, without exception,
develop enlightenment and together cultivate fortunate karma,
bringing it to pass that present existences will lead to happy future
lives, that the sustained creation of good causation will carry us
one and all up to wondrous enlightenment.

Barely a year after issuing this declaration, this prayer for universal happiness, Emperor Wen launched his invasion of the south. Of this Hsi-wei spoke mordantly.

"Why trouble people who never threatened us?" he asked. "Only because centuries ago they were under our thumb? I blame the Emperor's victories in the west. They made him over-confident."

"In your opinion he overreached?"

Hsi-wei glanced skyward. "My Lord, victory is a stimulant; therefore it's intoxicating, and therefore often a poison."

"A poison?" I asked.

"It wasn't just the victories over the Turks. Those just inspired rashness. It was actually the army's victories in the south that led to their defeat."

I had an idea. "Ah. Is that the theme of your poem—the one called 'The War in the South'?"

The Master shrugged. "I suppose so," he muttered.

"That's a letter-poem, isn't it?"

"True. That was its form."

"And, if my memory is good, it's addressed to a person mentioned only at the end. Forgive me, Master, but I can't recall his name."

"Yuan Boling."

"Who was this Yuan? A friend?"

"A friend? Yes, in a way. Or a classmate—also in a way. For a time we were both pupils under Master Shen Kuo."

"Oh, the stern Master Shen."

Hsi-wei could not help smiling as he always did when recalling his teacher. "There was no other Master Shen *but* the stern one."

I asked if Hsi-wei could tell me something of Yuan Boling. This he was more than willing to do; he spoke at length. It seemed to me that in telling me about his old schoolmate the Master was feeling that peculiar pleasure one sometimes gets from recollected pain.

"The Yuans were a military family. Boling's father served the Emperor with loyalty and distinction in his earliest battles to take the throne and unite North and South. When I knew his son, General Yuan occupied the post of commander of all the troops in Lungyu and Chiennan, those charged with guarding the border with Tibet. Though his headquarters were in Ch'engtu, Boling said his father was so diligent, and so fond of hardship, that he was always in the field."

"A good commander, then?"

"Oh, yes. There was no trouble from the Tibetans while he was there. However, the General didn't want a military career for his only son. He forced Boling to be a scholar, to prepare for the examinations so he could enter the civil service, to practice the arts of peace, and become a minister."

"A noble aim."

"Boling was a good fellow, one of the few pupils of Master Shen who didn't treat me—the upstart interloper, the filthy peasant—with disdain. He wasn't in the least haughty. Perhaps it was because he'd spent his childhood in garrisons. In fact, Boling made me his confidant. He told me he didn't care for his studies—which, to tell the truth, was obvious to everyone. No, he said that what he yearned for was to emulate his father; he wanted to become an officer, dreamed of being a commander. He excelled at horsemanship, fighting with staves, at all military exercises. He neglected his scrolls and brushes to practice with the gong and qiang. Master Shen upbraided him ceaselessly, though he didn't dare beat the boy. It wouldn't have made any difference if he had. Boling was stubborn and, in the end, the General gave in. When we said farewell, Boling was so filled with elation he forgot himself and embraced me."

"Did you hear from him again?"

Master Hsi-wei was quiet for a bit before resuming.

"One day, about twenty years ago, I decided to see the river with which I share a name and made my way to Kwangsi. I had not gone south since I carried the message to General Fu, put off less by the memory of my dangers than the sultry climate. This was about a year into the southern campaign. As so many of the Kwangsi men had been conscripted, the war was the talk of the province. At first I heard only of victories—how quickly the army had taken Tong Binh and all its surrounding tributary kingdoms. The old men and the women spoke with joy and relief of how their sons and husbands would be home in a month, two at the most, returning in triumph, back in time for planting.

"But then I came to a village where the mood was just the opposite. The bad news was brought back by the few who had survived the ruinous thrust into Champa and it spread quickly. These stragglers also spoke of victories, and proudly, as soldiers will. In a village by the Hsi River I myself met one of these men. Though he couldn't pay I made him a pair of straw sandals and told him it was to honor his service to the Emperor. He was only about nineteen, terribly thin and weak, and struggled to bear himself upright like the veteran he was. It was he who told me how they had defeated the war elephants and then pursued the enemy deep into the pestilential forests. 'We were invincible,' he insisted harshly, as if I had denied it. 'Our officers were smart, the archers sharp as nails, morale high as Heaven's gates. Until,' he said, 'the sickness began, the terrible fevers.'

"I asked this man if he had ever heard of an officer named Yuan.

"'Captain Yuan? I never met the man but he was known to everybody,' he said sadly. 'He was one of our best officers, trusted by the commanders. His men must have loved him because they mourned him for a whole day. Not long, you'll say, but by then all of them were either sick or dying.'"

We were quiet for a time, watching the sun go down. "And the letter-poem?" I asked.

"Written to my friend whose father wanted him to become a minister."

Not knowing how to respond, I said I was sorry.

Hsi-wei sighed. "Only a year later the Emperor died, or was killed by a son who lacked his father's vision and decency but had all his worst impulses in abundance—who launched still bigger projects and even more disastrous wars."

"I believe our new dynasty will fare better and last longer," I said confidently. "With fewer wars."

Hsi-wei smiled wearily. "So I hope too, and with better poems."

With that my host humbly begged my pardon, saying he was drowsy and needed to sleep.

Thanking Master Hsi-wei for his hospitality and openness, I quickly took my leave and returned to Chiangling.

The War in the South

Were you ready for them? People say you weren't warned.
What a shock it must have been after the easy triumphs,
the delicious exotic food I picture you wolfing down
as you lounged in the abandoned palaces of Tong Binh.

Was the food as good as they say? Are the women of
Linyi really slim as willow branches, shy as fawns?

Champa must have beckoned like a crimson pomegranate
hanging so low you only needed to raise your hand, tug,
and drop it in the basket of the Emperor's swelling glory.

But how terrifying they must have been, the war elephants,
their tusks and exultation, the thick trunks rearing back
like giant pythons seeking prey, the cracking of their
rush through the forest. The biggest trees would
be nothing to them, mere twigs and splinters.

Many must have been crushed, broken, shouldered aside.
But you officers, steady men and crafty, didn't panic, not you.
You passed the order to feign retreat, found soft earth and
arrayed the ranks of crossbowmen, set the men to digging.
Elephants are no fools. I imagine only the first stumbled into
the traps; the others wheeled slowly and fled, harried by bolts,
stamping on the infantry of Champa. What a paean the
men must have raised, seeing war's fortune turn.

They say many victories drew you deeper into the poisonous
southern forests. First a few fell ill, crying pitiably for
water. Then more and yet more until the whole army was
wasted by fevers. The news has come home but few of you.
Old men and boys, mothers and young girls, weep as they plant this
year's rice and till brown fields, missing your strength.

They say that in Daxing the Emperor has met with his ministers.

I know we parted six years ago. Only in dreams do
we still drink under the new moon, joking, reciting verses;
yet to me also the world feels like a forsaken field.

Yuan Boling, you triumphed over the enormous but fell to
the invisible. Surely there must be some lesson in that.

Hsi-wei and the Village of Xingyun

Early in the reign of Emperor Yang, the peasant/poet Chen Hsi-wei was making his way through Jizhou. He had no particular destination but thought he might visit the city of Dingxiang. It was a wet November. Hsi-wei was drenched and cold and a long way from the prefectural capital when he found shelter with a peasant family. Like so many families Hsi-wei encountered on his travels, the Huans were missing men, both a father and an uncle. Though he knew what she would say, Hsi-wei felt it proper to give Mrs. Huan a chance to speak about what concerned her most. He asked after her husband.

"The army," said Mrs. Huan in a tone that might have signified, "in the grave."

Mei, her younger daughter, a girl of eleven or twelve, took her mother's hand and disagreed with forced cheerfulness. "They said it could be the canal, the Grand Canal, Mother. They said people come back after a year, two at the most."

Mrs. Huan scoffed, gave a shrug.

"It must be difficult to manage."

Bao, the older daughter, who was fifteen or sixteen, spoke sharply and with pride. "We manage as you see. But what I'd like to know is how *you* manage, sir. I mean, why haven't they taken *you*?" Suddenly, her tone changed from accusing to hopeful. "Or *did* they take you, and you've actually returned, is that it? Or have you *escaped*? I've never heard of anyone returning. Is it possible?"

Bao had struck him in a vulnerable spot. Hsi-wei felt embarrassed and pained.

"No, I was never taken. It's probably because I'm always on

the move. The Empire likes to do things methodically and, you see, I'm not registered in any prefecture."

"So you hide from the roving conscription gangs—the ones that aren't so 'methodical'?" asked Bao.

Hsi-wei nodded. "I confess that I have, once or twice."

"Then I say good for you!" Mei exclaimed, clapping her hands. "I wish that's what Father and Uncle had done."

Bao was entitled to be proud of how they had managed. Though it was not growing season, Hsi-wei could see that the land had been well tended. The house was in need of some repairs and paint, but it was neat, the floors swept and washed.

When he arrived at their door in the late afternoon, tired and wet, Mrs. Huan looked at Hsi-wei almost fearfully. Her daughters stood behind her, Mei expectant, Bao looking almost put out. Mrs. Huan became less suspicious when he told her their elderly neighbor, Mr. Chen, with whom he happened to share a family name, had directed him to her. "Mr. Chen said he regretted he had nothing suitable for me and suggested you might be able to put me up for the night," explained the poet. He offered to make Mrs. Huan, Bao, and Mei fine straw sandals if they could spare a corner for him to sleep in, and perhaps a little rice with a vegetable or two, a small cup of tea.

"I think we can do that," said Mrs. Huan.

Hsi-wei bowed, thanked her, and said he'd noticed a broken barrow by the door. He offered to fix it.

"We'd prefer help with the roof," said practical Bao, pointing up to a damp spot on the ceiling.

Emperor Wen initiated vast projects, restoring and extending the Great Wall and digging the Grand Canal. He had begun wars to secure and extend the Empire. He raised taxes; the peasants could pay in kind, with labor, or military service. Staggering numbers died at the works and in the wars. The people grumbled and, here and there, rebelled. However, when they considered all the good Wendi had done, for the most part they submitted. And Emperor Wen did accomplish a great deal, beginning with the reunification of the country after three centuries of disorder. He reformed the state's antiquated and corrupt administration. He simplified the Empire's political structure and re-allocated land in a way that was more fair and productive. For the first time in memory, the cities had surpluses of food. Wendi brought back the examination system and centralized all government appointments, at once raising the quality of the civil service and freeing people from the system of nepotism under which officials were drawn from the richest, best connected local families. Wendi's first reform was to replace the system of traditional punishments—which included dismemberment and even the execution of three generations of a criminal's family—with the humane Kaihuang Code. His second was to standardize the currency by minting new Wu Zhu coins to replace the old private and local currencies.

Emperor Wen was succeeded by his tyrannical, sybaritic, and vicious son, the Emperor Yang who, according to rumor, assassinated his father. In his travels, Hsi-wei observed how conditions worsened under Yangdi. Taxes were further increased and with them conscription. Millions lay under the Great Wall; and more than half the workers sent to the Grand Canal died by drowning, mudslide, exhaustion, hunger, or exposure. The new Emperor's military ambitions exceeded even his father's. He sent vast armies to invade Champa in the south and Goguryeo in the north. All these campaigns failed with colossal losses.

Like many others, Hsi-wei missed Emperor Wen.

Bao sent Hsi-wei back to Mr. Chen to fetch straw from his late-wheat harvest. The sun was down when he returned, and Mrs. Huan prepared a dinner of rice with bok choy, mushrooms, and some dried pork. Mei made a pot of tea of which she was quite proud.

The meal ran late because the Huans had so many questions. It seemed to them that the guest who had come from nowhere had been everywhere. Mrs. Huan was amazed that he had lived in the old capital of Chang'an when it was still known as Daxing and had also visited the new one, Luoyang. She wanted to know all about both. How wide were the streets? Had he seen the Rotating Pavilion? What were the Buddhist temples like—simple or very grand? Did all the people in the capital dress in silk? Were the women as haughty as they were said to be? He had trekked through the southern provinces and climbed the Yellow Mountains. He had visited the Grand Canal and had even seen the ocean. Bao refused to believe that he had really been to all these places; yet she had more questions than either her mother or her little sister. Hsi-wei was glad to answer. He described the new temples erected by Wendi and the old Buddhist monastery at which he had stayed. He told them how poverty and wealth pushed up against each other in the cities and how the countryside suffered through ferocious droughts and relentless floods.

Mei wanted to know more about Hsi-wei himself. What adventures had he had? Hsi-wei obliged by telling her a few of his experiences, and Mei, her eyes shining, begged for more stories. He never mentioned his poetry or how the little fame they had won him led to his being well received in this or that province. It delighted him, as it always did, to be among good people who knew nothing of his writing and took him for what he truly was—a vagabond peasant who, as a boy, had learned the craft of sandal-making from an uncle.

It grew late and Mei began to yawn.

Hsi-wei asked Mrs. Huan if it would be possible for him to stay an extra day. "If not," he said, "I'm sure I could find other lodging nearby. But it will take me two days to make your sandals."

"And to repair that leak," Bao reminded him.

"Oh, please let him stay, Mama," pleaded Mei. Enthralled by his stories, she hoped to hear more.

Mrs. Huan agreed with a smile and told the drowsy child to go to bed.

Bao reminded Hsi-wei about the repair to the roof.

"Tell me," asked Mei as she got to her feet, "did you ever visit that wonderful village, the one in Liangzhou, the one—" She turned impatiently to her sister. "Oh, Bao, what's its name? You know the one I mean."

"Xingyun," said Bao.

"Yes, Xingyun. Have you seen it?"

Hsi-wei had heard at least a dozen versions of the story of Xingyun. The tale had been circulating for years. It had to date from early in the rule of Emperor Wen since it involved two of his earliest reforms. Hsi-wei had noted that, wherever the story was told, the teller always placed the village of Xingyun in some distant province. As Mei was sure it was in Liangzhou, the people of Liangzhou were just as certain the village was in Ba-Han, while the peasant from whom Hsi-wei had heard the story in Ba-Han situated the village in Henan.

Hsi-wei thought that perhaps there was some truth to the story of Xingyun but, over time, it had become a legend, a folk tale of pluck, peace, hope, and justice, just the kind of story to appeal to children like Mei.

According to all the versions of the story Hsi-wei had heard, the local prefect—whose name could be Fung or Chang or Shui—was one of the old sort, nephew of a local landlord, cruel, biased, quick to demand a bribe. His family had held the position for generations.

When the order came from the capital to begin conscripting peasants and increase their taxes, this Fung or Chang or Shui threw himself into the work, anticipating a rise in graft to match the one in taxes. It was also an excellent opportunity to rid himself of malcontents. Those out of favor or who could not pay were taken away, men and women alike, until many villages in the region were left with only young children and elderly grandparents.

At the same time that Emperor Wen ordered the conscriptions, he began the process of standardizing the Empire's currency. He had five mints built in various provinces to strike the new Wu Zhu coins. In accord with a schedule worked out in Daxing, armed convoys would be sent out from these mints to distribute the new coins through the Empire and to confiscate the old, privately minted ones. It was estimated the task would take two to three years to complete.

Conditions in the prefecture run by Fung, Chang, or Shui were particularly harsh. Young men stole away before they could be conscripted. Some went to relatives in other jurisdictions; others became bandits.

Some versions of the story include the unlikely exploits of the young bandits. Whether they are kidnapping the prefect's son and teaching him to despise his father, stealing pigs from the prefect's family compound, or outsmarting Turkic mercenaries, the outlaws are always presented as clever, down-to-earth, decent heroes who enjoy the sort of camaraderie that is irresistible to children, especially if the heroes are children themselves. In some versions, the bandit gang includes women who are just as brave and clever as the men. The bandits are always young, healthy, witty, and indifferent to the risk of torture and beheading. Hsi-wei recognized all these bandit stories as elaborations, digressions to please the public, but distractions from the story's proper subject.

The tale really begins when bandits ambush an armed convoy carrying the Emperor's new Wu Zhu coins. After a short, sharp fight, the outlaws kill the officers and drive off the guards. All this is witnessed by four ragged but fascinated children who are foraging for mushrooms and happen to be at the side of the road. Three of the bandits take hold of the children and warn their leader.

"They've seen everything. They can identify us. Maybe we should—"

But their captain cut the man off with a laugh. "There must be forty caskets in this wagon. I say we give one of them to these children."

Some of the bandits objected and the captain let them speak. But once they were done, he made a short speech.

"These children are just what you would be, if you had been born only a few years later. They're poor and hungry; they're without parents and hopeless." From his horse, with his hand on his hip, he looked over the gang. "Do you withdraw your objections?"

There was silence.

"Good," said the captain. "Now, the casket's heavy—make them a litter so they can carry it back to their village."

In the morning, Mei sat watching Hsi-wei work at the sandals. "You've never been to Xingyun? Really?"

"Never heard of it," he said. The poet pretended not to know the story so that Mei could have the pleasure of telling it to him.

Mei said her favorite part was when the four children arrived in the village of Xingun with the casket full of bright new coins. They shouted, "Good news! Good news!" And everybody came out to see, young and old. The littlest children jumped up and down and clapped their hands.

"But everyone was *very* thin," said Mei seriously.

Hsi-wei saw no need to point out that Mei and her sister were hardly fat.

"When they saw the casket full of money, everybody was so happy. They began talking about the wonderful things they could buy. Only one old man looked on with a frown." Mei also frowned and made her voice as low as she could. 'Where did you get these coins?'

"So, the children told everything that happened—the looking for mushrooms, the attack on the convoy, the bandits grabbing hold of them and then how their captain gave them the casket of money to bring back to Xingyun.

"The children said, 'It's for everyone.' But the old man shook his head and said there was going to be trouble."

All versions of the story agree that, when he heard about the casket of coins in Xingyun and how they had come to be there, the prefect ordered a detachment of cavalry to place the children of the village under arrest. And this was done. They were taken to the local capital, put in jail, and would have suffered hunger and cold if the local women had not taken pity and brought food and blankets.

A date was set for the trial. Everybody was sure the prefect, who had been unable to recover the shipment of coins or find the bandits, would impose the most severe punishment on the children.

But then something unexpected happened. In accord with his reform of the civil service, Emperor Wen sent out a new prefect who took over just days before the trial of the children. The deposed prefect was furious but could do nothing except to insist that his successor, who knew so little of the region and its problems, permit him to prosecute the thieves who had stolen the Emperor's new coins. The new prefect, who had been well informed as to the character of his predecessor, courteously agreed, and the trial went forward as scheduled.

The former prefect turned prosecutor delivered a speech packed with fury, indignation, and innuendo. He asserted without proof that the children—indeed the entire population of Xingyun—had been working hand in glove with the bandits, spying for them, letting them know when the Wu Zhu convoy would be coming through the region, warning them of the authorities' pursuit. "How else can we explain why the bandits are still at large? My Lord, the guilt of these children is self-evident. We found the casket and the coins in the village. They didn't even deny where they had come from. Judgment must be swift and severe. We all know how precarious our current stability is. The Emperor needs to deter anyone who would undermine his divine plans or subvert his projects. These children should be sent to work on the Grand Canal. What's more, the village of Xingyun should be razed and its remaining denizens scattered, exiled to distant provinces."

Mei's second favorite part of the story was what happened next.

The new prefect courteously thanked his predecessor for so forcefully presenting the prosecution's case. He then turned to the four children and, in a tone that was not unkind, asked if they could defend themselves.

The oldest child (in Mei's version, it was a girl) spoke up in an even, clear voice.

"My Lord, what he just said about finding the coins in the village is true; but other things he said are not true. We have three arguments to offer before we submit ourselves to your judgment, as we have to do."

"Go on," said the new prefect with an encouraging smile.

"First, we didn't have anything to do with the bandits. We didn't tell them about the coin wagon. We couldn't have since we knew nothing about it ourselves. We didn't steal anything. The casket of coins might as well have been found by us beside the road."

The prefect cocked his head at this last assertion. "Your defense is that you didn't steal but that you received stolen goods?"

"Stolen, My Lord? Only moved from one place to another, which was exactly what the Emperor is trying to do. In fact, that's our second argument."

"It is? Well, let's hear it."

"Second, the Emperor's aim is to spread the new coins over the whole Empire. And to do that, people need the coins to spend, to give one another. For example, the people of Xingyun want to buy six pigs from the people of Haoqin and ten geese from the people of Luangxi and now we can. Isn't that fulfilling the purpose of the Son of Heaven?"

The prefect smiled. "And the third argument?"

"Third and last. Let's say that we obtained the coins because of a theft—though we didn't commit it. Let's also say that this theft was from the State—even though the State didn't want to keep the coins but to distribute them as widely as possible.

213

Now, because we accepted a casket of these coins, we're accused of stealing from the State. But, My Lord, what if we look at the ledger? My aunt told me that a good bookkeeper must have more than a single column."

"What do you mean?"

The child stood up even straighter and looked bravely at the new prefect, a man who may have seen the Emperor himself, who may even have heard his voice, a man of real authority, come from the Imperial capital. "Just this, My Lord: if we have stolen from the State, what has the State stolen from us? What have we children lost because of the Grand Canal and the Great Wall and the war in the south and the ones north? What has the Empire stolen from us, My Lord? Hasn't it taken our parents, our aunts and uncles, our cousins, our rice, our future, our hope...." The child broke off, overcome.

"Is that all?

"Yes," said the child in a shaking voice but standing firm. "That's all we have to say."

It was the next day when the prefect announced his decision. So many gathered to hear it that the reading of the verdict had to be moved to the marketplace.

"It is our judgment that the village of Xingyun may lawfully spend the Wu Zhu coins which came into their possession by accident rather than theft. In return, the people shall hand over to the government all other abolished currency they may have in their possession. In addition, we declare the village of Xingyun exempt from all taxes and conscriptions for a period of five years."

"The cheering was loud and it lasted a long time," declared Mei with satisfaction.

When Hsi-wei was ready to depart, he thanked Mrs. Huan, Bao, and Mei for their hospitality. Bowing before each, he handed them their fine new sandals. Inside one of Mei's, Hsi-wei had put a small scroll on which he had copied out the verses written over the two nights of his stay. This poem was later banned by Emperor Yang but nonetheless continued to circulate among the people who called it "The Village of Xingyun."

When a new owner takes over a neglected villa
He wants everything set to rights at once:
The cobwebs cleaned from the corners, the broken tiles
From the courtyard, the scarlet pillars freshly painted, the garden
Planted with peonies for springtime and chrysanthemums for fall.

With light hearts the servants set to work to make
The house spotless and beautiful, with peonies in springtime,
Chrysanthemums in autumn, and rice the whole year through.
A promising start indeed, if only the master didn't long
For a larger house, for water gardens, and thicker walls.

High in the Yellow Mountains or down in the Yangtze valley,
In the arid air of Jizhou or the humid haze of Yangzhou,
In Mizhou, Liangzhou, or perhaps in Ba-Han,
The village saved by children and a humane prefect, still stands
Under Heaven. There all are safe and fed, awaiting the return
Of loved exiles. Huan Mei, who wouldn't wish to visit Xingyun?

Hsi-wei and The Three Threes

Before retiring to his cottage outside Chiangling, the peasant-poet Chen Hsi-wei had always been on the move. When the news spread that he was able to receive visitors, several came. Among the most welcome was Liu Qing-sheng, who, before his own retirement, had been a second minister in the last years of the Sui dynasty. Liu and Hsi-wei had been pupils together under Shen Kuo, an exacting and formidable master. As the two friends shared recollections, both noted that the pains of their youth were somehow more delightful to recall than the pleasures. "The alchemy of age," Hsi-wei mused, "is magical. It seems to have transmuted resentment of our Master's sarcasm and fear of his bamboo cane into something almost like affection."

Liu had brought along with him two large jars of Sogdian wine, a recent and prized import. Hsi-wei thanked his guest and reminded him of what his namesake, the Daoist poet Liu Ling, had written of himself. *I was born Liu Ling, and wine is my name. Each time I drink I down a hundred liters. Then, to sober up, I drink another fifty.*

The two old men laughed and patted each other on the shoulder. Liu suggested that they honor his namesake by polishing off both jars before they parted and they vowed to do so. With nostalgia exhausted and his tongue loosened by the wine, Liu discarded all discretion and regaled his host through the afternoon and evening with stories of a decade of court scandals. When he had finished, he asked the poet to tell him a story in recompense. Hsi-wei smiled and said such a debt deserved to be repaid with interest. "So, tomorrow I'll tell you a story with one story inside of it and another on the outside."

What follows is the account of Hsi-wei's tale as Liu Qing-sheng recorded it in his memoirs.

❧

Many years ago, Master Hsi-wei began, I spent a memorable night in Ch'engtu as the guest of a jade merchant by the name of Fong Cheng-li. We had met at an inn on the road near the border of Chiennan province. It was wintertime and the demand for straw sandals had fallen as rapidly as the snow and as low as the temperature. I hadn't enough money for a room, but I needed to find something; it was too cold to sleep out of doors. Fong and I arrived at the inn at almost the same time. He was a heavy-set man, twenty years my senior, with two servants and a loud voice. He tramped into the inn, shouted for the proprietor, demanded the inn's best room for himself and something suitable for his servants. The innkeeper quailed before him; perhaps he was deafened. As for me, I promised the innkeeper two pairs of sandals if he would let me to bed down; anywhere would do. He took pity and said I could have the small pantry behind the kitchen, but I would have to be up at dawn.

Fong sent his servants to see to the horses, ordered wine for himself and looked around for company. The innkeeper was preparing the rooms so there was no one but me.

"Well, come and join me." It was more a command than an invitation. "Your company can't be worse than this wine."

"Very well," I said.

"Tell me about yourself? No, let me guess. Rice farmer? Pigs? No? I wouldn't call you big but you look strong enough to be a porter."

"I make straw-sandals. I'm an itinerant."

Fong looked disappointed. "As for me, I deal in jade, the finest. I just wound up a buying trip. Now I'm taking my wares home where I'll sell them for considerably more than I paid."

"That is the work of a successful merchant."

Fong looked askance at me. "You're a sensible man."

"I too am a merchant, sir."

"A merchant of *straw*," he scoffed.

"Not of straw, sir, but of sandals made from straw. The work is what creates value. I presume you look for good workmanship when you're buying jade carvings?"

"That's true. The jade has to be of good quality but it's the workmanship that sells."

"It's the same with poetry," I said. "Words are common enough; it's putting them in the right order that counts."

Fong laughed like a donkey. "So, you like poetry?"

"Without poetry, life would feel like a mistake," I said simply.

This drew a curious look. "A peasant who sells cheap sandals yet cares about poetry. Not something found every day. You know how to read, then?"

"I do."

"A peasant who reads—that's like one of those birds that are trained to talk."

I pointed to the bottle. "A parrot is like this wine jar; it can't put out what isn't put in. But, as a craftsman transforms jade into maidens and tigers, learning can change a peasant," I said sharply. "A trained bird doesn't write poems."

Fong laughed again. "What? You *write* poems too? Now this is something unexpected indeed! Recite one of your poems for me."

I recited for him.

Fong struck the table. "But I know that poem. It's called 'Yellow Moon at Lake Weishan'."

I was surprised. "You know it?"

"*Every*body knows it. It's one of my daughter's favorites. But *you* didn't write it."

"Who did?"

"Well, certainly not *you*, you scoundrel. The poet's a fellow named Chen Hsi-wei—not an educated peasant like you, but a magistrate somewhere up north. A business acquaintance told me he met the man himself, said he was just as fat as I am!"

I couldn't help feeling a little pleased that my poem had found admirers but I was disturbed by the news of this other Hsi-wei, the fat magistrate up north. Fong was drinking a lot; maybe he had gotten things mixed up. But then I had a nauseating thought. Perhaps there really was another Chen Hsi-wei, claiming to be the author of my verses. Maybe there were even more Hsi-weis. I felt as if the floor had opened up beneath me.

Fong laughed. "You claim to have written this poem everybody knows. If you're a poet, then recite a different poem for me."

I probably should have excused myself there and then and gone to sleep in the pantry. But I was indignant. I discovered that I had more vanity than I thought and felt compelled to answer the man's challenge. I thought for a moment then recited the poem that's become known as "The Cruelty of Springtime." I chose it because no one else knew of it at the time—it still felt too personal to circulate—and because of the comparison in the third verse.

Blossoms unfold overnight.
Hills change from ugly brown to
the pale green of Lingnan jade.
The weightless air bears intoxicating
scents of manure and turned soil.
Ducklings waddle behind their mothers,
plop into ponds refreshed by rain.
Horses stamp on the dried-out roads.
Armies begin to march.

I too take to the road in springtime,
indifferent to peril, ineptly sealing up
a heart fissured by departure.
I suppose in springtime all men must
go to war, each in his own way.

Fong put down his cup and stared at me, his mouth gaping.

I was ashamed of trying to prove myself and yet I went on doing so, perhaps because of the wine. "I wrote that poem when I was leaving the capital, when I first took to the road."

Fong's brow furrowed and he scratched his head. "This isn't the sort of conversation I was expecting," he said.

"What were you expecting?"

He chuckled. "Oh, something about the weather. The usual complaints about the government."

"Sorry to have disappointed you," I said curtly and got to my feet. I wished him a good night and thanked him for the wine, then excused myself and headed for the pantry.

I was up at first light but, as I was preparing to leave, the proprietor came and told me that one of the jade merchant's servants had asked to have me wait. His master wanted to see me. I was in no hurry to get out into the cold and so I sat myself on a stool in the kitchen.

Fong stuck his head in. "There you are," he said.

"It's warm here. Why not?"

"Look, there's no doubt that you're a remarkable specimen," he said. "*All men must go to war, each in his own way.* That's not bad. I confess it caught me. And some Lingnan jade really *is* just the color of hills when the first leaves come out. I thought about it last night. You could be giving me somebody else's poem, like that trained bird we spoke of. So, I still don't believe you're this poet Chen Hsi-wei. He's that magistrate up north."

I shrugged. "As you wish, sir. We can leave it at that. But, before I go, I'd like to tell you a little story about a magistrate. It might interest you."

"Fine. I don't mind letting the world warm itself a little. Let's have some tea, then, before we go our ways."

He shouted for the innkeeper to bring tea then hollered to his servants. "Take your time getting the horses ready."

Here is the story I told the jade merchant.

Once, in Shun, a magistrate had a problem. It was a case of robbery and assault. As he came out of a tavern, Bao Zhu-sing was struck from behind with an iron bar; he never saw his attacker. Three witnesses came forward. All had been either in or just outside the tavern and claimed to have seen Bao's attacker. The problem was that each accused a different man. The magistrate ordered that all the accused men be arrested. He further directed the police chief to pursue certain inquiries.

Meanwhile, the magistrate questioned the three witnesses, one at a time and in private. He asked each three questions: Did your parents beat you? Have you ever broken a law? Would you call yourself wise or ignorant? Only one of the witnesses—with much blushing and staring at his feet—answered *yes*, *yes*, and *ignorant*. The magistrate thanked the man and told him he could be on his way. He ordered the other two witnesses held pending the result of his inquiries. Two days later, the magistrate was informed by the chief that, as he suspected, the two false witnesses were friends of the man accused by the third witness.

"So, you see, sir," I said to the merchant, "three accused robbers, three witnesses, but only one of the former was guilty just as only one of the latter told the truth."

Fong said nothing for a minute then broke into a half-comprehending, uncertain smile and got to his feet.

"Hmm. You're an unusual young man, even if you *are* a word-thief. If your travels take you to Ch'engtu, you may come to visit. We could enjoy a good dinner and, if you want to spend the night, I promise not to stuff you in the pantry.'"

Here Hsi-wei paused and took a long pull of Sogdian wine.

"And that, I take it, is your story inside a story?" I asked.

Hsi-wei wiped his mouth. "Yes, but I promised you something more."

"That's right, there was to be an *outside* story as well. Good. There's plenty of wine left, and I'm eager to hear the rest."

Hsi-wei resumed in a speculative mood.

A certain cynical sage once observed to another that the greatest part of people's thinking is devoted to rationalizing their needs. The other sage replied that the secret of success is convincing oneself that what is necessary is also virtuous. I can't say that I agree with either; however, some weeks after the encounter at the inn, I arrived in Ch'engtu. I was shivering, hungry, and had sold three pairs of sandals in the previous ten days. I suppose accepting Fong's invitation amounted to a necessity; and, though I didn't care for the man's arrogance, loud voice, or how he had provoked in me a shameful vanity, I did try to make a virtue of necessity, to rationalize my needs. I told myself that it would be impolite to refuse an offer of hospitality that was, after all, graciously extended.

After making a few inquiries in the marketplace, I found my way to Fong's home. It was a rather showy villa, with much gold paint and a brace of stone lions at the gate that were both hideous and pretentious. I knocked and the door was opened by a young woman, modestly dressed and quite pretty. She looked me up and down with a mixture of contempt and interest. I explained why I was there.

"I'd better fetch the Master," she said and turned, then casting a suspicious look over her shoulder, she told me to wait outside the door, which she closed.

Fong appeared soon after.

"Ah," he said, "so it's the peasant who makes sandals out of straw and a poet out of himself. You've come, then." It was obvious that he hadn't expected I would.

"Brrr," he said rubbing his hands together, "it's cold. You'd better come in." He pointed to a corner. "Put your bag over there. Chunhua!"

The serving girl returned at once. "Master?"

"It appears we'll have a guest for dinner. Tell Cook to prepare something a little special. Leave the choice to him." He turned to me. "Will you be staying the night?"

I explained that I had just arrived in the city and had as yet no lodging. I told him frankly that I would be grateful for any warm space.

Fong told the girl, who was staring at me with perplexed interest, which room to prepare and she ran off.

Fong called for his wife. She was a slim woman, dressed rather like a child's doll, and much younger than her husband. This didn't surprise me. She didn't look happy. Even the modest smile she gave me was melancholy.

"Her parents named her Qiao, but I call her Meifen, because she's sweet and fragrant as a plum. Aren't you, my dear?" Fong said this the way he might have praised a jade carving to one of his customers.

"Meifen, this fellow is our guest for the evening. I met him on the road. I know he looks like a common peasant but he's an educated one, if you please. He even claims to be a poet. And not just *any* poet, my little plum, but the author of that poem about Lake Weishan everybody was talking about last year—you know, the one Shuchun liked so much." He laughed. "I wouldn't believe much any poet has to say, mind you, but still less one who isn't really a poet but a vagabond who makes straw sandals. Still, he's a clever fellow. We were drinking and I invited him to visit and he took me at my word."

Meifen bowed to me. "You are welcome," she whispered modestly.

After she left us, Fong told me that Meifen was his second wife. "The first one died and this one is young enough to see me through. And, if not, I can always get another."

Just then the door opened and another young woman appeared, followed by a servant carrying two long boxes wrapped in burlap.

"My daughter Shuchun, the apple of my eye," said Fong, who was evidently in the habit of comparing women to fruit.

"Who's this, Father?" the girl demanded, looking hard at my clothes.

"A guest. And what are those? More silk gowns?"

"Only two, Father. The colors are new and anyway I needed them. So, who's our dusty guest?"

As Fong explained, Shuchun looked at me pertly. She was perhaps two or three years younger than the wife, about the same age as the serving girl. "Ah, I've always longed to meet a poet," she said merrily. "I'd have loved to spend an afternoon chatting in a garden with Tao Yuanming, for instance, just listening to him talk about trees and grass. But I suppose even a pretend poet is better than no poet at all." She threw me a challenge. "You know Tao's poetry?"

I replied with a bow and these verses:

Only by wine one's heart is lit,
only a poem calms a soul that's torn.

"Ah," she said with wide eyes, obviously surprised and pleased. "Father, I know how improbable it is, but perhaps you're wrong. Maybe he really is a poet."

Fong scoffed. "Why? Because he can recite somebody else's lines? He did the same with 'Lake Weishan' when we met. He even claimed to have written it."

"Well," said Shuchun casting me a sympathetic look, "just as you say, Father. As always, I bow before your wisdom."

Fong growled, but not angrily. "Go put your things away, child. Our guest will be staying to dinner."

"Oh, good! I'll put on one of my new gowns! The peach one, I think." And she was gone.

The dinner was a feast, with both fish and pork dishes, five different sauces, as well a plate of mushrooms and tiny bok choi. The serving girl, Chunhua, was attentive and made sure that I tasted everything. The daughter, Shuchun, commended the fish and ate a great deal of it. Meifen, the wife, was quiet, but appeared a little less miserable.

Perhaps Fong was showing off for the women or trying to impress me; he dominated the table talk. He spoke of his close friendship with the governor and the sound advice he'd given him about building a new bridge. He recalled youthful adventures in which he appeared both brave and able. He even attempted to quote the masters—but did so incorrectly. His daughter ventured to correct him, earning a paternal frown and an indulgent growl.

Meifen urged me to tell something of myself. I told how, as a boy, I had carried the Emperor's message to the southern army and how this service led to my education. The women, who had scarcely paid attention to Fong, seemed keenly interested. They asked me all sorts of questions about the South, the court, the dangers I had passed through, what the Prime Minister had looked like, my village, and why I had chosen to go on the road making straw sandals. When Shuchun wanted to know if I had left a sweetheart in the capital her father interrupted.

"Enough," he declared. "It's time you women retired."

As soon as they were gone, he brought out the wine. Fong continued talking about himself for at least an hour before he noticed my yawning and half-closed eyes.

"Can't be the company," Fong snapped, "must be the hour."

And so, I was dismissed to the spare room at the back of the house. Chunhua had thoughtfully lit a fire in a small brazier and made up a bed with many cushions. In minutes, exhausted and a little drunk, I fell asleep.

Here Hsi-wei paused and rubbed his chin. "I wonder. Do you think if we could see inside our minds there would be any difference between a dream and an actual event? Isn't it only when we wake, when we look around and see a chair, our foot, the sky, that we make the distinction? But then we don't *always* wake, not fully, do we? And then the distinction turns into a muddle."

"You mean like Zhuangzi's dream of being a butterfly and the butterfly's dream of being Zhuangzi?"

"Yes. Well, something of the sort happened to me in the middle of that night. I felt my shirt lifted and warm hands on my stomach—or it was a dream of hands and stomach. There was a smell of fruit, too. Plums, apples, apricots. I thought I

225

glimpsed a half moon with winter clouds drifting across it like cobwebs. But that too could have been part of a dream. Then there was a rustling of clothing and more than hands were on me. My trousers seemed to fall away and then there was quick breathing, breasts, a low moan, smooth, entangling legs, an urgent mouth. The room was unnaturally dark—or, just as likely, I never opened my eyes. In any case, when I woke at dawn and looked about me, the cushions were scattered over the floor and under my blanket I was only half-dressed.

"I was drenched in shame. I knew what had happened but not exactly how, or with whom. Was it Chunhua the servant who had come in the night, Shuchun the daughter, or the young and unhappy wife, Meifen? Or was it none of them?

"While the household still slept, I gathered up my things and, without leaving even a short note of thanks, I fled the house and then the city... Liu, you're looking amused."

I said I was amused. Hsi-wei's chastity was well known. I thanked him for the story.

"Oh, he said, *that's* not the story. Not the *outside* one. That I made later, when I was back tramping on the road—truly outside. I wonder if you'll see the connection. Pour out the rest of that wine and, if you like, I'll tell it to you."

And then Hsi-wei told me the following tale which I've titled *Licking Dragons*.

When he was little, the landlord Lin's mother cautioned him sternly. "Changpu, you were born in winter. You must never forget that you have a Major Yin nature and so the Year of the Rat will always be dangerous, the most likely to heap misfortunes on your head."

Lin had reason to recall his mother's warning. It was during the last Year of the Rat that his beloved wife caught a fever and died.

Now, as the new year approached, Lin grew anxious. Bad enough that it would be a Rat Year; worse still, he was about to turn forty-four and, as everybody knows, four is the unluckiest of numbers.

Normally, Lin was not superstitious—less than most, at least. Though he could be soft-hearted, he was a hard-headed man. He was deemed a good landlord, fair-minded and never mean; he was proud of that. So, he was worried not just for himself, but for his household and tenants as well. He was also anxious about his son, off in the capital preparing to take his examinations.

Lin's oldest servant, Deshi, who had served Lin's father, observed how his Master cringed at the sound of thunder, the way he stared fearfully at the sky. He was troubled when Lin forbade the cook to prepare dishes with mushrooms, as mushrooms were formerly among his favorite foods. He also noted that his master was constantly asking the women to check the outbuildings for signs of fire.

Though he had known his master since his infancy, Deshi always preserved the formalities. He asked Lin for permission to speak with him privately.

"But of course," said Changpu, who felt affection and respect for the old man and indulged his ways. He invited Deshi into the little study where he kept his accounts.

"What's the matter? I hope you're not unwell."

"*Some*one's not well, Master."

"Who is it? Not the cook? Oh, it's not little Meiling?"

"No, sir. It's you."

"Me?"

"Forgive my forwardness, but you haven't been yourself of late, Master. I can see something's got you worried. Perhaps I can help."

Lin was embarrassed to confess to the old man his worries concerning the coming year and the bad fortune it was likely to bring. There was no one else to whom he would do so and he found it a relief.

Though not himself given to superstitions, Deshi knew all about their power. "I believe I have a remedy," he said.

"You do?" asked Changpu hopefully.

The old man nodded. "The best way to provide against bad luck is to ensure the good. When I was young, I heard a wise woman say that to possess a dragon made of green jade can avert both flood and drought, that it brings gentle rain and good harvests."

Lin looked at Deshi hopefully. "Really? Must it be a big dragon?"

"No, Master. The size of the statue doesn't matter, but it must be made of genuine Lingnan jade, solid through and through."

If Lin was skeptical, he gave no sign of it. The next day he dispatched a messenger to his agent in Ch'engtu. A week later three merchants arrived at his home, each offering a green dragon. The sizes and prices were different and so were the dragons—one looked ferocious, another indifferent, the third was smiling. Changpu was uncertain which to buy. The old servant begged permission to offer his assistance.

"Please do," said Lin.

Deshi hefted the first statue and made a disapproving face. "Too light," he said, then licked it. "Too light and not from Lingnan either."

The merchant swore it was from Lingnan and not hollow at all.

Deshi ignored him and picked up the second statue. He licked it as well. Again, he frowned.

"Not from Lingnan?" asked Lin.

"But I found it there myself," said the merchant indignantly.

By way of reply, Deshi took a small knife from beneath his shirt and, over the protests of the merchant, scraped the statue. Flakes of green paint fell to the floor.

Deshi picked up the third carving, the smallest and most expensive, the one of the smiling dragon. He weighed it in his hand, gave it a friendly rub, then a good lick. Smiling, he presented it to Lin.

"Choose this one, Master."

Hsi-wei stopped there.

The story made me laugh—the story and a quantity of Sogdian wine.

"You see the connection, then?" the poet asked.

"Three witnesses, three women, three dragons," I replied. "And jade merchants from Ch'engtu."

My old friend laughed, pleased. "And, Liu—who knows?—maybe there are three Hsi-weis as well."

The Empire is vast, its population beyond counting; nevertheless, in my opinion, there is only one Chen Hsi-wei.

Hsi-wei's Last Poem

From the Memoirs of The Tang Dynasty Minister, Fang Xu-an-ling:

In his last years, the poet Chen Hsi-wei gave up his travels and lived in a house given him by the Governor of Chiangling, a decent man though not over-generous. The place was made of warped planks salvaged from other edifices, had only two rooms, and just enough land for a small vegetable garden. There was also a tiny walled patio at the front which the poet, expressing gratitude rather than irony, was pleased to call his courtyard. This modest dwelling was not in the city but three li outside the gates of Chiangling in the middle of a plain of farmland planted mostly with rice and onions. Nearby was a village so insignificant that it did not appear on any official register or map. Because of the single mountain that appeared to have been dropped on the land by some whimsical god, the locals referred to their region Xia Shan (Under the Mountain) and that was what they called the village as well.

Hsi-wei's settled mode of life was as simple and unvarying as his diet, but he was not completely isolated. From time to time visitors would seek him out, admirers, poetry-loving pilgrims who knew his work, or bored travelers to whom he was pointed out as a local curiosity. The poet entertained all sorts as best he could and in the same manner: he offered his visitors tea and asked them about themselves. Thanks to these callers, Hsi-wei was fairly well informed about conditions throughout the Empire. These were the years of Yang Guang whose reign of disasters brought the Sui dynasty to an abrupt end after only two generations. Hsi-wei knew the rumors that Yang had conspired with his mother to poison his father, Emperor Wen. Now he was saddened to learn of the repression of the

Buddhist monasteries, the corruption of the rigid Confucian examination system, and he saw for himself the consequences of the new emperor's mass conscription of troops for his four ruinous wars with the Goguryeo and of laborers for his colossal engineering projects, the Grand Canal and the reconstruction of the Great Wall, the ever-rising taxes to support it all. These depredations left the land short of men, the peasants destitute and often starving. The Emperor's own luxurious ways were spoken of with disgust, and they were shameful indeed, even allowing for the exaggerations of his enemies. Unlike his faithful father, Yang kept a large number of official concubines and was said to have had scores of unofficial ones.

During his last years, Hsi-wei wrote little; it seemed to him as if his verses needed to be composed on the move. So there were few poems, yet he still made straw sandals to barter for food or to give as presents to his neighbors. The poet made good sandals; people prized them. Though he was content to live a solitary life, when he felt the need of company Hsi-wei walked into the village. Here he sat with the old men by the well but he preferred chatting with the old women, whose complaints were more eloquent and gossip much livelier. But both the men and the women feared for the future and lamented the absence of so many young men. The old fellows told stories about their youth, the wars in which they had fought or cleverly avoided, the hardships they had endured. They glorified their romances and bragged about how strong they had been. The old women told tales too, stories of intrigue, envy, and hypocrisy; but what they liked best was to speak of their grandchildren, who were either preternaturally bright, precociously robust toddlers or lazy, disrespectful, ungrateful good-for-nothing teenagers. Hsi-wei reflected that people see history much as these peasants did their descendants. It was either a long slog steadily uphill or a chute from a golden age straight to the dung heap. People like things to have shapes. It was only the very old who could look on history as they did on nature, a steady thing punctuated by seasons of peace and war, plenty and famine, yet fundamentally unchanging and unchangeable.

All this I learned in my youth when I myself was one of those who traveled to Chiangling and visited Chen Hsi-wei. In those days I dreamed of becoming a great poet, not a minister of state—or better still, a poet who amused himself with statecraft. Hsi-wei's verses had inspired me in part because I foolishly believed I could do as well as he. After all, he was born a peasant, I told myself, whereas my father and grandfather had both filled the high post of Chief Registrar of Sung. As I write this I can feel my face turning red with shame.

Hsi-wei did not speak directly of how bad conditions had become under the new emperor. However, I do recall him telling me the following story.

"Last week I had a painful conversation with Mrs. Fung. Her given name is Hua, Fung Hua, and she's a widow, so far as she can tell. A year and a half ago armed men came here and took away her husband Fung Bao along with some twenty other men. I understand it was to work on the canal, and it's said that few ever return from that work. Anyway, it's been a struggle for Mrs. Fung without her husband. She said that but for her oldest son, Gang, she and the other children might have starved over the winter. Though he is only thirteen, each day he made his way up the mountain and cut wood to sell. Mrs. Fung wanted my advice on a difficult matter." Here Hsi-wei paused and looked at me almost sternly, gesturing lightly to the silk robe I had put on for my visit. "You come from the capital, from Daxing?"

I said I did but reminded him the new dynasty had restored its old name, Chang'an. I was proud to live in the great city but even more of having undertaken the journey to Chiangling.

"I wonder," he mused. "Have you ever heard the expressions 'propitious paw' and 'fortunate feet'?"

I said that these were phrases with which I was unfamiliar.

"No? Well, perhaps they haven't made their way to the capital, but they are common among the peasants. Well, then, tell me, sir, what do you suppose they mean?"

I wanted to show Hsi-wei that I was not empty-headed. "The peasants are terribly superstitious. With them everything is a token of either good luck or bad. These phrases sound like some old wives' tale. They examine a newborn's hands and feet as a method of foretelling the infant's future."

Hsi-wei looked down and smiled in a way that felt like a reproach. "A propitious paw is a broken hand," he explained. "Fortunate feet are fractured ones." By then dusk had fallen and the poet turned his eyes on the black mass of the mountain young Gang had climbed the previous winter, hatchet in his unbroken hand, struggling upward on his two sound feet. It seemed to me that Hsi-wei was speaking to the mountain rather than to me when he said, "Unhappy is the land whose mothers must decide to cripple their sons' limbs."

After that we settled down and spoke far into the night of our mutual admiration for the ancient masters.

Before taking my leave, I asked Hsi-wei if I could possibly have a memento of my visit. What I wanted was something written in his own hand—anything, his name, only a single word. With the devoted enthusiasm of my years I promised I would treasure it always as the most prized of all my possessions.

Hsi-wei rose with a small groan. "When will you be leaving? Surely not tonight?"

"In the morning, Master."

"Very well. If you could come by before taking to the road I'll try to have something for you then. I fear it will be too little to acknowledge my gratitude for your kind visit, young sir."

I was at Hsi-wei's house at first light. He awaited me in his courtyard, greeted me warmly, wished me a safe journey back to the capital, then handed over a scroll wrapped tightly in braided straw. It contained the verses which follow, a gift infinitely more precious than I had requested. He spoke with typical humility—so different from the poets I had known in Chang'an—saying he wished he had been able to produce something more worthy for me but, as it had been many months since he had taken up his brush, these lines were the best he could manage. "Please forgive my wretched calligraphy—what my old master Shen Kuo used to call my 'bird's-foot characters.'"

The poem itself appears to be entirely personal, the thoughts and feelings of a man approaching his end. Its theme is a common one, that all passes away. However, whenever I read this poem—very likely Hsi-wei's last—I recall his story of the propitious paws and fortunate feet. I believe it was not only the end of his own life Hsi-wei contemplated that night but the fall of the Sui dynasty in which he and his generation had invested so much hope, seeing in Emperor Wen the salvation of the country. Looked at this way, Hsi-wei's poem is a prophecy, a peasant's judgment on the Emperor Yang who had embroiled the state in four ruinous wars with the Goguryeo, neglected to deal with incursions from the west, squandered the support his father had won from the nomads, and recklessly poured men and treasure into the Grand Canal and the Great Wall, as if one were the dynasty's grave and the other its headstone.

Two years later, the military situation had become untenable. Emperor Yang was forced by Li Yuan to flee to the south where he was done away with by his own generals. As poison could not be found, a soldier named Linghu Xingda was commanded to strangle the detested emperor.

As for the poems of Chen Hsi-wei, despite what he wrote that night, they have outlasted his straw sandals.

I'm told that his grave can still be seen in the region of Xia Shan but that it requires considerable exertion to see it. His neighbors buried the poet's body at the summit of the mountain.

This is the poem that I was given by Hsi-wei.

Yesterday I had a visitor, a young lord declaring he wants
to become a poet. His well-fed body was bent with humility,
yet his eyes glittered with intelligence and ambition.
"Come sit," I said to calm him but he stood and recited
one poem, then another. "Not bad at all," I said appreciatively,
not wishing to discourage the lad. Embarrassed, he bowed
and in a voice like that of a mother's putting her child to bed,
said, "But Master, they are yours." Then I made tea and we
sat watching the moon rise, talking of the Shijing masters.

How strange now to think of all those li I walked,
the provinces I traversed. By now, all my straw sandals
will have turned to dust, worn out by the feet of hard-working
peasants. Strange too to think of the poems I wrote long ago
and can no longer remember. They too will become so
much wind-borne chaff, having also served their uses.
Poems and sandals are all I made, workman-like things,
so many footsteps on dry roads, waiting for the rain.

From my little courtyard I used to watch the sun and moon,
then it was the days I observed; now it is whole seasons
marching in review. Like rainwater as it nears a drain,
time has begun to race, each year a smaller fraction of
my life. The mountain turns from green to brown to
white so swiftly that I believe a pair of old monks
beginning their ascent in springtime would be lost in
snow banks long before they glimpsed the top.

Acknowledgments

"Hsi-wei's Skull" first appeared in *Sou'wester*

"How Hsi-wei Became a Vagabond" first appeared in *The Montréal Review*

"Hsi-wei's Famous Letter," "Hsi-wei's Letter to Ko Qing-zhao," "Hsi-wei, the Monk, and the Landlord," and "Hsi-wei and the Three Threes" first appeared in *Amarillo Bay*

"Hsi-wei's Justice" first appeared *Otis Nebula*

"Hsi-wei's Grandfather" first appeared in *Write From Wrong*

"Yellow Moon at Lake Weishan," "The Bronze Lantern," "The Sadness of Emperor Wen," "Hsi-wei and the Exile," "Hsi-wei and the Rotating Pavilion," and "Hsi-wei and the Witch of Wei Dung" first appeared in *Mouse Tales*

"Hsi-wei and the Hermit," "Hsi-wei and Mai Ling's Good Idea," "Hsi-wei and the Funeral," "Hsi-wei's Last Poem," "Hsi-wei and the Grand Canal," "Hsi-wei and the Duke of Shun," and "Hsi-wei and the Southern War" first appeared in *Eastlit*

"Hsi-wei and the Magistrate" first appeared in *Peacock Journal*

"Hsi-wei Cured" first appeared in *Indiana Voice Journal*

"Hsi-wei and the Good" and "Hsi-wei's Visit to Ko Qing-zhao" first appeared in *Lowestoft Chronicle*

"Hsi-wei and the Twin Disasters" first appeared in *Bangalore Review*

"Hsi-wei and the Liuqin Player" first appeared in *Ginosko*

"Hsi-wei and the Village of Xingyun" first appeared in *Indian Review*